About the Author

Louis R. Spickett was born in 1924. He served on various ships in the Royal Navy during WW2 including those involved in the Allied invasions of North Africa and Sicily. Immediately after the war he joined the Merchant Navy as a Radio Officer and was on the famous *RMS AQUITANIA*, Cunard's last Four Funnel Liner, during her last year in service before being scrapped. She was under construction on the Clyde in 1912 when her 'sister', another Four Funnel Liner, the infamous *TITANIC*, struck an iceberg and sank during her maiden voyage.

At the age of 32 he met his lifelong partner, Leslie, and they were together for around 50 years, until Leslie died. Louis became Financial Director with an Electronics firm, a Contracts Manager with another, then finally spent many happy years with his partner, running an Antique Shop in Harpenden in Hertfordshire. He now lives in North West London.

To the memory of Leslie

L. R. Spickett

MAURICE
A NEW BEGINNING

Copyright © L. R. Spickett (2016)

The right of L. R. Spickett to be identified as author of this work has been asserted by him in accordance with section 77 and 78 of the Copyright, Designs and Patents Act 1988.

All rights reserved. No part of this publication may be reproduced, stored in a retrieval system, or transmitted in any form or by any means, electronic, mechanical, photocopying, recording, or otherwise, without the prior permission of the publishers.

Any person who commits any unauthorized act in relation to this publication may be liable to criminal prosecution and civil claims for damages.

A CIP catalogue record for this title is available from the British Library.

ISBN 9871786123015 (Paperback)
ISBN 9871786123022 (Hardback)
ISBN 9871786123039 (E-Book)

www.austinmacauley.com

First published in 2006 and 2011 by Heritage House Press on behalf of L.R. Spickett

This edition published (2016)
Austin Macauley Publishers Ltd.
25 Canada Square
Canary Wharf
London
E14 5LQ

OXFORDSHIRE LIBRARY SERVICE

3303270867	
Askews & Holts	20-Feb-2017
AF	£7.99

E.M. Forster wrote *Maurice* between 1913 and 1914, at that time homosexual acts between men were a criminal offence. It is understandable, therefore, that Forster only permitted a few copies of his story to be distributed. Not until after the author's death in 1971, and Parliaments' implementation of the Wolfenden recommendations on homosexuality, was his novel finally released for general publication.

I believe that Forster's novel, *Maurice*, ends around 1914. A sequel, which encompassed the First World War, was a non-starter. The chances of any of the main characters surviving that 'catastrophe' are remote and, without them, there is no story. I have taken the liberty, therefore, of advancing Forster's ending to a shadowy summer night in 1920.

For the benefit of those who have not read *Maurice* I offer, as best I can, a brief résumé. (See Introduction.)

Introduction

Forster's original tale, set in the first quarter of the twentieth century, is a story of homosexual love.

Clive Durham and Maurice Hall first meet while students at Cambridge University. Both are from upper-class families, each with a widowed mother.

Clive's sexual orientation is already established when he meets Maurice. Maurice's feelings are initially inhibited, but his reticence is short lived and their affair flourishes. The trial and imprisonment of Clive's friend, Risley, also homosexual, follows his entrapment by the police. His appeal to Clive for help falls on deaf ears. Clive now fears discovery of his own affair and his reason is overturned by conventionality, with marriage offering an escape route. Maurice's sister Ada becomes innocently embroiled in the debate, over which brother and sister become estranged. In desperation Clive marries Anne, a girl he meets in Greece. Maurice's visits to Clive's home continue, though are less frequent.

It is during one of these visits that his luck changes. Alec Scudder, Clive's under-gamekeeper, enters the story. His desires and passion turn in a similar fashion and his heart is set on Maurice. His unorthodox appearance in Maurice's bedroom on a wet and windy night is where their relationship is forged. Alec provides the catalyst which forces the action dramatically forward towards Forster's concluding chapter. Forster's beautiful novel follows many diverse tangents. We encounter Alec's bluff at blackmailing Maurice and its passionate resolution outside the British Museum; Alec's planned emigration to Argentina following Maurice's apparent ineptitude towards their relationship. Finally, Maurice's stormy meeting with Clive when he admits to his love for Alec.

From about here, in the gardens of Clive's Penge estate, does my story begin.

MAURICE – A New Beginning
Finished 2011 Begun 1994

Dedicated to the birth of Gay freedom also
In memory of my partner, Leslie

Hope Springs Eternal in the Human Breast Man ever
is, but always to be blessed.

Alexander Pope 1688-1744

The perpetual energy that drives the human spirit might be called Hope. It provides us with the momentum to reach out for that supreme nirvana of our imagination. Sadly, as the unsung sands of time drop to the lower sphere, so often with it does our optimism disappear. Hope battles endlessly with that interloper called Fate, which is constantly disrupting the cornerstone of life. Despite such adversities, however, there always appears a crowd of optimists at the summit.

Louis Spickett

Chapter One

Penge, an estate inherited by Clive Durham from his father, is situated in the West Country not far from the sea. It is a warm September and the year is 1920. The evening is drawing late.

The birth of life's emerging maturity, with its excitement and passion, had, for Maurice, both come and gone and, like many others, he had experienced the bitter taste of failure in his search for lasting happiness and love. One can try to fashion the future but our fate is often turned by events. The discovery of an ugly side of fate's fickleness had been Maurice's misfortune.

Since then, whether by accident, luck, or whatever, everything miraculously changed. The rekindled flame of love, unmistakable even to Maurice's wounded and disillusioned heart, gradually flickered back into life again. It grew, unhesitatingly, into a brilliance of joyful incandescence. Maurice likened it to a rainbow, unexpected, sudden, and from out of nowhere, but unlike the rainbow it would not fade for it was within the compass of Maurice's control. That golden chalice of life, with its special and rare elixir, was, once again, being offered to him. Another chance: a new beginning.

Maurice would like to believe that some ancient God with humanitarian wit had intervened. He might just as well have hoped that the same Deity would focus on the violence and dogmatic ignorance of many of His human creatures, cleansing their maladjusted minds and enabling them to recognise another of nature's creations, homosexual love. Maurice sighed, "Such, was unlikely," he concluded sadly.

Whatever the magic, Maurice was amazed by the sheer momentum of what was happening to him. It was as if he had been blasted into another world, a survivor from the wreckage of the old.

At this cherished moment there were many departing memories. Some Maurice still wished to enjoy, many of them pleasant memories from the past, which of course involved Clive. Why, he insisted, should he ever want to forget his very first, and precious, encounter with requited love; a love long in identifying itself for the very reason that it was not listed in the vocabulary of his mentors. He could afford to entertain these reflections of the past for the promise of much greater things was within a moment of his grasp. This was a momentous time for Maurice where both sides of the scales reflected happiness, and all was calm once more.

He happily remembered that first experience up at Cambridge, the crossroads where his and Clive's emotions had converged. A friend, Maurice resolved, Clive would always remain, though he was in some doubt whether their paths would ever cross again. He recalled that initial baptism of excitement, which had hurtled them forward on a roller coaster of gaiety and passion. How crazily it travelled, sometimes bruising, but joyful in most other ways. He remembered with sadness how, as the last year ended and the new began, their love affair disintegrated. He was now fully cognisant of the reasons why the magic of their union was so short lived. That tyrant called conventionality was to blame, for it was that which had prised love's reciprocity off its perch, wounding it so effectively and mortally. Maurice could never ever accept Clive's justification for behaving as he did. In truth both knew it to be just an excuse, a response to Clive's perpetual fear of the established yet uncivilised order of things in this England of theirs, his surrender to those old enemies, prejudice and hate, and his ultimate and final action against all his natural instincts, marriage to Anne. For just a few moments he thought again of the man he had just left. There had stood reluctance, a creature of uncertainty. Poor Clive, he had been so utterly stunned by Maurice's revelations concerning Alec and more particularly of his declaration once more on that forbidden topic. Maurice allowed these already receding memories to depart with a little sorrow. They were far too entrenched, too deeply etched in his mind for them ever to disappear completely but the pain their crippled love had caused was rapidly becoming overshadowed by the very real and positive present.

He could now look back dispassionately on those events. It was history, just that, history, and in the way of all things, beginning to fade. Maurice looked up towards the sky. The blackness of the night had suddenly changed as the radiance of a full moon, swept clear from behind a cloud, shone out. Coincident with this came a luxurious feeling of peace – blissful, heavenly peace.

Alec's intended destination as he left home that morning had been Argentina, to begin a new life! This resolution was destined to fail – a journey never to be, for fate had decreed otherwise. Meeting Maurice had triggered an awareness in Alec's sharp and receptive mind. For him it was writ clear and concise, without ambiguity. Understanding came swiftly to Alec, both the realisation, then the acceptance of that most powerful force, love, but love of a different and more difficult kind, love of another man, love so intense. He had suffered a disturbed night thinking primarily about Maurice. Argentina, his brother's destination, and supposedly his, had got hitched to Alec's confused thinking, but did not sit easily there. There was really no contest, for that very morning, when it was nearly too late, his mind did a metaphorical 'volte-face'. "Damn it all," he swore defiantly to himself, "what the hell am I doing? My life's here, with Maurice." The strength and determination with which this was uttered, unreservedly resolved the tug of war, which had been going on in his mind. This honest reaction to his true instincts meant that at least one misguided voyage in his life had been avoided.

Right from the first day, Alec had tried to make sense of the sudden surge of excitement, which began this journey with Maurice. He recalled it once more.

That day, with a sun not yet at noon, Alec had spotted Maurice strolling idly in the garden. Alec was only a short distance away. He had experienced an unaccountable desire, as if some magnetic force was propelling him forward, and, within moments, found himself walking alongside Maurice. Maurice had not shown any displeasure, or encouragement for that matter, and they walked side by side for some distance. Alec, carrying an empty canvas bag felt his hand accidentally brush lightly against Maurice's. He was so aware of the touch, desirous in fact, that he felt the light hairs on Maurice's wrist brush against his. The sensation was electric, something he had never before experienced. Alec allowed his hand to touch again, this time with purpose, and the sensation was there again. He felt a warmth transmitted from Maurice, if only for a fleeting moment. As they moved on through the garden Alec became excited at what was happening to him. The sensations made him kind of shiver. He was responding to something new, for nothing of its kind had ever affected him in this way. He became immediately aware of the sexual stimulation this provided. Remarkably, it did not strike him as strange that this man could affect him so violently. He gave little thought to its cause. This obvious homosexual event did not register in his mind as being wrong. Prejudices of the nature to produce guilt were not resident in his mind and had they appeared would have been ignored, such was the nature of his temper. Whether telepathic waves or some other unknown device made Alec instinctively aware of Maurice's sympathies, we shall never know. Enough to say that their union was settled very shortly after that – on a wet and windy night.

Alec had joined in the usual activities young men of his generation did, albeit within his social class. He knew that the girls he had met never pleased or excited him even though there had been many who sought his company. He did not consider this unusual. Ignoring tales of perdition, as most young men did, masturbation had been his prime route to sexual gratification. This routine he had accepted as the ritual nature intended. Whatever thoughts or visions came to mind during those times is hard to know. Suffice it to say that the opposite sex did not feature significantly, if at all. Now, following that first encounter with Maurice, the violence of emerging mental and physiological changes were making themselves felt. The visitor to Penge, one Maurice Hall, now became his idol, worshipping merely the prelude. It overshadowed all else and Alec began to include that demon called lust in his imagination. He was determined to find and capture the cause for this new craving whose intensity began to rage like an inferno. The difference in their respective positions in society caused him no great anguish, for he reasoned that once together, once their bodies combined, the rest would follow naturally. This reasoning was no less original than might be composed by a more educated man, for instincts, desire, and love follow no academic laws.

Maurice had moved quickly away from the house, which had witnessed a very tense and charged encounter with his old friend, Clive. All of a sudden he felt the air grow cold, and his shoulders screwed up to will a frightening shudder, a ghost of the past? This thought momentarily chilled him. Then, as suddenly, he relaxed and admitted to the sensation of some strange spirit protecting him. In his dreamlike imagination he heard music from far off, clear enough and of such striking intensity as to give climate to his present humour. Some unrecognisable force appeared to be propelling him effortlessly towards Clive's boathouse, which lay but a short distance away, hidden by trees.

He conjured, momentarily, with thoughts that all this was just a dream. But no, the reality was there, the sweet and the precious reality of his encounter, yet three months old, with the loving untarnished soul of dear Alec. During that time there had been fleeting doubts, on both sides, questioning the sincerity of the other's feelings, often occurring through misunderstandings. The class divide came in for a storm of criticism for the misery it could cause. They schooled their minds to overcome this and other difficulties which might arise.

Maurice moved across a familiar meadow, which formed part of Clive's estate. He began to reflect on his past fight against the bitterness, which had begun to blight his field of vision, and understanding. He remembered how he had distressed his Mother with his ever-changing behaviour, how he had gravely alienated the affection of his sisters, particularly Ada with false accusations concerning Clive. Even in his city office, he could not escape the great swathes of never ending misery, perhaps self-pity, which constantly engulfed him.

Now, with the name Alec finely tuned to his brain, that mountainous wave of depression had ebbed, and with its turning began the formation of a new horizon. Life's wheel of fortune had finally tilted in his favour. It had cleared his mind as effectively as a breeze might disperse a cloud of murky fog.

As the evening drew ever longer, Maurice experienced the lifting of even the smallest wisps of lingering doubts and fears. Exhilaration, a heady tonic, replaced it. He paced hurriedly forward. The vibrancy of his highly charged emotions seemed to exaggerate every sound, every smell, even the minute variations of light as the moon danced with escaping clouds. He moved impatiently through brushwood with thorny bushes clawing at his flowing coat, firm footed as never before.

A fine rain, hardly perceptible at first, fell lightly onto Maurice's head. The wetness on his forehead soon turned into droplets, which, as they fell limply from eyebrows raised in expectation, began to splice with tears now forming and falling from wide anticipatory eyes. Fern-like lashes shielded his eyes as they peered urgently ahead, seeking the route to the boathouse where he knew Alec had to be. His legs never faltered once and seemed confidently aware of the path with its rough and uneven surface. It was as if they were independent of the rest of his body, and yet, somehow, remained completely in sympathy.

Maurice neared the entrance to the boathouse, to that familiar porch supported by two columns, where first he and Clive had dared to kiss and embrace in broad daylight. He smiled at the memory, he remembered it well. Maurice's breathlessness and racing pulse witnessed his mounting impatience. Like some mystic he could instinctively feel the presence and strength of his – yes, by God, at last his – Alec, who, he was certain, sheltered in the building ahead. With such thoughts he was calmed.

Maurice tantalised fate by prevailing upon 'reluctance' to further delay the moment. He saw the inner door ahead. It would have been the simplest thing in the world to have just reached out and pushed it wide open. But this simple action had to mean more to him than just the opening of a wooden door. To Maurice the door had a symbolic significance of immeasurable importance, for beyond it lay his future, his life, and all that he had sought since his year of understanding.

The door creaked, and the small gap revealed reflected light from a blazing log fire, final proof of his lover's presence. He hesitated and felt suddenly afraid. Fears of disappointment born of past experience momentarily reared up like ugly spirits from some unearthly abyss. Then, with a finality which surprised him, these sparks of depression just as quickly dissolved – as might a shaft of prying light be extinguished by a friendly shadow.

A warm glow began to spread throughout his body, shaking out the damp and cold. This harmonised with the log fire before which, in total tranquillity, lay his beautiful and precious lover, one Alec Scudder, resting peacefully. It took all his willpower to stop himself from rushing crazily over and lifting Alec bodily into his arms. Alec, he murmured the magic name, Alec he repeated, as he leant over the body, which lay curled upon the old threadbare couch. Even in that relaxed and quiescent pose, it anticipated, no, it demanded, communion with one other.

In this high emotional state, he walked around the couch, then knelt, as if in prayer, before the sleeping figure. He dared not touch just yet; he wanted to take in all that innocence and beauty which now lay in evident harmony with the world. The tousled black hair, parted in the centre, long and caught in the collar of the jacket he still wore. Maurice remembered that same jacket from their sorry encounter, several weeks before, in front of the columned entrance to the British Museum. The jacket, carelessly resting across Alec's shoulders, now drooped towards the floor. One sleeved arm lay curved and moulded for the firm young neck, which nestled comfortably against it. Maurice watched and marvelled at the even movement of his lover's muscular chest as it rose with each new breath. The brightly coloured shirt, pulled carelessly from unbuttoned trousers, lay partly open, exposing nipples, which Maurice found sexually exciting. The shirt, newly pressed, was one of the items Alec had recently purchased for his voyage to the new world. A shirt he had put on that very morning, before starting out to join his brother at the dockside.

Maurice marvelled at Alec's decision to forego the adventures Argentina offered in order to remain with him. He considered it the very pinnacle of unselfishness. Alec on the other hand now realised that he could never have sacrificed the love he had for Maurice. Alec's final decision, influenced by love's overpowering effect, was inevitable. Maurice knew this unexpected turn of events would entirely reshape both their lives. Thoughts of some hypothetical consequence of pursuing a life which, to some, might appear unorthodox, a lifestyle others might not approve of, did not bother either of them. Alec was strong in determination. Maurice had no fears either for he had been down that path before. He viewed this newborn relationship as impregnable, a partnership, which would last from now to eternity. This was no 'pie in the sky' illusion. The reality of it all was right here, even if it was something, which a few months ago he would never have believed possible. How lucky, Maurice now urgently realised, that his recent encounter with psychology, which sought to manipulate and alter nature's intent, had been the failure it deserved to be. He shuddered at the memory of it all, the couch and the American psychologist's kindly advice.

The creature upon whom Maurice now looked with such possessiveness had, by a single action, by just a simple smile, flooded his whole universe with hope and finally, understanding, of what the world of despair of the clerics and their miserable followers would never, in a thousand centuries, be able to comprehend.

He leaned further forward and kissed lips that remained parted as if in waiting. He felt the heat of Alec's body as they touched. With moisture in his eyes reflecting unimaginable joy, lungs expanding with slow deep breaths, he looked down at the still sleeping figure.

"And about bloody time too." came Alec's deep and resonant voice. "Wherever have you been, Maurice?"

Alec's eyes were now wide open, and with a smile that would have touched a thousand hearts, drew his arms quickly around Maurice, drawing him even nearer, a crushing nearness as if to merge body and soul each with the other. The closeness of their lips prescribed no further conversation, and so, with passionate accord, naked and with decided purpose, they reached a blissful exhaustion, which came as naturally as night follows day. Drawing scattered garments over cooling bodies, they fell into a unified sleep in each other's embracing and protective arms, daring the world to keep its distance from their sanctuary.

Chapter Two

At the far end of a large meadow in an idyllic setting, and standing alone, is a wood-beamed, white-washed cottage. There is a dirt track that runs nearby and eventually joins the main road to the village. The front garden extends to a wrought iron gate which gives access to the meadow. At the back is a small paddock in which a mottled brown and white Shetland pony tugs at tufts of grass as it endlessly moves around. A couple of dilapidated wooden outbuildings are nearby. One shelters a small two wheeled trap which, when attached to the pony, makes occasional trips into the village.

Dotted over the surrounding fields one can see sheep munching away at the shower enhanced pasture. Equally conspicuous are the dark entrances to burrows where the army of rabbits hide and copulate. Sometimes they crouch, still-like statues, then suddenly flash past in the blink of an eye. The crowded shrub boundary of Clive Durham's estate can be seen in the distance.

George and his partner, John, bought the cottage shortly after they met. They were roughly the same age – near fifty. George is of medium height, fit, yet stocky. John on the other hand is tall, six foot odd, and slim. Their relationship had endured for many years and is endowed with intellectual maturity in both the physical and spiritual sense. They are, of course, homosexual. George works for Clive as his butler. John, or Professor John Jenkins to his students, teaches archaeology at Cambridge University. They had developed no significant friendships while living here. They owned a studio flat in London where they stayed when visiting the theatre or meeting their close friends. John often stayed over at university but this weekend had joined George at the cottage. The contemplation of a holiday had occupied their minds over lunch.

It is early afternoon of the same day and both are sitting relaxed in Windsor chairs before a blazing log fire. John is reading a newspaper. He lowers the paper, leans back on his chair and looks towards George.

"By the way, whatever happened to the two lads you were telling me about, George, you know, Maurice, er, what's his name, and the other lad, Alec?"

George looks up, his voice reflecting disappointment,

"Yes, such a shame. God knows what went wrong. Sad, very sad. Alec, bless 'im, sailed from Bristol this very day – immigrating to Argentina. I did mention it. Showed such promise, so intense, what on earth happened, I wonder? Big social difference 'tween 'em, I know, but, no, that couldn't have been the reason. Maurice Hall will be terribly upset, that's for sure, what with Durham and now Alec. Frightening! Hope he doesn't get suicidal – I might in his situation." George gives a sigh.

"George!" exclaims John.

"Well, perhaps not, but you must admit 'tis a fearful business."

"Yes, it's a sad old world, George. Pity we couldn't have helped. On our doorstep too. Shame, great shame. No doubt the class difference would have caused a few headaches. Bet Bernard Shaw would have something to say on that. If only we could have got involved somehow. They weren't aware of us of course. Don't usually see situations such as ours in the pastoral shades of England." John smiles at George. "Maybe we should start a missionary for lost homosexuals." George laughs.

"As for Clive Durham, well, from what you tell me, George, he's another with big problems. To get married! What an idiot. My guess is that a little more honesty with himself at the very beginning would have saved him a hell of a lot of trouble. Too blasted proud by half and a bit of a snob from what I can make out – now to be a Member of Parliament." Sounding exasperated, "heavens alive! Why can't people behave like us?"

"Well, John, I can't claim immunity for not seeing the obvious. God, look what I went through before meeting you – and that bastard up at the school. Thankfully, that's all in the past."

George gets up and walks over to John, reaches down and in a show of affection places an arm over his shoulder. John looks up, their eyes meet.

"You've such a kind heart, George."

"We are just so lucky, John." He sighs. "I just wish we could have passed on some of our happiness to the boys. Wonder if we shall see young Hall down here again?"

George stands then moves back to his chair, remarking casually,

"I'm up at the House tonight, John. Just imagine having to contend with all their claptrap, especially over dinner, and that religious crank wittering on." George pauses, then says,

"Durham's still canvassing. Lost cause I'd say. World's changing. Heap of paperwork to clear up so I shall probably stay over. Is that OK?"

John nods. "Uh, huh."

George laughs as he remarks, "Shan't make a habit of it."

The distant chimes from the tower clock over at the manse woke Alec with a start. His alertness to the slightest movement or sound had become a by-word in the village. His success as an under-gamekeeper had partly depended on it. He stretched his arms and legs as if breaking out of a chrysalis and at the moment felt Maurice increase his hold. He brushed his face sensually against Maurice's and his tongue followed a line down the prickly chin and neck, finally nipping a bare shoulder, causing Maurice to wince.

"Sorry, beard too rough, Maurice?" he said with a grin.

For several minutes their bodies remained locked together, secured by entwined arms and legs like a human octopus. They were frantic not to let the enduring excitement escape, not to miss this first real baptism of faultless passion. Maurice, particularly, realised how easily it could have passed them by. Awakening to these new found emotions – Alec's especially, for no love of this kind, or any other for that matter, had ever intruded like this – made their possessiveness, at this moment, diminish all else in the world. In this overwhelming need for each other, they became utterly tactile, fervently clawing for sensations so vital, so necessary. Though in the very flower of youth, they determined that there was so much time to recover, and for Maurice so many hurts to make well, that haste seemed essential to validating their union.

Suddenly, fully awake, Maurice lifted his face. "My God! Alec, what on earth is the time?" he said urgently.

Alec's teeth gleamed as he smiled. "Don't you worry, Maurice, 'tis but five o'clock."

Maurice looked down at his sleepy bedfellow. "Come on, my beauty," he said lifting himself from the couch and attempting to reach for his shirt. "We must get out of here before Clive's servants are about."

Reluctantly they both moved from the creaking settee. Alec slowly dressed, and then fell backwards onto the settee as one leg became caught in his trousers, laughing loudly as he revelled in the situation. A look of devilment matched his grin as he looked lovingly towards Maurice. Leaning forward he began slowly to lace up his boots. When they were both at last dressed Maurice suddenly grasped Alec by the waist, holding on firmly lest he should escape. He stood for a while staring into Alec's clear blue eyes, not searching for lurking doubts, but merely seeking further confirmation of the love reflected there.

As if reading his thoughts, Alec remarked hastily, "You know, Maurice, all the fucking shilly-shallying, 'til all over." Nodding his head, he continued.

"As that silly ol' bugger, Bor...anus or whatever 'is stupid name is, said at Fanny Allsops's wedding, we two is now one, one, us, just you and me, because," here Alec hesitates, then rushes on, "because, well, what do yer say, Maurice, love. Yes, that's it – Jesus Christ – I love you, Maurice!"

Strange as such a declaration was from Alec's lips, it was said with a firmness that dared no contradiction, a determination that spoke it all.

The Right Reverend Borenius was a perpetual visitor to the house of Durham, particularly at the dining table where Clive's mother reigned supreme.

For a moment, recalling his brief encounter with the gentleman in question, Maurice contemplated the Reverend Borenius's 'apparent' righteousness. On the subject of sex, Maurice had no doubt that the Reverend would offer a vigorous denial of its existence, except perhaps in some holy vacuum. Now, he thought, just what would he make of their present situation? He conjectured on the condemnation that would assuredly fall from those thin waspish lips; lips, which, when drawn together were as narrow as a plucked eyebrow. All this was of little consequence, not worthy of serious thought. Thoughts such as these were an interruption, fleeting and of no import.

Maurice sighed deeply. "Alec, my dear, words escape me, I can't describe just how much you mean to me. I feel as if merged with your wonderful body, we have become so close. My touch is also an Alec touch. I feel as if joined, I'm not sure where or which part I like best, certainly the sensitive bits attract me a lot." Here Alec laughs. Maurice went on. "Amazing sensation, ghost-like, hard to fathom... then, who wants to analyse? You're a jewel, Alec, as rare as the proverbial needle, albeit a magical one and all mine!" he said with emphasis.

"Proverbal?" queried Alec.

"No, proverbial. A proverb, Alec, meaning that for me to have found you is as rare as finding a needle in a haystack. Chance in a million!"

"You've a funny way of putting things, Maurice, still, I gets yer meaning."

Maurice's mind probed the sentiment he had just expressed. He considered the remarkable way in which this second opportunity had presented itself and the series of events which followed. Given the enormous difference in their respective situations, class, education, society's preference for segregation, and so on, he was not blind to the possible difficulties arising from them in the future. The reality of emotion which attached to this relationship, something which he recognised as a dimension growing in magnitude, was potentially the spring which from now on would control their lives.

Pulling Alec to him once again he felt the ease with which the other responded, its simplicity was as it should be. They remained in this tight grip for some time. Time had presented them with a new world, a world crammed full of every possible sensation. Maurice considered man's insatiable appetite for seeking other stars while never stopping long enough to wonder and marvel at a single one. This he vowed would not happen to him and Alec. Elements of disruption, and there were bound to be a few, would receive short shrift, though such was Alec's commitment and pride in their relationship that his reaction to any criticism was likely to be somewhat violent. Maurice didn't mind, in fact he relished the thought, for this would be one of the markers to confirm their commitment to each other.

"Now," said Maurice releasing Alec, "we must get out of here, and quickly." He reached for his overcoat on the settee. "As I plan to be away for a while I must call in at the office. There is much to do, Alec." With enthusiasm and excitement, he went on.

"We've our future. You and I are, to all intents and purposes, married, and from now on, my love, we do everything together, you understand, Alec, everything." He studies Alec for a moment.

"We've to watch out for the righteous bastards, of course, but that's an irritation easily dealt with. Now and forever, I know, Alec, brave words, your life is mine and mine yours. You smile, Alec, but it has to be thus."

Alec nods his head, then appears impatient.

"Now, where to live? I suggest, for a time, that we stay at mothers in London." Maurice watches Alec looking away.

"Alec, my dear boy, don't look so sad. You'll be with me and, of course, share my bed." Maurice gives a laugh, but Alec sniffs and turns away.

"It's just for a short while, Alec," Maurice pleads and in a more serious voice continues, "just long enough for us to sort ourselves out."

Alec remains silent.

"Alec, Alec, we mustn't ever let anything or anyone come between us." Maurice voice strengthens. "We now share everything, our lives, everything, and by God, forever!"

Alec looks down, then in a voice showing concern,

"That's fine talk, but what about your folk then, eh, Maurice? You think they're going to be happy 'aving the likes of me 'anging around the place, eh? Their friends, and the servants. How about them? You might not worry but I do." Then somewhat passionately, "I'll not be 'aving any more to do with the 'yes' ma'am this and the yes fucking ma'am that and all the rest of it. Them in all their fine clothes and me, well, you know what I mean, Maurice.

Immediately Maurice was sad at his own thoughtlessness. Who was he to prescribe Alec's future in this way, without discussion or apparent consideration of the other's feelings? Maurice was determined that their different backgrounds should not be allowed to create barriers in any way. With fearful concern on his face Maurice went quickly to Alec. With love in his eyes he lifted the worried face with his hands.

"Dear Alec," he began softly. Suddenly both were struck by the sound of someone moving around outside. A moment later they heard the outer door being forced against its rusted hinges.

"Oh Gawd!" whispered Alec.

Maurice held a finger to Alec's lips. "Shush," murmured Maurice. Silently they stood together, each acutely aware of the comfort and security by contact with the other. Then they heard the sound of further movements. This was quickly followed by the clatter of leather soles striking the stone floor as the intruder moved slowly but inevitably in their direction. The agonising sound of each step rose, as did Maurice's concern. Instinctively he took Alec's hand, squeezing it tightly. Maurice was not afraid of meeting Clive again but felt guilty at being on his estate after their last and supposedly final conversation. There were several seconds when all was silent, then the inner door swung open to reveal, of all people, Simcox, Clive's butler.

George Simcox was a man of many mysteries, or so the staff up at the house were apt to believe, including Alec. Although Maurice had not previously made any particular note of the man now standing before them, he did at least remember thinking of him as having a somewhat vague indifference to his relationship with the people for whom he worked, albeit efficiently. Clive had once remarked that Simcox was 'out of place'. Embroiled as he was at that time in matters concerning his and Clive's 'affairs of the heart', Maurice had never consciously sought to analyse the meaning of that remark.

Maurice now began assessing the man standing before them. Shorter than him, must be about five eight, he thought. Simcox stood very erect, a proud head on broad upright shoulders. Hair, while still showing signs of a youthful chestnut, was, Maurice noticed, giving way to many strands of silver grey. The face, Maurice had never previously paid any particular attention to it, but now, isolated and alone in the boathouse, he looked purposely at him for the first time. Maurice noticed its fullness, with the occasional soft line of maturity, and a smile showing obvious gentleness. All this seemed to portray considerable friendliness. He had soft delicate hands, nails, as always, meticulously manicured.

Before either Maurice or Alec could utter a single word they heard Simcox say with the utmost clarity,

"I thought I'd find you here, Mr. Hall."

It was said in such a friendly manner, without censure and with a slight tremolo in the voice. It was in direct contrast to the well-controlled voice they remembered announcing visitors up at the house. There was a discernible softness in his tone.

"I think I should explain," Maurice began, intending as he progressed to establish some plausible reason for the presence of them both! He saw a problem in this. Here they were, at the very crack of dawn with the cock, as they say, having crowed the beginning of the dawn chorus, and what was their purpose. He speedily conjectured that excuses of any kind must appear suspiciously wide of the truth. It did not immediately cross his mind to question why Simcox should have arrived at the boathouse at this unearthly hour of the day.

"Please, Mr. Hall," interrupted Simcox, "there is no need," he said shaking his head and lowering his voice as if pleading to be heard. "Let me be the first to explain." He paused then looked first at Maurice then towards Alec.

"I imagined that you would make for the boat house last night."

Alec glanced at Maurice, who was beginning to lose his patience.

"I think, Simcox," Maurice proceeded warily, "that that is my business. Anyway, we were on the point of leaving so perhaps you would be good enough to return the key which Scudder has…"

"Oh! Scudder is it!" exploded Alec throwing all caution to the wind. "We're damn well back to that again are we, well," Alec rushed on, his face now flushed with anger. "We'll see about that."

"Alec! For God's sake," cried Maurice, alarmed.

With astonishment they heard the strong yet soothing voice of Simcox rise above them.

"Please, please, Alec, and you as well, Mr. Hall, there is no need for either of you to feel threatened. For you see I know, I know," he repeated, nodding his head again but this time with assured emphasis.

Maurice and Alec stared at him with unexpected feelings of guilt. This was a bad start. The guilt did not originate from any sense of wrongdoing, such interpretation was for twisted minds, and Maurice had long since discarded such nonsense. As for Alec, well, he viewed his friendship with Maurice both normal and proper. Guilt, such as there was, could, therefore, only relate to the small matter of trespass, for they were still on Clive's estate.

George Simcox's face broadened into a smile, which, in itself, was remarkable. Normally sedate or at best static, the changes they now witnessed were unfamiliar to Maurice, and certainly rare in Alec's experience. Both independently considered what it might possibly signify.

"You know! You know what?" Maurice said sharply, causing even Alec to flinch.

"Please, please," Simcox pleaded urgently, "I'm here as a friend. Don't you, of all people, reject me, reject my help."

"Reject you! In God's name, what is all this? Exactly what are you trying to say?" Maurice asked, unable to make sense of the conversation.

"I am simply trying to tell you that I am also homosexual and I'm here to help if I can, for, God knows, there's not much sympathy or encouragement for us out there" he said sadly.

He paused, and then astounded them once again by giving a small laugh, which was his reaction to their evident confusion and astonishment.

"Good Lord!" said Maurice utterly stunned by this dangerous yet honest admission. He looked at Simcox who now appeared relaxed and at once relieved at having declared his hand. This grey haired man standing before two young, relatively unknown men, had shared an intimacy, which, in other circumstances, could have been disastrous. His judgement and trust touched Maurice profoundly.

Maurice shook his head. "Well, I do apologise, though I'm sure you understand that it was something of a shock you appearing like that." Maurice paused for a moment then went on. "And now this. My old world seems to be collapsing around me and I'm beginning to see why, for the new one, well, oh hell, it's just wonderful and exciting. No man could ask for anything more."

"You can say that again, Maurice," said Alec, having now forgiven Maurice for his careless remark – Scudder indeed! Then, somewhat cheekily yet in a manner not set to offend, Alec asked, "Now I don't work up at the house no more, do you mind if I call you George?"

Simcox looked first at Maurice then at Alec. He grinned, then without hesitation, extended his hand. "You can, Alec, you most certainly can." he said warmly as the two of them shook hands. His thoughts went back to his earlier discussion with John, when he had expressed his belief that all was lost. That Alec was destined for the American continent, far away from any influence which might have guided him. Now, to his relief, he looked upon an Alec who had been saved by his own initiative, a commendation in itself, an action of great maturity.

"I am still puzzled" said Maurice. "Just when I thought we were on our own and about to move out, you materialize. Glad it wasn't anyone else. Explanations would have been difficult. Phew! What a relief." Maurice sighs. "I hope that no one saw you heading this way. Mind you, at this hour, unlikely. What intrigues me is how the deuce you found out about us."

It occurred to Maurice that perhaps he had been indiscreet – and yet, indiscretion had become a foreword to so much that he had done over the past couple of years, since Cambridge in fact.

"It's a longish story, are you sure you want to hear it?"

"Absolutely essential," replied Maurice, now beginning to feel more at ease. "Especially now that we, we are 'uncovered' so to speak," he replied, fumbling for words.

George sat on the edge of the bench table facing them. Alec and Maurice waited.

"It was some time ago, before you, and Alec." Here George paused, briefly hesitating before going on. "What I have to say, Alec, concerns Mr. Hall and Mr. Durham, at least in the beginning. It is difficult to avoid them. Would you rather I didn't talk of their friendship?"

"'Tis alright, George, Maurice told me all about them getting together, I'm OK with that. Anyway, 'twas all over before I met Maurice, so it don't really matter."

"Go ahead, George, there are no secrets between Alec and me."

"Some'ow can't see ol' Durham letting his 'air down – or anything else for that matter," Alec said with a chuckle.

"Alec!" protested Maurice. "Do go on, please," he said to George.

"I beg you not to take offence at anything I say," continued George, "for, believe me, all along I had your interests at heart.

"When you first came down here, Mr. Hall, Mr. Durham had arranged, insisted in fact, that you and he share rooms together on the top floor. For a long time now, rooms in that part of the building had been considered unsuitable for guests. They are small and rather tucked away from the rest of the house! With the intuition of an 'insider', if you like, I became somewhat suspicious, inquisitive, and alert for 'any' sign of... well, no matter.

"Even more surprising was Mr. Durham's enthusiasm. To put it mildly, it struck me, right from the very beginning, as, well, somewhat more than that normally shown by, shall we say, even the best of friends!" Here George grinned.

Maurice smiled as he remembered his first visit to Penge. He could recall the room, recall Clive's passionate embrace in its privacy.

"Because of my situation, I have to be particularly conscious of the behaviour of others. Here I am referring to the guests. Youthful high spirits may have satisfied others, but yours seemed to point to a special kind of affinity," said George with emphasis. "Even so, I could not really believe the thoughts beginning to claim my attention."

At this point George paused again, then, sensing their continued interest, went on.

"I freely admit that I took pleasure in observing you both. I could still look back and remember the terrible difficulties I had in coming to terms with the reality of being homosexual. It is all very well winning the intellectual argument, Mr. Hall, but the thought of a future life in the frame of current prejudice and misinformation was frightening. Then, I was on my own. The little courage I had in those days was not over-inclined to fight for what I knew to be my birthright. At one time I even considered the alternative to living in an unfriendly world – not very seriously I hasten to add."

"Terrible, bloody terrible," exclaimed Maurice amazed at what George had said.

"Then, thank God, I met John," George smiled, cherishing the memory. "From that moment, my life really began.

"John, yes," he said quietly as if calling the moment to mind. "You will meet him. He was quite the opposite of me. He shared none of my fears and certainly had none of my inhibitions. He loved me and clearly told me so. That was all it needed to jolt me back into life again, a life which had meaning and purpose, and by that, of course, I mean love. After that, other people's views and values were secondary or of no great consequence." George paused.

"Sorry, I digress, but then, that's inevitable when you have such a charming audience."

"Does that include you, Maurice?" Alec joked.

"Hush, Alec," said Maurice.

George Simcox rubbed his forehead with one hand trying to recall the recent events, which had started this conversation.

"Oh dear, now, where was I? Oh yes, as I was saying. One afternoon, on my way home to our cottage – which, by the way, lies on the edge of the village, not far from here – I witnessed a scene which focused my mind in no uncertain way. You may remember it, Mr. Hall," he said. It was George's sudden smile that began rekindling Maurice's memory of the occasion.

"I have a feeling you will remind me," Maurice remarked with a laugh.

"I passed this very boathouse," continued George, "how well I remember." Here George gave a chuckle. "My concentration, or sudden lack of it, caused me nearly to hit a tree as the bike went off the road. 'Tis a miracle that you and Mr. Hall weren't called to administer first-aid."

Alec laughed, as he had on several occasions when watching George on his rather dilapidated bicycle. His vivid memory now gave riot to some really raucous laughter. "You ain't very good on a bike at the best of times, George," he remarked.

George also smiled as he continued to recall the event. "I had good reason, Alec. There you both were, Maurice, clutching each other in an embrace which left nothing to the imagination. You were kissing, actually kissing. There were now no more doubts in my mind. In broad daylight too! You took a chance that no one else was around. It was no boyish peck either." Here George laughs at the recollection. "No, by Jove, this was a kiss of great passion. It's a wonder I didn't fall of the bike. Oh, such a great moment. It affected me deeply." George paused for a moment.

"No, my dear Alec, it was much more than that. The shock was not in seeing two young men clinging to one another as if their very lives depended on the moment. Oh, no," he went on hurriedly "it was just, well, the very first time that I had witnessed such a daring and open display in broad daylight – albeit on Mr. Clive's own estate – of homosexual expression. It was a revelation. It was a joy to my heart! My only concern was of it being witnessed by someone else, someone over in the house, particularly the 'gentleman of the Holy Order' who would possibly have made such terrible trouble out of it."

Maurice sounded astonished. "Thank God we didn't see you. I'm thankful the Rev. B. doesn't ride a bike. Imagine!" They all laugh at this. "In our excitement we probably got a bit careless. It could have been worse. If you'd been privy to what we did here in the boathouse – gracious, when I think of it! You weren't shocked, were you, George?"

"Heavens no. The rarity of such a moment is one to treasure." To general laughter they heard George say, "Just sorry I missed the finalé."

"Well, Durham, and Maurice, that be a thing of the past. Right, Maurice?" said Alec, pressing Maurice's hand for reassurance.

"Of course, you dear old rogue. Happened, as you rightly say, Alec, before we met."

They waited in silence for George to continue.

"I passed very close to you, Mr. Hall. The old bike wobbled even more, must have been as excited as I." Maurice was forced to laugh at George's words. "In fact," continued George, "I only just avoided another tree. The large cedar over by the fence. I was so afraid that you and Mr. Durham might spot me."

Maurice and Alec were both amused at George's description.

"But the picture you offered was, oh, so refreshing." Here George gave a sigh. "Mr. Durham's enthusiasm gave it all away, no doubt about it. You appeared a little apprehensive I thought, then given the circumstances I'm hardly surprised. Luckily there was no one else around." George had been going on and on and now paused for breath.

"My heart went out to you both. I saw happiness yet was somewhat fearful. Witnessing the event, however, made all around seem idyllic – for a few moments anyway. I was close enough, yet hidden from view, to see your eyes clearly, Mr. Hall. As now, they surely give you away, as well they might. Sadly, shortly after that you left for London."

"Did you see any of this, Alec?" asked Maurice nervously.

"No, 'course not, probably over at the house. Still, you 'adn't met me then, Maurice, so I couldn't be jealous, could I? But go on, George, let's 'ear the worst. Just what did the buggers get up to?" He said this with a laugh, yet there was a slight tenseness in his voice, which Maurice did not miss.

Looking at the various faces around the room one could observe a nervousness which reflected the different emotions through which each was passing. Maurice's initial interruption had bothered George. He was beginning to wonder if he should have revealed those intimate moments between Maurice and Clive. He decided not to dwell on it again. Alec had momentarily drawn a slightly troubled face on learning of this intimacy, which in turn caused poor Maurice to feel somewhat naked and defenceless.

As if to rectify the situation and bring about a mood, which reflected his true affection, Maurice now sought a safer haven and moved quickly over to seat himself next to Alec on the couch. He moved his hand up to the head that he loved and began stroking Alec's hair then turned to face him. Maurice felt his eyes misting over.

Alec leaned towards him, kissing him roughly on the lips. Then he encompassed him in his arms.

"Maurice, Maurice, you're mine now, and that's all that bloody matters," he said, defiance and danger in his voice.

George looked at them as they clung together. They were not acting in a scenario of desperation. George could see and understood the fervent strides they were taking towards finding the right degree of savage expression to show the depth of their love for one another. A situation as delicate as theirs, required, as George knew from experience, careful handling. The beauty of witnessing their dedication to one another touched him deeply. Later he might tell them of his and John's experience, tell them how their passion would overshadow all else, at least in the early stages, tell them to be ever vigilant, right from the beginning, of a wrong word said in haste or anger, or an action thoughtlessly timed. Ever watchful they must be of the direction they followed to maintain and protect this miracle of life, true love.

For a brief moment, George imagined his presence here might be construed as that of a voyeur, which was something furthermost from his mind. Such an idea did, however, produce a shadow of guilt, and raised the question of whether he should have intruded like this. It was his passionate hate towards their would-be persecutors that overcame this element of reticence. He was overwhelmed with a fiery passion, becoming more in the nature of a mission, to protect their relationship from the devil incarnate – thus did he view the would-be enemies of homosexual love. He had discussed his discovery, vis-à-vis Maurice and Alec, with John. Because of the risks – and hence danger – inherent in such a partnership, there evolved in George's mind, an overwhelming desire to give whatever support he could to promote and protect Maurice and Alec's happiness. Doubts on the integrity of his motives were dispelled as he waited in silence, watching this display of heart-rending tenderness. It was moments before he felt able to continue.

Finally, Maurice and Alec disentangled themselves.

"I'm sorry... er, George, may I also call you George? And do you mind dropping the Mr. Hall? A bit out of place in our situation. Please, Maurice from now on." George paused, then continued.

"You may recall that it was over a year before you came down again. Mr. er – Clive, was now spending a lot of his time away, in London, with you I believed. His long absences gave me reason to hope that, perhaps, there you are!" he said resignedly. "How terribly wrong one can be. Then a little later your mother and sisters came to stay. I did not attach any great significance to their visit until a week after they had returned home. It was an afternoon; I remember it well. You and Clive were in London. I had served tea and just as I was leaving the drawing room heard Mrs. Durham, Clive's mother; distinctly refer to the suitability of your sister as a daughter-in-law. Apart from anything else she made the poor girl sound like a commodity! Why can't they mind their own blasted business?" George turned to look directly at Maurice for fear that his last remark had been taken amiss. But no, Maurice gave a nod of understanding.

George continued. "Clive then returned home where he remained for several weeks. Judging from his behaviour, both to the staff and me in particular, it was obvious that he was decidedly unhappy. I now realise that they were unhappy times for you both."

"Unhappy, George?" exclaimed Maurice, "My God! Unhappy! That is the greatest understatement of the year. By then I had really begun to question the purpose of living. Alec, God bless him, has more than compensated for that, his love is beyond anything that has gone before and the world spinning in its orbit has no greater velocity of purpose than ours."

"My dear boy," George said with sadness in his voice, "I can well understand." He seemed lost for a few moments.

"Ssh," interrupted Alec taking Maurice's arm, "let George tell us what 'appened after that."

"Sorry, George."

"Well," George went on, "for reasons best known to herself, Clive's mother began to dwell upon the subject of Clive's unmarried state. She gave this matter great voice, not only to her guests but also more increasingly in front of Clive. Her approach was very subtle as only a woman can be. Oblique references to begin with, then the subject jokingly introduced. Towards the end she took on a more demanding tone. One began to wonder if she was, perhaps, subconsciously aware of the meaning behind your friendship with Clive. Whatever it was, that sacred cow called marriage, once raised, just wouldn't go away."

"I'm glad she didn't mention it to me," said Maurice, "I might have laughed. Poor old Clive, what a bitch."

"I suppose we can't really blame her," said George,

"Initially, Clive's reaction to all of this was one of irritation, but in a very short time there were signs, at least I thought so, that he was perhaps bending to the idea of marriage."

"News to me," interrupted Maurice. "But in retrospect nothing now surprises me." With a distance now between them, and Alec having occupied the void created, Maurice could now view the past more dispassionately. "Poor old Clive," he said with a degree of sympathy in his voice.

"Anyway," continued George, "whether in desperation or boredom I can't really say, but it was significant that, at about this time, he began isolating himself from the family. He spent less and less time dealing with affairs of the Estate and even resorted to having meals by himself in the library. Very depressing. It was as if he were fighting against some preordained destiny, one which included a wife, and presumably an heir."

"Oh, if only he had confided in me," cried Maurice. "Poor, poor fool," he said sadly.

"I know, I know," agreed George. "I also believed that if Clive weakened any further – and by his actions I assumed his battle in this conflict was not going well – then your relationship, Maurice, if such it had been, was on a rocky old patch. I found the situation profoundly upsetting."

"Then came the trial at the Old Bailey of young Risley, an old college friend of Clive's. He had stayed at Penge several times in the past."

Maurice also remembered Risley from Cambridge, for the superior chap he was supposed to be. In discussion Risley would take the floor and adopted a stance, which insisted on this superiority. It was at one of these meetings that Maurice had first met Clive – an historic moment.

For just a fleeting moment Alec felt Maurice tighten the grip on his hand. George's reference to that tragic event had brought back some of the horror Maurice had experienced at the time. The feeling of standing uncomfortably close to some other human's disaster, someone with whom both he, and Clive particularly, were acquainted. Although he now brushed these thoughts aside, it had not, initially, stopped him from remembering. Risley had sought Clive's help. He recalled, vividly in fact, the mental anguish Clive had suffered as he followed the proceeding in court on the last day of the trial. Maurice remembered with sadness how Clive, his face stained with tears, had described just why he had purposely hidden his face in his hands as he sat in the court to hear the verdict. He admitted to Maurice that he did this to avoid being recognised, especially by his friend who stood accused in the dock. For Clive, this admission to Maurice was like an act of confession. After the trial, Clive went through hell at the thought of not supporting his friend during that dreadful time. He had turned away, afraid of being tainted by association. Maurice was now sure that this was the moment when their relationship began to disintegrate. Clive had taken fright, magnifying beyond all reason the dangers, which he saw ahead.

The visit down memory lane was brief, very brief, for Maurice recovered as soon as he noticed the others looking at him.

"Sorry, George, day dreaming, memories are sometimes such a frightful nuisance."

"Don't worry, Maurice, just accept them for what they are – memories. They'll soon fade, particularly as you'll be far too occupied with young Alec here to have room for much of the past."

"Yes, of course, you're absolutely right, George. Please go on."

"Ah, yes, well, you can imagine the conversation or rather the indirect comments that were exchanged in the drawing room," continued George, "particularly as that 'beastly man' or the 'offending party' – to quote the Reverend – had previously been a guest at Penge. The nature of the 'offence' was far too delicate for Mrs. Durham and most of her friends to mention directly always assuming that they knew its meaning. They managed, however, quite adequately, to skirt between the lines and assume something of an obscene nature had occurred. The Reverend Borenius made ground as if on some crusade. Their behaviour, Maurice, was abysmal. I am ashamed to say that my thoughts on that occasion, for that shabby group of people, dwelt upon some pretty evil form of vengeance.

"On the very few occasions that Clive was present the subject, though not ignored, was certainly somewhat muted."

Maurice shook his head. "I can't say that I am surprised. Disappointed? Yes. I would have thought Clive's mother capable of greater compassion."

George spread his hands in despair. "I agree," he said, "but it happened just as I have described."

"On the day after the verdict of guilty had been brought in, and when Clive, his mother and guests were having lunch, Clive, after a remark by the Reverend, suddenly erupted." A look of great satisfaction crossed George's face.

"A violent explosion would be more accurate, for, with both fists clenched Clive struck the table such a blow that for a moment I thought the candelabra would topple over. Then, his face white with anger and eyes blazing, he leaned across the table towards his mother and Borenius and shouted angrily, 'I will not tolerate this. I forbid you ever, do you hear, ever, to mention the subject again in my presence, or in this house.' The confusion at the table after this outburst was a joy to witness. First there was Mrs. Durham who gave every appearance of being on the verge of fainting. When I looked over at Borenius, his face had turned a dark purple. Then he started to choke on a radish he was eating at the time, causing him further distress. I can imagine that he would now worry at the risk of losing the Durham patronage, a benefit Clive could terminate if he so wished. The two other guests ended up by turning their eyes downwards towards their plates, in the hope, maybe, that their presence had not been noticed."

"Gawd, what a to-do," remarked Alec. "Miserable buggers."

"Well, Maurice, very shortly after that, and with precious little notice, Clive left for Greece. I believe that he was in great distress at the time."

"That made two of us," interrupted Maurice.

Maurice was reminded of Clive's inconsistent behaviour at the time. Maurice had tried, hopelessly as it turned out, to recreate the bond of affection which Clive first declared in his room up at Cambridge. Clive now obstructed him at every turn. These passing thoughts had no purpose and Maurice shook them off. He turned his attention back to George.

George looked at him, and then smiled sadly.

"I'm sorry, Maurice. Perhaps you would rather I didn't talk about it."

"Oh, no, George, I'm well over that now. Please, do go on."

"Well, as you know, Maurice, Clive was away a month. When he finally returned home," George paused, "he... he announced that he was engaged to be married. It surprised everyone. Watching him after that was like seeing two shadows. One apparently relieved and contented, the other, well, you could see from the heavy anxious eyes and the Napoleonic frown just how suspect were his motives. The news delighted his mother, of course. Needless to say I was very unhappy for him. Remembering all that I had previously witnessed, it came as something of a disappointment. Tragic. I had not really believed events would turn out in this way."

George paused a while. "I thought of you then, Maurice, and, in truth, began to wonder how you would take the news. I doubted if we would ever see you down here again. Then, lo and behold, you turn up at the wedding. I tell you, Maurice, I was dumbfounded."

"I was a fool," Maurice remarked, "a stupid fool."

George shook his head. "No, Maurice, you can't take the blame. By the same token, nor can Clive, for the pressures were enormous. Poor chap, a terrible shame. One hears of it time and time again. It was the final crisis that did it. That obscene judgement from the bench and prison for his friend. The effect of this on Clive was somewhat predictable."

"Oscar Wilde all over again," interjected Maurice mournfully.

George nodded. "It broke Clive, completely, and led him to that," he said sadly, pointing in the direction of the house. "And now, as Shakespeare might have said, his rationality is conveniently out of joint. Clive will live, and die, as so many others, unfulfilled, and all because of prejudice. Sad, oh so very sad," he said shaking his head.

Maurice sat staring at George, amazed at his knowledge of the relationship with Clive. Amazed also at the genuine concern and understanding which George expressed.

"Maybe some of it was my fault after all," he said somewhat sadly.

"No, Maurice. And I doubt if Clive's true feelings changed. He just happens to live in a country where our right to love is prohibited. And fear can be destructive – a quicksand, dragging you down. Risley's was the Oscar Wilde scenario all over again and undoubtedly tipped Clive Durham over the edge. You will understand why John and I are always keen to help others in our situation. I'm sure you would do the same." Maurice nodded.

"What a fool," said Alec, suddenly coming to life. "Still, if Clive hadn't got married where would I be?" He shuddered then, rapidly, said, "Don't make excuses for him, George."

"The choices, Alec, for Clive at least, weighed heavily against him," remarked George.

"George," said Maurice suddenly, "you really are a surprise, and philosophic to boot. But that doesn't explain why you are here and how you discovered us."

George smiled. "Ah! That. Yes, well. It all started with the storm two or three months ago." George hesitated. "If Alec can contain his impetuosity I will tell you."

Maurice and Alec remained silent yet impatient, as if waiting for the curtain to rise on their own little drama.

"If you remember, Maurice, and I'm sure you do," George said with a laugh, "it poured and pelted from the heavens that morning you left for the station. As you drove away I spotted young Alec here, racing across the lawns and along the track after your carriage. Quite mad, I thought. He managed to keep pace with you for a short while, then, as quickly, turned, and walked slowly back, not seeming to care what the sky was chucking down. 'Very odd, what on earth made him do that? I thought to myself.'"

"Wasn't odd to me," said Alec suddenly. "I thought Maurice was going away for good. It wouldn't 'ave been fair. I knew then that I 'ad to see him again and I thought this might be me last chance."

"Yes, Alec, I can understand that now, but at the time I didn't associate it with anything other than a brain storm, something which motivates young men like you to do crazy things." Alec gave a laugh.

George went on. "Later, I did reflect on Alec's behaviour but certainly had no notion that you, Maurice, were the prime cause. I thought of a number of possibilities but ended up thinking it was just high spirits. I mentioned it to John by the way. It was he who suggested that perhaps someone on the coach had something to do with Alec's marathon in the rain."

Wisely, George did not mention his reaction to John's proposition. He had, in fact, dismissed it as extremely unlikely. George had witnessed Alec's refusal of Maurice's tip. Yet to him it implied nothing more than bad grace on Alec's part. The two passengers on the coach were also of a class who, George was confident, would be shocked at any such suggestion.

"Briefly I toyed with any number of fanciful ideas but finally gave up. John said that I am too obsessed with romantic dreams and fantasies."

"I remember that incident so well," said Maurice, interrupting. "I even remonstrated with this young scamp before I got into the coach. He dared to refuse my offered tip." Here he laughed. "I remember seeing that face through the coach window. My first thought, Alec, was that you were a 'cheeky young devil'. Then," continued Maurice quietly and savouring the memory, "I saw that mud streaked face with hair dripping from the drenching rain. You could simply not ignore it, at least I couldn't, and I turned to look again at the rascal, this time more purposefully."

"I saw you look, Maurice, I saw it all, but I couldn't run no faster," said Alec.

"I'm sure you did, my love," Maurice answered affectionately.

"It was really quite weird, George, for I felt compelled to continue peering out of the window at Alec until he fell way behind and out of view. My travelling companion Archie thought it decidedly strange, putting it down to an 'odd' quirk of one of the staff. It troubled me slightly, I have to admit, though at the time I couldn't think why. It was the day, or rather the morning, that I had an appointment to see my psychiatrist. Whether, subconsciously, Alec had in some way influenced my responses to the psychiatrist's questions, I'm unsure. In the final analysis I was given up as a hopeless case and told to accept myself for what I was, and, if life became untenable here, then to go abroad and live."

"It troubled me an' all, don't forget," Alec interjected. "I knew how I felt, weren't nothing clever in that. I just wanted you, Maurice, and, what's more, meant to bloody well 'ave you."

Maurice actually blushed at Alec's outspokenness but through this slight veil of embarrassment recognised the sincerity in Alec's words. George also sensed it.

"Sorry, George," said Maurice, "I've interrupted you yet again."

George smiled, "It is all very, very interesting, Maurice." Then he went on.

"Soon after that, as tea was being served, I heard Clive's wife, Anne, excitedly telling Clive's mother of your impending marriage, Maurice. I just couldn't believe it.

Clive was bad enough but you, Maurice, no, I couldn't believe it to be true."

"In fact I spoke of it as a possibility, not as a fact," replied Maurice, angry at the memory, "It is what everyone wanted to hear – including Clive. It was said to escape from all the boring questions routinely asked of my future intentions. I had no such plans, of course, but it made for a settlement of their inquisitiveness. It was stupid of me."

"Well," continued George, "It distressed me at the time though I began to question its validity when one of the maids said young Mrs. Durham had virtually led you into saying it because of her nosiness. Incidentally, the staff are pretty au fait, as Alec will know, of what goes on in the house. Their 'downstairs reports' can be quite outrageous sometimes, even for me," he said laughing. "Clive's activities in the bedroom, for instance, or lack of them, has given them a field day."

George thought it unfair to enlarge on Clive's marital problems even though he judged from these reports that all was not well in the Clive Durham domain.

The more Maurice listened to George the more puzzled he became. Something was not quite right.

"George," Maurice said interrupting once again, "may I ask you something which has been baffling me throughout this conversation? It's not that I mean to be inquisitive but, listening to you, George, I'm struck by – I hope you will not take this amiss, George, or think me rude – but, well, there's something in your style, or put another way, your fluency, your manner, oh, so many things that just don't add up, and certainly out of step with your, er, situation here." George listened and smiled across at Maurice.

"Maybe because of what has been said I see you differently. Your resemblance, George, to the image of a butler is not now very convincing, and I have known a few," he said with authority.

George looked at Maurice and laughed.

"So, George," insisted Maurice, "what dark secret is there lurking behind those serious eyes of yours?"

Almost immediately Maurice felt a sense of guilt.

"Hell, that was very rude of me. Forgive me, George, I got carried away."

"I don't understand what you're on about, Maurice. Butler? Of course George's a bloody butler, and a good one at that," remarked Alec generously, yet having completely misunderstood Maurice's remarks.

George looked serious for a moment, which quickly gave way to a beaming smile. "Good Lord, Maurice," he chuckled, "am I that transparent? It's all quite simple, really."

Alec and Maurice waited for George to continue. After a few seconds George went on.

"Several years ago, Maurice, I was, believe it or not, the history master of a preparatory school in Norwich."

It amused George no end to see the look of surprise on Maurice's face. To Alec, this sudden declaration had very little impact.

"All right, Maurice, I see by your face that you want more of my history. It will have to be potted, for the time is not right for a long dissertation."

After a brief rest, George began.

"It was about five years ago and we were nearing the end of our summer term. The night before I'd been to the Palace Theatre in Norwich to see Wilde's 'The Importance of being Earnest'. During lunch the next day I was discussing the production with other masters and the Head happened to be there. He was a dour looking fellow who always wore pin stripe trousers. After a while he launched a tirade of vitriolic and abusive remarks, not so much about the play but about its author, poor old Oscar."

"Must have known a bit about our persecuted friend," Maurice observed.

"I'm sure about that, Maurice. The discussion, having ripened into an argument between him and me, became somewhat heated – and he got very angry."

"I can well imagine," said Maurice.

"Anyway, I felt I had a right to defend the poor old chap. I've enjoyed most of his work and it was that which I was really defending. I like to think that I won the day, but of course I was to pay heavily for my success, if that was what it was."

"Why?" asked Alec, taking a sudden interest, "What 'appened?"

"Well," continued George, "the Head, whose face was by this time several shades darker than the dining room's pink walls," George laughed at the memory, "as he was leaving the table turned to me and remarked, 'I do not like your attitude one little bit, Simcox'. I was certainly surprised at his attitude for we had never had any disagreement previously. Nor did I anticipate what was to follow."

"That sounds ominous," said Maurice interrupting.

"It was, Maurice. A week later, a friend, another master, told me that the Head had been questioning some of the others about my character and more particularly about my marital intentions – when you reach a certain age a wife is often considered a prerequisite for the job. Of course you wouldn't know that, Alec."

"But why?" queried Alec, "What's a wife got to do with it? 'Ole Durham never asked me when I first come to Penge."

"You were probably too young, Alec," said Maurice with a laugh.

"Well," continued George, "he achieved little, if any, satisfaction from that quarter. But the Head had obviously formed ideas and accepted conclusions which he wanted to believe. Maybe the suspicion had been there all along and our argument had merely reinforced his beliefs." George looked at them as they waited patiently for him to continue.

"To end this sad old tale, Maurice, I hasten to tell you that within less than a week, the sum total of his judgement on my suitability as a tutor was contained in the short letter I received which terminated my employment at the school at the end of term. I don't usually swear, Maurice, but he was a bastard. Wouldn't even see me to discuss the matter. I never saw him again. There was no question of 'impropriety' so he was forced to provide a reference, in which, I might add, he gave the minimum of recommendation."

"I was very, very fortunate in having John with me at the time, my vital prop, who helped me through that traumatic time. John, you will recall, I mentioned earlier." He saw a smile of recognition cross their faces. "Looking back maybe the head was more intuitive than I gave him credit for. Abysmal behaviour, nevertheless."

"Why a butler? And how did I end up at here? Well, Maurice, that is another story, which will have to keep for another day. Suffice it to say that a degree of subterfuge was necessary."

Maurice's thoughts at this point began to wander ahead. He recognised that he and Alec were entering a situation similar to that of George and his friend. The initial shock of being discovered together in the boathouse would have unnerved the sturdiest. In fact, it nearly did just that. Thankfully the shock wave turned into ripples of comfort, for which Maurice was more than grateful. In their new situation he believed that George and his friend might provide some guidance.

George watched for Maurice to recover from his thoughts.

"Sorry, George."

George smiled in understanding, then, "John," he continued "well, as I mentioned before, we have been friends and lovers for a very long time. He is the one and same John that I keep mentioning. He is my 'dark secret' – my raison d'être. I think that says it all."

"By, God, you're a dark 'orse, George. Wish I'd known earlier," exclaimed Alec.

"Me, too," concurred Maurice.

"Yes, that would have been interesting," said George, though doubting if he could have helped Clive or Maurice in any practical way. "As I said before, we are not unique. We visit friends in London and elsewhere. Some are homosexual but many are not. One must not always assume that everyone believes in the inhuman and draconian laws, which would have us all hung drawn and quartered. I can even count a bishop amongst our homosexual acquaintances and in the Catholic Church there are, so I'm told, many. Parliament houses quite a few, which is where weird fetishes also flourish, particularly in the Lords." Maurice laughed. "Living on the continent is a wise alternative but that option is only open to a few. John and I do not spend time worrying over our lifestyle, though we are alert to problem-makers. Naturally we take care in choosing our friends. Incidentally, we do not have any in this area. More often than not the house is empty. Nervous about our situation? Not in the least." He said defensively. "I very much doubt if the Head even knew of John's existence. But the tiniest suspicion resulting, in this case, from a single discussion, was enough. Once a seed is sown in the jungle of prejudice, the opportunity for reason rarely prevails. Well, there you have it, boys," he concluded.

"My God!" exploded Maurice, genuinely surprised by what he had heard. "What a dreadful experience. Thanks, George, for telling us. I am just beginning to get a measure of the things Alec and I will have to cope with. Sorry to interrupt, George."

"Don't worry, I've drifted somewhat anyway. Back to you, Maurice, and Alec – who, no doubt, thinks we are all quite mad.

"Well, that day I shall always remember. Seeing you disappear to London in the morning I was naturally surprised to hear that you had returned to Penge. I heard the carriage. It was young Alec's sudden and obvious excitement which puzzled me." George laughed at his recollection of the scene.

"It was like an imitation of one of his rabbits. Ha, Ha," he chortled, "funny when I look back. He shot out from the kitchen where, moments before, he had been polishing boots. I shortly followed, in a more dignified manner, I might add," he said with a smile.

Alec thought the very idea of George shooting out of anywhere, extremely funny, and fell onto Maurice's shoulder laughing continuously.

Once Alec recovered, George began again.

"I was forestalled from going into the drawing room to serve afternoon tea by the sudden appearance of Clive, who remarked that there would be another 'cup' needed. He was hanging affectionately from your arm. 'Off speech making', I heard him say. Then he was apologising for having to be away that night. 'The election you know.' I did get the impression, Maurice, that you were not greatly pleased." Maurice nodded in agreement.

"After supper I went straight from the kitchen to my room which is on the top floor beneath a flat roof. It serves as an office as well as a bedroom for when I stay over. As Alec well knows, I usually cycle home after serving dinner. Our home is about half a mile from here.

"It was terribly humid that evening. You may remember, Maurice?"

Maurice smiled. "God, how could I ever forget!" he remarked.

George had good cause to remember for it was to be the beginning of his interest in their romance, a memory he would always treasure for it ultimately allowed him to see, first hand, the coming together of two young men seeking the happiness which he and John enjoyed and valued beyond all else. Against all the odds he was witnessing another victory over the anti-Christ and their shoddy, iniquitous, laws He felt enormous pleasure at the way things were turning out. Maurice observed the changing expressions on George's face, which he assumed reflected the various emotions he was going through in recounting the saga.

"Please, George," Maurice remarked feeling at once embarked on a similar journey.

"Sorry, Maurice, thinking once again, it's a joy to recall what has happened. Oh, yes," he said without hesitation, then, "for a while I tried to read, but the blasted rain pelting the flat roof completely ruined any chance of that. Although tired, I couldn't get off to sleep. The rain, persistent against the window, was made worse by the strong wind. There was little chance of sleep right then, so, for some obscure reason, which even now I cannot really understand, perhaps out of sheer frustration, who knows," he said shrugging his shoulders, "I decided to take a walk in the grounds.

"Considering that it was past midnight it was a pretty rum sort of thing to have done. Anyway, I got up, and collecting my brolly on the way along the hall, walked out onto the driveway.

"I remember just idly walking away from the house, there was no plan or anything in particular to motivate me. It just happened that I ended up walking towards the front of the house.

"Turning the corner my attention was drawn to the bay of the dining room, or rather the ladder, which had been left against it by the workmen, or so I thought at the time. Then, to my utter astonishment I saw Alec; at least I thought it to be him. He had just stepped off the top rung and, after pausing for a second – at least that's how it seemed to me – he climbed in through the open window of your room, Maurice. I couldn't believe my eyes."

"Frightful coincidence," said Maurice.

"Yes, indeed, Maurice. But had I noticed that he carried a gun my reaction may have been very different. Whatever prompted me I shall never know, but I actually started climbing the same ladder."

"Heavens alive!" exclaimed Maurice in surprise.

"You're absolutely right, Maurice, I must have been off my head to do such a thing, utter folly at my age, especially as it was still raining. What I intended doing when I reached the top, God only knows. Whether instinct carried me this far, I've no idea. I do not have the stature for acts of bravado and heroics do not sit easily in my repertoire of talents." Here George gave a laugh. "It is fortunate that I did not consider waking the household – luckily fortune was on my side and yours as well. I was pretty breathless by the time I reached the outside of your window, Maurice." George paused.

"I expected to hear you calling for help, Maurice, instead I heard Alec's voice, completely out of character – at least to me – soft and in a tone unfamiliar to me, and those profound words of his, pleading, comforting, 'It's alright, Sir, it's alright now'. There were no angry words from you, Maurice, no signs of an affray, then, although you were both invisible to me, the barely audible sounds coming from the room made the situation abundantly clear."

"Well, I'll be damned," said Alec voicing both their astonishment.

"I very nearly was, Alec, for my heart was racing faster than it should; my position on the ladder ridiculous to say the least; and I was getting drenched. I got a leg caught in the ladder and when I got it free scampered, well, not quite, down as quickly as I dare. Despite all of that, I really believe my happiness at that moment was possibly as great as yours. How am I doing?"

"Crikey," exploded Alec, "if I'd known you were there."

"Thank God, Alec, you didn't. That might have ruined everything," said Maurice.

"Well", continued George "after that I had to behave as if nothing had happened; a butler normally has plenty of practice – utter decorum and all that rubbish. I was limited in this respect but in my very amateurish way I contrived to do just that, for it was extremely important that you should be totally unaware of this 'invasion' of your privacy."

George looked over at them both and considered how fortunate he had been in seeing it all come together.

"From then on I watched over you as might some guardian angel – well, perhaps not the winged variety," he said, causing both Alec and Maurice to laugh.

"I swore that, within my power, I would make damn sure that nothing impaired the progress of this relationship, something that had become very important to me, as John will verify. Then came the cricket match." George smiled at the memory.

"Who could forget it? You had immediately insisted that Alec captain our team. I could have hugged you, Maurice, for that to me was a sure sign that, whatever was developing between you, was heading in the right direction. On the pitch you batted together. It was like a ballet. If only I could have encapsulated and retained forever the sheer joy reflected in your faces – a picture of outrageous happiness – a photograph should have captured the moment for you both to treasure for the rest of your lives."

"You put it so beautifully, George, though I suppose we were somewhat reckless," said Maurice.

"Hilariously funny, really, when I consider all those frivolous women clapping you on, Maurice, their interest in cricket as great as your interest in their applause. You wouldn't have been very popular, Maurice, if they could have guessed at the nature of the feelings between one scamp called Alec and yourself. Every stroke, every run, seemed to be an expression of love at least that's how I viewed it. It was all so terribly obvious and gratifyingly outrageous."

"They are memories we will always want to remember. Isn't that so, Alec?" said Maurice.

"Of course," Alec replied.

Even now, Maurice marvelled at the incredulous and unusual beginning to their relationship, at the rapidity with which reciprocal love cemented it. He savoured the memory of their outrageous display of it, albeit surreptitiously, on the cricket pitch the following day. He smiled to himself.

"Shortly afterwards, for some obscure reason, Maurice," continued George, "you suddenly rushed from the field where minutes before you had been playing, and left almost immediately for London. This foxed me completely".

"A misunderstanding, George." said Maurice without explanation and looking across at Alec who just grinned.

"Then I had it confirmed that Alec was leaving and would be emigrating, along with his brother, to Argentina. They were leaving within a fortnight, in fact yesterday. It was a dreadful shock and I was terribly upset with the news. I really couldn't understand why this was happening. What was going on? It made me very sad. Alec was unsettled, that was obvious. To those wishing him a final farewell he showed no enthusiasm whatsoever, his face downcast in fact.

"A couple of nights before he was to leave, I became aware of his midnight vigil here in the boat-house. Yes, Alec, you were not alone. My heart was there with you."

Alec smiled, then reflected more sadly, "That was Maurice's fault – didn't come when I asked him to. Nearly didn't get me."

"Well I've got you now alright, Alec," said Maurice grabbing him. They embraced a while, then, with arms linked allowed George to continue.

"The final episode," George went on, "covers last night. I would compare it to that of some dramatic theatrical drama with love, the controversial variety of course, the theme. Add music and you've grand opera." This made Maurice laugh.

"Last night, I had some housekeeping to sort out, and as John was away, decided to stay over at the house. After dinner Mr. Durham asked me to fetch some notepaper from his study. When I got back to the drawing room I found he had gone out onto the terrace and was leaning against the rail rehearsing his acceptance speech. Very optimistic, I thought."

George looked over at them, anticipating an interruption, but they remained quiet, intent on what he was saying.

"Maurice, have you ever felt the need, for no reason at all, to pause suddenly in the middle of what you are doing?"

"With Alec, very frequently," joked Maurice with a laugh. "Seriously though, I once experienced what might be called the restraining hand of providence. Remarkable when I think back. It happened in the British Museum of all places. It was where Alec and I nearly came to blows – well, not exactly, but something or someone quietened our tempers, preventing what could have been an embarrassing situation. Certainly saved the day for us, and our future. Remember, Alec?"

Alec nodded and moved to pull Maurice closer to him.

"Well, that was one of those occasions," said George. "It was as if some force was restraining me. Sounds crazy, but that's how it was, and very fortunate too. My hand was actually on the handle of the outer door, yet I hesitated. Suddenly a shaft of light from the room reflected on someone in the garden, over near the hedge. I pressed my face close to the glazed panel and recognised you immediately, Maurice. I then noticed Clive lean over and begin talking to you. You must have moved, Maurice, for only your outline was now visible. Clive then went down the steps into the garden where darkness finally enveloped you both."

"I certainly didn't see you, George." exclaimed Maurice, "should probably have run away if I had," he said laughing.

George smiled. "I pulled back quickly and virtually ran downstairs to the dining room. Fortunately, it was unlit. As you probably remember, Maurice, the dining room has a bay, which sits further out into the garden. The luck of finding the window already open was a bonus. What a picture I must have presented with the upper part of my body hanging halfway out of the window. I was not the most dignified of people at that moment, I'm afraid, but I just didn't give a damn at the time," he said laughingly.

"I might mention that I am not in the habit of eavesdropping, contrary to what my behaviour might suggest, but ever since our interest and concern began over your relationship, a rare event in our calendar of experience, the dialogue between you and Clive was something I had to witness. The conversation between you, even though dulled by the night air, was plain enough. Your words, Maurice, were like music from a futuristic age. I could hardly believe what I was hearing. And, to my immense joy, Alec, still here!"

At this point George looked unhappy as he recalled also the sadness.

"Poor Clive. He returned to the terrace and stood, as if in a trance, looking towards where you had disappeared into the darkness. I saw his head sag heavily into his hands and his piteous plaintive cry echoed softly on the slight evening breeze.

It was one of those rare moments when I cried. I cried for you both."

George held this picture in his mind for a moment then quickly recovered.

"I was so sure the boathouse was your destination, Maurice, I wanted to help if I could, but knew instinctively that early morning would be a better time. I returned to my room and waited for daybreak. I was so sure that you would both be in the boathouse, and it turned out that I was right."

"My, my, George, what a grand story," exclaimed Maurice. "I am very grateful that it was you, George. Alec, we have been under surveillance, what do you say to that?"

Alec just smiled then nodded his head, as might a sage contented that the conclusion of events matched his prediction.

"Well, George," Maurice said after a brief pause, "simple though our aims now are, reality requires a bit of planning. I think a move to London is in our best interests right now, which means getting to the station."

"Hey! Not so fast, Maurice," interjected an alarmed Alec. "Don't I get a say?"

"Oh, yes, of course, but Alec, my dear love, you must know that we can't stay here in the boathouse. Apart from anything else Clive would not take kindly to finding us ensconced here, like a couple of gypsies – and at the height of his election campaign." Here Maurice chuckled at the thought.

"'Course not, I'm not asking that," said Alec, as if he were speaking the obvious, "but we could at least find a room at a lodging house somewhere, just so we can 'ave a bit o' time together before, well, before."

"Before facing the real world," finished Maurice. It was a careless remark, which he immediately regretted

"Maurice," shouted Alec, "that's bloody unfair."

"Please, please calm down, Alec," said Maurice alarmed, "I'm sorry, but just where do you suggest we go?"

In the silence that followed, George recalled a conversation with John the previous day. They had talked of the problems Alec would face in Argentina. They considered the depression which would undoubtedly fall on Maurice, and their fears of how he might respond to this second failure. Within a few hours, all had changed, dramatically. Knowing that John would agree, George said,

"Why not stay at our cottage, with John and me? It's only a suggestion, but there is a room for you both. And John, I can vouch, would also be delighted with your company."

Maurice, amazed yet delighted at the offer, was impatient to accept, but paused and turned his face towards Alec. Having been presumptuous earlier in taking the lead he knew that the decision must now come from Alec.

"What do you say, Alec?"

"I think 'tis a good idea. But are you sure? Are you really sure, George? I'm good around the 'ouse, enough for both Maurice and me. And I'll pay for what we eat, honestly." George laughed at this.

"Absolutely, Alec. You are both welcome to stay for as long as you like."

"That is terribly generous of you, George. If we can stay for a short while that would be of tremendous help. Give me a chance to catch up with this rogue!" he said looking at Alec with a loving smile.

"Thanks, George," said Alec warmly, "now I'm 'appy. 'Bout time I 'ad an 'oliday."

The satisfaction on their faces was ample reward in itself for George. He was cheered at the thought of their company.

"At least Alec and I can start our new life in the very right environment," said Maurice thoughtfully, "But I must go home today." He put up his hand as Alec began to object.

"It's alright, Alec, don't worry, I'll catch the midday train and return this evening. In the meantime, why don't you collect your things from home?"

"I've got all me 'things' as you call 'em, Maurice, with me. I was emigrating, remember? Me bag was with me when I went to the station to catch the train to Bristol." There was silence as they waited for Alec to continue. He suddenly remembered, and raced ahead.

"It was no good, Maurice, I couldn't go away. I'd known for a week or two that I 'ad to be with you. No choice really. Brother, 'e'll be mad as 'ell. But I tell you, Maurice, now that I had made up me mind finally, it was a real relief. I shouted your name, Maurice, out bloody loud, then I jumped up and down on the station platform, laughing and shouting. People looked at me as if I was barmy, but I didn't care, I went crazy, laughing and even crying, Maurice, as I watched the 'ol train steam out of the station. No, Maurice," continued Alec, now quite worked up, "I don't need to go anywhere, except with you. There's my bag," he said finally, pointing to a canvas bag tied up with rope that lay in the corner, "That's all I own except for you."

This demonstration of loyalty and love overwhelmed Maurice completely. It was the very strength of Alec's words that left him speechless, he felt dizzy with the potency of it all.

George looked on, experiencing untold pleasure in witnessing the beauty of this unique moment.

Chapter Three

Mrs. Hall had more talent in the world of wisdom than her children gave her credit for. Unfairly, timidity seemed to hitch itself to her reputation.

A year or so before her husband died she had accompanied him to Paris where they stayed for about a year. He had been sent over to oversee an agency associated with the League of Nations. After the Great War there were a great many displaced persons, many of them young and destitute. It was in this particular field and environment that her husband worked. She would accompany him on many of his tours into other countries and witnessed despair and depravation on a grand scale and in all its grotesque forms. She had seen young children in rags begging at the curb side, she had witnessed girls as well as boys and men importuning on the streets for the price of a meal. She had been horrified at the sight of crushed and disfigured men, women and children who had been injured because of the war or had suffered terrible brutality. She saw the result of man's inhumanity to man at first hand and became mellowed by the experience. It would remain with her forever for its imprint was now etched in her memory. Prior to this, her social world had been narrow, as had her education. Her judgements were now less jaundiced. Maurice, her son, had offered as prime suspects for the world's problems, politicians, rulers and clergy in that order. He was young, she thought, but had not completely discounted his views. At the moment her main concern was her daughter, Ada who was shortly to get married

During his boyhood and early adolescence Maurice had formed an abounding affection for his mother. It was said that she had considerably influenced the development of her children, but she had never over indulged any of them. Maurice viewed her as a late Victorian who had inherited some of the odd traits from that era. When he proposed this to her, she had laughed and replied that he had an awful lot to learn about life. He also knew that there had been some transformation following the carnage of the Great War and her subsequent experiences of the aftermath. During the last two years, or more precisely since he departed for Cambridge, Maurice had been somewhat neglectful of her and certainly less communicative. Of the reasons he was quite clear, yet it saddened him.

Maurice arrived home in the early afternoon. He walked into the entrance hall just as his mother was coming down the stairs. She looked flustered.

"Maurice, my dear," she said somewhat breathlessly but obviously pleased to see him, "I was hoping to see you earlier. We've had such an exciting morning. What with the fitting for Ada's wedding dress – the wedding is only a fortnight away you know. Most of the invitations have yet to be sent out. Which reminds me, Clive telephoned about eleven."

Maurice was suddenly alarmed. "What on earth can he want with me?" he muttered to himself.

"Sounded very strange, very strange indeed," said Mrs. Hall. "He kept repeating himself. Very odd. He wanted to know where you could be contacted. I was surprised as I thought you were staying with him at Penge. All I could suggest was that you were probably at your club in town. Where were you, dear?"

"Yes," replied Maurice not having heard the latter part of the conversation.

"Were you at your club?" she repeated.

"Yes, no," he said, raising his voice and becoming irritated.

"Really, Maurice! There is no need to speak to me in that tone of voice. I don't know what is coming over everyone. So very touchy these days. Must be the weather."

"I'm sorry, mother, but work has been hectic and, apart from that I have had so many other things on my mind, and," he continued somewhat gruffly, "Clive Durham is not one of them."

"Oh!" she exclaimed surprised.

"As Clive is such a close friend I thought you would want to know straight away. Apparently not," she said somewhat disappointed, "anyway," continued Mrs. Hall, "Clive asked you to telephone him. It sounded important. So now I have told you," she said rather dismissively.

Maurice did not reply.

"There is something else, Maurice, over which I am fraught with worry. Maurice!" she said raising her voice. "Are you listening?"

"Yes, Mother."

"It is about the wedding. Ada is being frightfully difficult over the arrangements. Have you fallen out with her recently?" Without waiting for Maurice to answer, she went on.

"I will, of course, expect you to give her away. I know that church is an anathema to you at the moment," she said as if it were an indisposition, which a Beecham's powder would quickly put right, "but that is not the problem." At this point Mrs. Hall gave a cough, a signal to call Maurice's attention to what she was saying.

"But Ada is so difficult and that's the trouble. She is saying, no insisting, that she doesn't want you to attend her. Her remarks on the subject were a little more coloured than that, which I did not like one bit. Always her father's favourite," she said as if that were a crime, "but even he would not have countenanced this."

Maurice's mother moved closer to him.

"I spoke to her about it just this morning and she still insists on going against my wishes. To refuse her own brother!" she said, aghast at the very idea.

Mrs. Hall was, mentally at least, continuously analysing the social effects of such an event without her son as escort. She was not overawed with society's decorative ideas and beliefs, and had not submerged her own ideas of what was right and wrong – that interval in France with her husband had extended her vision – but she lived in their world and with such a non-controversial issue as a wedding, and it being the first of her children, conformity with all its razzmatazz was what she asked for.

"Well, Maurice," she said becoming more agitated, her voice showing signs of wavering, "I can do without all this worry, and my friends will gossip – they always do! I have pleaded with her, begged her not to be so silly – so selfish. You will have to talk to her, Maurice and make her see how disgraceful it would be. 'How could you ever think of doing such a thing', I told her. You can imagine, Maurice what some of the guests will think."

Maurice listened, not in the least surprised at what his mother was saying.

"You must speak to her, Maurice," she repeated, "Tell her that it is her duty – as well as yours. She must be made to come to her senses. There must be no more of this nonsense." Mrs. Hall said finally, concluding that the matter was now finally resolved.

Maurice was not sure that he wanted to be involved with Ada just now, and especially in advising her on what her duties were. Knowing his sister as well as he did it was likely that she would, in the present circumstances, inform him of just where to take his advice. Ada's independent spirit made him smile, and in this flippant mood he asked, "Who then, might I enquire, has she asked to perambulate her up the aisle?" he said with a slight chuckle.

"Oh, Maurice, please don't make light of it. If you must know, she has already asked Dr Barry to perform the office. And to make matters even worse he has agreed!" she said astounded at the very idea.

"I have not seen him recently but, no doubt, he imagines that he has a duty to the memory of your dear father. He will, of course, understand when I tell him that you will be there to give her away, and that it was all a silly misunderstanding."

"I wouldn't be in too much of a hurry," said Maurice, then, "Old Barry, that touchy old hypocrite."

"Maurice," she said, seemingly shocked, "how can you talk that way? He has been so kind to the family since dear father died."

"I say that he is a narrow minded old quack who, if he weren't retired, should be struck off the register or whatever it is."

"Maurice," she cried in horror, "what on earth has happened to you? You have never spoken ill of him before."

"Only because I have been too polite, but not anymore. I simply do not like the man," he said decisively.

"However," Maurice went on, "I have absolutely no doubt that he is very happy to act the surrogate father bit, and Ada obviously desires it. So, good luck to them all, I say. Anyway, I shall not be there," Maurice said conclusively.

"What on earth is happening to this family?" Mrs. Hall began to weep. "What has happened to you, Maurice? You were so happy up at Cambridge. In going around with your friend Clive you seemed so settled," she said unaware of the significance of the remark.

"Now you appear so, so much older somehow, so unhappy, and for some reason at odds with everyone."

"Who on earth told you that?" Maurice asked sounding annoyed. He shrugs his shoulders. "It doesn't matter," he said with resignation in his voice.

"Oh, well" she said, dabbing her eyes on a small lace handkerchief.

Mrs. Hall looked over at her son, her instinct told a story of conflict or confusion yet she detected in his face an air of contentment, which made her instinct swing around. There was more behind that brow, she believed, than was evident to the eye. In a strange way he appeared different from the boy she had known a few years back. There was a maturity of a kind she could not quite comprehend. In trying to decide what it might be she went out of her depth. It disturbed her considerably. Eventually, she thought, he will tell me. Meantime and more immediately she had Ada on her mind. Her thoughts had routed her away. Now she turned quickly back to listen to Maurice.

"So the old devil wants to give her away – well let him. I have urgent business to attend to over the next couple of months anyway, and will be away most of that time. Dr Barry, the old rascal, is unwittingly doing us all a service."

"You mean that you will not be at your very own sister's wedding!" she burst out. "Oh, the shame, the disgrace, how will I bear it? And your friend Clive and his wife have been invited and are sure to be there. How will I face them? Look what you are doing to me." She was now crying openly.

Maurice was distressed to see her like this. He moved over and placed an arm over her shoulders.

"Mother, please Mother, don't cry. You will never really know, my dear, just how difficult life has been for me during the past couple of years."

"The business?" she said recovering slightly. "But I thought it was going so well."

"No, Mother, it has nothing whatsoever to do with the business. No, my troubles have been personal ones."

"A girl? A woman?" she quizzed.

"No," he said with a cautious smile.

"What then?" she insisted.

"As I said, Mother, it is personal."

"Oh come, Maurice, am I not your mother?" she said as she drew a small handkerchief from an invisible pocket and delicately traced her moist eyes.

"It is because you are my mother. And I love you."

Mrs. Hall gave a great sigh then smiled as she looked lovingly at Maurice.

Maurice considered carefully what he intended telling his mother.

"I have no intention of burdening you with details of some of the things that have happened to me over the past couple of months. Some of them, personal in the extreme, you would not approve of. In fact, I'm sure you wouldn't. Enough to say that I am happy with the way things now are."

"Maurice, I have absolutely no idea what you are talking about," she said sounding exasperated.

"Why do young people speak in such riddles these days? You confuse me. Surely we shall never reach a situation where you no longer believe that I can be trusted; to be sympathetic, whatever your problem might be. It is a mother's duty to share in the troubles of her children." She did not quite believe this yet at the same time wanted to find out the cause of his present reluctance to tell her more.

"Mother," continued Maurice patiently, "As you well know, even between parents there are always certain confidences, secrets if you will, which are never shared with their children, or for that matter with their friends. So is it with people the world over. There are sometimes issues which are far too sensitive to divulge to another, even to one's own mother. And it so happens that this is one of them. No, Mother, please don't press me on this," he said as she tried to interrupt.

"I will, however, tell you this much," he went on. "You must have noticed that I have been extremely unhappy during this past year. Miserably so," he emphasised.

"Yes, yes, my dear, I am not totally blind to what happens around me. Your happiness is all I ask for. I am so sorry, Maurice, that you have been so down," cried his mother, "perhaps I could have done more."

"No, Mother, it had nothing to do with you. It was of my own making. But I'm glad to say that the problems I had are now all behind me," he said relishing the relief which these words gave him.

"Looking back, Mother, it was similar to that of someone suffering from claustrophobia and being forced to live in some dark prison. My escape, if that is the phrase, has been caused by the most fantastic piece of good luck, fantastic in that it should have come my way. Words to describe the absolute joy it has given me are hard to find. But I can tell you this, Mother, it has charted my voyage in this life, forever."

"Good gracious," said his mother quite astonished. For one moment she began wondering just what this burst of exuberance could possibly mean. She shook her head as well as shrugging her shoulders, very pointedly showing her frustration at not knowing its cause. She took comfort in the fact that she would eventually win his confidence, she usually did.

With unconcealed excitement Maurice went on.

"It has taken me to new heights which I still find hard to believe. And all within the last few weeks! It is something I would like to enjoy with the whole world, yet even if that were possible, I would be reluctant to share even one jot."

With a frown on her face his mother asked.

"You're not becoming a Roman Catholic, are you?" she said warily.

Maurice laughed out loud. "No, Mother, it is much more sacred and realistic than that."

"Maurice! Don't blaspheme," she said appearing shocked. A disillusioning smile spoilt its effect. Then, after a pause, "Can't you tell me, Maurice?" she pleaded.

"No, mother. Now please let the matter rest," he said with authoritative finality.

Mrs. Hall's mind became unusually active as it played with the usual options before finally coming down on the side of some obscure-ism for which she felt he had developed a passion.

"I am leaving this afternoon and shall probably not be home for a week or two. I had better pack a suitcase. No, I think a trunk would be better. I shall send for it in a day or two."

"Will you being staying with Clive?"

"No, Mother, I will not," he said. "I shall be staying with friends in the country."

"Oh," remarked his mother, with a feeling of rejection, "and is that also a secret?"

Maurice smiled. "No, my dear, it is not. At the moment I am not sure of their address myself. I shall write to you tomorrow, after I arrive there."

Maurice walked over to his mother and kissed her lightly on the cheek. All at once he felt close to her; it was an emotion reminiscent of his childhood. His mature emotions lay in the direction of his heart, which now belonged to Alec. There also rested his first priority.

"All this mystery," she said, now smiling. "Youth must have its secrets I suppose, otherwise they might think their lives dull or mundane."

"Something like that, Mother," Maurice said, laughing and giving her a hug.

Chapter Four

Maurice was now in his bedroom. A large heavy trunk had been brought up from the basement and now sat, rather precariously, on a couple of low stools in front of his dressing table. Its lid, bearing many exotic labels from various countries around the world, was held open by two supporting chains.

Having returned from the other side of the room where he had collected two suits from the wardrobe, he was just in the process of placing them into the trunk when he heard the voice of his sister Ada. She was talking with his mother. Next came the sound of her light feet climbing the stairs. The door to his room was partly open. He did not stop or turn but when he stood up from the trunk and peered into the dressing mirror he saw, reflected there, his sister looking directly across at him. She had not actually entered the room, but instead stood hesitatingly in the doorway.

He had not seen Ada for several months. For one thing he had been spending a lot of his time either at Clive's or at his club in town. It was also obvious to Maurice that of late she had made an even more determined effort to avoid him whenever possible. Her appearance now may have something to do with her impending marriage to Arthur. But perhaps, thought Maurice hopefully, she brings the olive branch of peace.

Maurice was well aware that he had once, out of jealousy and the fear of losing Clive, been grossly unfair to her. He remembered the evening very clearly. He had, falsely as it turned out, accused her of actively supporting a liaison with Clive. Although it had all happened some time ago the memory of that night still rankled with her, as well it might. Maurice, however, could still not understand why she had not forgiven him. Time had not dimmed his recollection of the event, nor apparently, hers.

On the day of this violent disagreement with Ada, his concern and possessiveness over Clive had reached a pitch, as had Clive's determination to prevent it. Now that he was able to look back more dispassionately, he realised how unreasonable he had been.

It had all begun with the sudden realisation that his relationship with Clive was on the brink of some almighty disaster. He had looked desperately for anyone on whom to vent his frustration. Unfortunately, and unfairly, Ada looked a suitable candidate. His verbal onslaught was as one demented. In his passion he accused her of flirting with Clive, of ruining their friendship. The hurt caused by this outburst was so great at the time that she had been unable to offer little in her own defence. She had rushed from the room in tears. From then on Ada treated him as a stranger, leaving him in no doubt as to her extreme anger at what she had been accused of.

Since then very little water had swept under the bridge of reconciliation and, now, Ada was soon to be married to Arthur, an old acquaintance of both Clive and Maurice. Until now Ada had been firm in her refusal to discuss their row over Clive, let alone accept Maurice's apologies. Her distress had been considerable.

'Well, at least she looks friendly enough,' thought Maurice. The last time their paths had crossed no words had been exchanged. In fact, since then, neither had so much as acknowledged the other.

'Maybe the omens are good!' Maurice thought.

As Ada had entered his territory, as it were, he felt it was an invitation to speak. Her face did not show the old sparkle, which he had always associated with it.

"How are you, Ada?" he said as pleasantly as he dared. He was not anticipating any great improvement in their cordiality.

"Quite well, thank you, Maurice."

The tone of her voice lacked enthusiasm yet it was apparent that she had something further to say.

"More than that, actually," she went on, "for one could say that I have every reason to be very contented with my life. The only blight is you and even that is now of no great consequence."

Maurice could hardly equate her contentment with the present look on her face. It probably reflected her bitter feeling towards him. Seeing him again had probably brought it all back.

"Arthur," she continued "is, as you know, to marry me shortly. I understand from mother that you approve." Before Maurice could answer she hurried on.

"Well, Maurice, let me tell you that I really don't give a tinker's curse whether you approve or not, for it will make no difference to me at all."

"Heavens," said Maurice somewhat disappointed, "I would have thought that by now we might have got over our misunderstanding."

"It was not a misunderstanding at all," she replied curtly.

"Ada, please believe me when I say that I am happy, very happy indeed, that love has drawn you and Arthur together. Arthur I like immensely, as you already know."

"Do you," pondered Ada for a moment, "I wonder? Love, well, we have never spoken much on the subject, Maurice, except when Clive made such a fiasco at entering the matrimonial stakes."

Maurice winced.

"You probably did me a favour, Maurice, by upsetting that particular melodrama, or at least my very small and innocent part in it."

"Ada, I have apologised on so many occasions, surely I am in purgatory long enough, or is there some pleasure you derive from my discomfort?"

"No, Maurice, I do not. You are yet my brother, Maurice, but I have not forgiven you for the harm you did me."

"Then there is little to be said," he replied rather sulkily. Immediately he decided that he was being unfair and changing the temper of his voice, went on, "Except that I am sorry, Ada, for what has passed. That we part, with you still harbouring ill feelings is, for me, sad."

Ada did not respond.

"I understand from Mother that after the wedding, you and Arthur will be moving to a house in Tunbridge. In the circumstances it would perhaps be better for me to keep out of your way 'til then." He looked over at Ada but there was still no sign of interest.

"I am, in any event, leaving within the hour. But I give you my word, Ada," he said with emphasis yet with noticeable grief in his voice, "that I will not make any attempt to return to this house again until after the wedding. Mother has already made clear your wishes regarding the wedding. I can understand you not wanting me to be anywhere near you or the church. You must do whatever suits you both."

"You make it all sound so simple, Maurice," she said, her voice softening without her consciously intending it to.

"You really do not understand me, do you? Or have you just forgotten? As children, and even when we grew up, we lived pretty happily here, under the same roof, in fact there were some wonderful times, and yet, and yet, now," she said with growing emotion, "intimacy between us is as far removed as that of distant cousins."

Maurice stared at her for a moment.

"I have often been told, especially by my girl friends, that closeness between brother and sister is rare. I used to believe otherwise, that we were different, Maurice." Maurice continued to listen.

"Why," she said defiantly, her voice gaining strength and demanding attention, "because of the difference in sex, does there have to be such a lot of barriers between men and women? Makes it seem like a gender war, which in reality I suppose it is."

Maurice shook his head wondering where all this was leading.

"Why," continued Ada, "does society, or at least that in this country, persist in imposing different values for woman and, where there is opposition, treat us like whores of the street?"

"My, my," began Maurice. Ada pretended not to hear.

"Sadly for many women," she went on, now quiet calm, "the profession of the street is the only one on offer."

Maurice stood spellbound at Ada's outburst, waiting a chance to make some comment and at the same time wondering what it all had to do with their original quarrel.

Ada looked over at Maurice for a moment, then, "I really get angry when I consider who the authors are of most of the so called moral principles enshrined in our laws and customs. Yes, of course, Maurice, it is the men, few of whom have any scruples or principles whatsoever. Am I boring you, Maurice?" Ada said with a slight smile, said also with a touch of sarcasm to express her continued displeasure with him. "Hate is so decisive a term, yet it so nearly expresses what I have felt towards you. But my purpose here is to dispel any ideas you may have concerning my wedding. Mother cannot understand." It was at this point that she turned to leave having completed the purpose of her visit.

"Please, please Ada, do not leave," begged Maurice, "I am honestly distraught at what has passed, there can be no-one more contrite than I, but the views you were expressing a moment ago really interest me."

"Well," came the indecisive reply, though Maurice did not miss the softening tone in her voice, "I'm not sure."

"Please," pleaded Maurice," do stay a little longer, Ada, I really am interested in what you were saying."

"Well, perhaps," she said giving way, "but don't imagine that I have forgotten the purpose of my coming here."

"I won't, I promise." he said quietly yet hoping this was the beginning of the end of their separation.

"Yes, well, oh yes," she began, "well, only the other day, at a Pankhurst Humanist meeting." She saw a sudden look of surprise on Maurice's face. "Yes, Maurice, the same, the suffragettes. The discussion concerned the ineptitude of some of those from the stronger sex, men!" Ada smiles, gives a chuckle, then goes on.

"A number of us were already aware of the stinking hypocrisy of many of them. The politicians who have the audacity to enact laws on morality, business men occupying the best seats in the 'synagogue', bishops and clergy offering gifts from the altar, judges, tongue in cheek, offering moral judgements; Oh, I could go on, the list of villains is endless. It did not take much imagination to understand how women, in low circumstances particularly, fare so badly and are so easily exploited."

"You express strong views, Ada," Maurice said gently.

"'Tis common knowledge that some of these b... bastards, in their clubs, revel in recounting their most recent 'conquests'. I tell you, Maurice," she said in a voice now resounding with bitterness, "there is more honesty in a single whore's existence than in the lives of many of these upper class bigots.

Ada paused to regain her breath then, now safely in her stride, raced ahead.

"But times are changing, Maurice, you mark my words. Revolution is in the air. Feminists out there, writers and so on, are beginning a revolt against these injustices," she said, sweeping her hands as if encompassing the whole universe. "Writers, such as George Eliot from the Victorian past, give impetus for change. There are of course men, as well as women, involved in this fight for changes in our society."

"Ada, I have never ever heard you talk in this way before," commented Maurice, amazed at her enthusiasm.

"Maybe not, Maurice. And your behaviour towards me when you were confronted with a situation not to your liking followed a similar pattern, one of commanding authoritarianism where the wrong done just had to be that of the woman." Ada was still angry when focusing on the memories of that day. She now put them to one side wishing to continue with her freewheeling thoughts on democracy.

"I plead guilty, my dear," said Maurice in a subdued voice.

"Everywhere you look there are examples of their most callous behaviour. Go back thirty or so years and study some of the Victorian painters, for example. You discover illustrated examples of man's bestiality. Women often portrayed either as pretty things, empty headed and 'righteous', offering no threat to those dominant scoundrels, or alternatively as fallen women, displayed in finite misery; the painters tribute to their fate for flouting the rules of man. The old queen, Victoria, during her lifetime never once lifted a finger to promote the cause of her own sex. Well-read she may have been but well-intentioned, never." She said with emphasis.

By this time Maurice was flabbergasted by Ada's continuing diatribe.

"Maurice," Ada said, sounding exasperated, "it is to my eternal sorrow that these revolting attitudes prevail. I am not Victorian, thank God! And I will not accept their dreadful double standards of morality."

By this time she had become quite exhausted, but by no means finished. She paused but briefly, not intending that Maurice should disrupt the flow of ideas reaching for expression. This may be her last chance to inform him of her mind. He just looked at her, amazed, not only at her views but also at the vehement way in which she expressed them.

"And I am pleased to say," she went on, "that my contemporaries are not all, of necessity, virgins. Necessity has a different meaning to them!" She said intending to shock.

"My God, Ada," said Maurice, surprised yet somewhat bemused, "talk like that to Arthur and you'll have another problem on your hands."

"You think so do you, well, that's where you are quite wrong. It may interest you to know that he largely shares my views. In fact, I am thinking of joining Pankhurst's suffragettes, somewhat late in the day I know but better late than never – and, my dear Maurice," she said, using an old familiar term, "with Arthur's full support," she said fiercely.

They had both ventured a long away from the original discussion, which, Ada had intended, would ensure that the gulf between them remained.

"I am very impressed, Ada, honestly."

Maurice was indeed impressed, overwhelmed in fact, by Ada's unexpected yet forthright views.

"I view the imposition of morals as a questionable pursuit, particularly when offered by undemocratic institutions, such as Parliament. I believe we must be our own judge of what is morally right or wrong. Although the thought will appal you, my dear, we are closer than you might imagine, Ada."

Ada moved into the bedroom. She looked across at Maurice. It pleased her that he had not interrupted until now.

"I also share your concerns, Ada. The perpetual encouragement for social inequality and oppression is a grim reality in undemocratic countries, as ours. As for the church, which, incidentally, you didn't specifically mention, all humbug," he said emphatically, "but there, you already know my views on that subject." Maurice shook his head as if to confirm this indictment.

"As for the rest of this wicked world, well humanity lives on and on and on and we can but grovel around with the rest trying to find a bit of happiness here and there," he said sadly.

"We are somewhat fortunate, Ada. We can propagate with purpose and energy all of our liberated views while trying to contain that horror called conventionality. We have enjoyed a privileged education; inherited an adequate purse, so, barring accidents, those of us so favoured will be able to survive better than the unfortunate multitude of poor bastards in this world!" Maurice said vehemently and raising his voice.

Ada looked towards Maurice, her frown having disappeared. She now favoured the way he spoke. It had not been her intention to allow a relaxation in her attitude towards him, but something had happened to him, which alerted her to find out more. Her pride had inclined towards not allowing this to happen. At least that is how it had been until this moment.

Now, she was puzzled, uncertain. He looked different somehow. The lines of worry that seemed to have developed during the past couple of years were now mere shadows. His manner had softened. He had listened to her as if eager to share in her development. She suddenly recalled their days as children, of the many carefree moments, the constant laughter. This recollection amended her mood, causing her so say, quite spontaneously, "Maurice, I think for once in a very long time I get to know you better. Is it possible that you improve on knowing?" she said with a sudden smile.

He looked towards her, somewhat uncertain of how to proceed. Her voice; what she had said; her final unexpected smile; all of these made for a changing atmosphere and began to remove shadows which now permitted his love to shine through.

"Ada, my dear," he said affectionately, "It all depends on what you get to know."

Choosing his words carefully, he went on.

"Do not jump too hastily, Ada, for I can be cussed at times. A little socialism may make me appear more tolerable, but my dear," Maurice pauses, fearful of giving too much away. "I fear for you to know too much about me. Unjustifiable prejudice comes cheap and like a virus can infect anyone, and there are certain facts about my life which might easily destroy what affection you have for me." Maurice pauses again, wondering if Ada had any idea of what he was talking about.

"If you have any affection for me, Ada, and it is probably presumptuous of me to assume that you have, then knowing me somewhat more than you do could change all of that. It could turn affection into distaste and possibly disgust. I can talk freely on most things, Ada, but there is one on which I must keep my own council. Uncovering one's soul, even to those nearest to you could leave one vulnerable and risk rejection, and I would hate that." Here Maurice stops for a moment, then in a voice strong with passion.

"Prejudice invariable results in violence or hurt to the subject. These are words, just words, Ada, but I must be cautious."

"My dear Maurice," Ada suddenly whispered, "if mother were to hear us now she might seriously seek religious guidance on how to redeem her offspring, or at least to bring them back into that spiritual fold you so abhor."

With this Ada's eyes began to light up, and she burst, unexpectedly, into laughter. This in spite of her earlier resolution!

"Against all that I vowed to myself, Maurice, I have allowed you to occupy my thoughts again. In truth I am happy that this has happened. From what you have just said, Maurice, I detect something which is not quite straightforward, a mystery in fact." Here she frowned. "It is a mystery which I could not hope to fathom, one which yet appears to isolate us," she said looking serious once again.

"I hear great anxiety in your voice, Maurice. Perhaps if I get nearer to you, to understand you better, it may provide more fertile ground. God knows I have untangled a lot about my own mixed up self, Maurice, so what say I vex you with a few questions? Who knows, they may untangle some of yours. Or will it upset you?"

"No, why should it, Ada?" Maurice replied though he feared even a mild inquisition.

"Well," continued Ada, now more solemnly, "before I begin I must tell you at once how I felt before this discussion. It is important for me to clear the air once and for all." Ada paused, and then looking directly at Maurice, began.

"I felt devastated when you accused me of interfering and spoiling your friendship with Clive – something which in itself was so intense as to mobilise my thoughts, which incidentally came to no conclusion. It is fair to say, though now somewhat irrelevant, that at the time I might have reciprocated any approach Clive made. But as you know, Maurice, Clive made none, then or ever, though you would not believe it at the time.

You proceeded to judge me most harshly, perhaps you now realise just how badly you behaved. Even now I cannot understand the depth of a friendship which would provoke such a reaction as yours. Anyway, the distress I experienced at the time was profound and my anger extreme. At the time, it seriously affected the deep affection I had held for you all my life."

"Ada," said Maurice, "oh, Ada, it is all so bloody," he said, his voice breaking. "If only I were able to completely explain, but it is just not possible."

She looked at him in silence for several moments, then went on.

"In this last year, Maurice, I have also grown significantly in understanding. I suppose I have Arthur partly to thank for that. He brought his intellect to bear on this rather stunted tree that he has promised to nurture."

"You do yourself an injustice," Maurice said with considerable conviction.

"Maybe, Maurice, who knows. What matters in the end, however, is whether one's conscience can live with one's conduct. Judgement is a treacherous field for it can support prejudices, in laws and actions, which contain no force in honesty or reason. The important thing for me is to direct my censure on those who directly or indirectly impose pain and suffering on others."

"You have certainly developed a rare outlook on this tragedy of life," commented Maurice, proud of his sister's compassionate outlook.

"Why do you say tragedy, Maurice? I look forward to my partnership with Arthur. There will be limitations, intellectual ones mainly, but there's the challenge. There will be obstacles, people mainly, but one steers a course to avoid them. I may not be much of a navigator just now but, by God, watch me try."

"Where do you get all this verve?"

"It has been there all along. Arthur has pricked the shell and I am experiencing a new birth, you might say."

"Sounds grand," said Maurice feeling more at ease with his sister than at the beginning of this unusual discourse. "I thought I detected an imposing influence somewhere along the line." Lowering his voice, he asked, "Are you really as one with Arthur?"

"Maurice," laughed Ada, "I thought that I was supposed to be asking the questions.

"Arthur, bless him," she said with feeling.

"I wasn't at first, Maurice, even though Arthur had been paying calls on us for some time. We got on very well together, as friends. Then it became clear, even to innocent me," she said with a chuckle, "that his affections were much stronger than that of just a friend. He proclaimed his love for me. Just before that, Maurice, you and I had that frightful... well, that's all over now," Ada said with a finality which pleased him.

"Well," she went on, "one day soon after that, Arthur called unexpectedly. Mother, if I remember correctly, was out – I think she was down at the Deer-Smyth's. Arthur was so shy, bless him. I knew before he spoke what he intended asking. It was quite comical in a way though I would not have dreamt of laughing. That would have been so unkind. I was certainly unsure of what I wanted. Then again my mind was in a pretty confused state. Mad? No, Maurice, not mad – except with you. So I said yes, I would marry him.

"Afterwards I was angry with myself for responding so quickly. It is true that I was fond of him, but to be his wife! Even now I don't remember anything clearly and have to rely on Arthur for revisiting that particular scenario. One thing stands clearly in my mind, that of Arthur clasping my hands in his, then, oh, so like Arthur, so gallant and courteous, kissing them. He did blush so, as if caught in some unseemly act.

"Over time I grew to know him better, and the more time we shared together, the more thoughts we exchanged, the greater our affinity. Finally I instinctively knew that our life together was 'well writ' as the saying goes. I fell in love with him more and more and the old blinkers of my life fell away.

"Independence, in thoughts and ideas, was no longer a one sided luxury. We began as equal and, we believe, civilised parties to a debate. Sharing as well as examining and questioning each other's ideas and values. So you see, Maurice, the answer to your question is very much a 'yes', oh such a big yes."

"You make me feel very humble, Ada my dear. Your arrival at this plateau of happiness pleases me much more than I can say."

Ada looked over at Maurice, her heart captured once again.

"And you, Maurice," she said gently, "now quiet and secretive in your enclosed shell. The once volatile boy who was in love with the world. One who dared to defy the deity at Cambridge. To the near exclusion of all others, one who appeared to contribute so much to a single friendship." Here she paused. "That in itself is a conundrum which Arthur and I have pondered over time and time again." At this Maurice became fearful lest Ada pursued the point. Ada continued, "The violence shown at one particular time and over one particular issue must have had its origin somewhere, for there is a reason for everything. Arthur believed he could hazard a guess but said it was unfair to mention it as it was merely an idea."

Maurice was horrified at the thought of what Arthur might have conjectured.

"Good Lord, Ada, was I so utterly beastly, so utterly selfish?"

"On one occasion, yes, but generally, no. It's just, well," here Ada hesitated, "well, Maurice, in one respect your concentration, shall we say, has traced a very narrow path, at least that's how it has seemed to me. I have to accept that my 'rebirth', as Arthur calls it, was initiated by him, well and truly." Here Ada consented to laugh quite unashamedly, "Having time on my side also enabled me to delve into many courses and causes. You would be surprised at some of them. Amazingly, you have occupied a lot of my time, Maurice, though a moment or two ago I would not have admitted it."

"Was it worth it?" Maurice asked hopefully.

"Now, yes, I'm sure it is. As I said, there are reasons and meanings in everything, though I don't always like to admit it, or at least I don't always immediately like what I see – then until I really see I must be considered blind. Ignorance can be a blight. The essence of understanding is in listening and learning. Not I hasten to add, to jaundiced views, but to those who seriously wish to understand human behaviour, in all its facets."

Maurice remained silent for some moments. He could see Ada watching for his reaction, could see her looking for some identification of what was bothering him. This close scrutiny made him nervous, it was as if she were stripping him of the silent guard of secrecy, which protected him.

"And what do you see with me? A selfish, unkind, self-opinionated..."

"No, no, Maurice," she insisted firmly. "Your soul is displayed enough for me to think otherwise. There is also something about you now that makes me inclined to believe that you also have reached the tranquillity most of us search for."

"Inclined! Now there's a word. Well, yes, Ada what you say is so, though the very nature of my tranquillity is not one which I would dare to broadcast, even though its cause I will always treasure." Maurice suddenly realised the danger of pursuing this line and quickly changed the subject.

"Are you still 'inclined' for Dr Barry to give you away?" he said with a laugh.

"If you really don't mind, Maurice. I would rather not upset him."

Ada quickly continued. "But you don't get away that lightly, Maurice. May I not know what it is that you treasure so much yet cannot speak of."

"No, Ada, I think 'tis best you do not know. I say this only because I am sensitive of your feelings. We are friends once again and I want it to remain so."

"Maurice, I cannot conceive you purposely doing anything harmful or wrong."

"Ada, my dear," he said affectionately, "all could so easily be undone if I were to tell you. No, no," he persisted when his sister attempted to speak, "it is much better that we remember this moment, ending in happiness and reconciliation."

Ada, who until then had been resting against the wall just inside the door, walked across the room to Maurice who was still leaning on the half-filled trunk. She stood just shoulder high to him. She stared up at him for a moment then put her arm through his. "We've not done this for a very long time, Maurice, and it's now overdue."

Maurice now felt totally helpless following this sudden contact. He feared that his resolution would falter. He smiled wanly at Ada, knowing more was to come, and knew that he was so emotionally charged that he would be unable to resist her.

"I do hope, Maurice, that you will not become isolated from us. For all our differences in the past I would hate to lose you. Do not underrate my intellect and capacity for understanding. I have subjected the contents of my cranium," here she gave a chuckle, which also made her brother smile at the expression, "to the most express course in the humanities – thanks to Arthur. And although I leave you without knowing more, I am no fool. Do not shut me out of your life because you think I am timid in understanding. Promise to test me."

As Maurice silently studied her face in that brief moment he knew that he could not hold out against her for long. Was this the frail creature he thought he had left in limbo a few years back? No one else had changed, yet Ada had a confidence quite new to him. How fast the world was changing about him. Should he tell her? That was the big question. She may hate me after this. Would she understand? Was Arthur's guess on the mark? He pondered for a moment then concluded that at the very worst she may never want to see him again though that somehow didn't ring true. But then, maybe, 'oh, to hell with it, I'll take a chance,' he thought to himself. What had he to lose?

"Alright, Ada," he said briskly, "you want the truth, for which you're willing to be shocked and, no doubt, horrified. Damn it all, why shouldn't you know? You are, I believe, the one in the family who might just understand. Well, my dear," he said, proudly raising his chin, "I have nothing to be ashamed of and everything to be pleased about. In the beginning it was, for me, one of the hardest things in my life to have to come to terms with. The prejudice and hate we spoke of earlier would feed rabidly on its knowledge. But for me it is all terribly simple, one of nature's spawning variations. I am in love, too."

Ada looked at him quizzically, somewhat fearfully, knowing that he had not completed what he had to tell her.

"I have no doubt that Arthur guessed my problem. Badly put, Ada, for it is not a problem. No, predisposition would be more accurate. Yes, my dear sister, I am in love, and…" here he paused, then, lest his courage desert him, went swiftly on.

"Yes, Ada, in love, and with another man."

He looked up quickly, expecting to see a frozen or agonised face. But his eyes recorded a different picture. There was the dignified human countenance of his sister Ada, a single tear welling up in the corner of one of her beautiful cornflower blue eyes.

Neither spoke for several minutes. During this time Ada made a quick review of events leading up to their original quarrel and the light of understanding began immediately to dawn on her.

"I am shocked, surprised," she began, at which Maurice covered his face with both hands, "No, no, Maurice, let me finish, I am also pleased, my dear," she said after considering what he had told her. "That it is indeed a surprise, I have to admit. I shall speak severely to Arthur for keeping me in the dark." Here she gave a small laugh. "I know little about such arrangements but then I am just at the beginning of my battle with the humanities. My dear, dear Maurice, don't look so glum." With that she took his hand in hers. "Now, where do I begin? I have read some of the classics including Grecian history not to be totally unaware of such things. There is very little said, or read for that matter, on the subject. One hears occasionally unpleasant people saying unpleasant things but then that is always the case where lack of knowledge prevails." At this point Ada gained strength in her determination to show support for her brother. She had set her pitch on the path to understanding, on a path to avoid contagion from the hypocrite. She turned towards him.

"Now understand this, Maurice; to me, you are my brother, my dear, dear brother and I love you all the more for being so terribly brave in confiding in me as you have. To me, my dear, your happiness is all. As I said previously, Maurice, and I believe it fervently, my censure is restricted to those who inflict pain and suffering on others. Now, if I dare to use an expression of my own choosing, my dear Maurice, then you have my blessing.

"Now, after all that, where is he? And who is he? I know it can't be Clive, not any more anyway, although I now believe it could have been. Maurice, you know that you have my trust, but I must know more, my dear."

"Ada," began Maurice, "It is a long and torturous story hellishly long and hellishly torturous. It began during my first month at Cambridge, when I first met Clive. If you insist I will give you a brief outline of the various twists and turns that my journey took."

"Maurice, I need to know, I need to understand and perhaps, I need to forgive. Please, my dear brother, tell me just what happened," she said kindly. Maurice closed the lid of the trunk and Ada sat down on it waiting for Maurice to begin. Maurice began the long saga, beginning with the discovery through Clive of his homosexuality, until finally meeting up with Alec. He described accurately Alec's social position. He made no excuses for him nor did he patronize or demean him in any way. By the time Maurice had finished telling his tale Ada had a good measure of the strength of feeling between Maurice and his friend. She recognised the difficulties he would encounter along the way, but again, with the stubbornness of a Hall, swore she would do her very utmost to promote and defend their relationship.

"My, my, Maurice, and I thought I had been to hell and back. You deserved my sympathy earlier, then how could I have known. This is also a new beginning for me, you know, my dear."

They both heard their mother calling from the hall below. "Ada, Ada, where are you?"

"I had better go down," said Ada, "but remember this, Maurice. I love you all the more for confiding in me." Speaking with confidence and complete honesty, Ada went on, "I am anxious for your happiness, and, more to the point, if your love for another man achieves that end, then that, Maurice, makes me happy as well.

"I do hope that you will introduce me to him, Maurice, and soon. Once again, please don't stay out of reach – either of you – ever."

With that she reached up and kissed him, and before he had time to recover she was passing through the door calling, "coming, mother, coming." He wept for a few moments, he wept for the intensity of compassion she had shown.

Chapter Five

On the train to the City, Maurice had time to reflect on the outcome of his exchange with Ada. Before he arrived home he had not given thought to the consequences of meeting his sister. He assumed that she would avoid him as she had previously. It was the immediacy of Ada's wedding and his mother's supposed problems with the 'giving away' rite that ended with him having a surprising dialogue with his sister. Least of all did he contemplate reconciliation. The sustained honesty throughout their conversation had come as a great relief. Right from the beginning, her forthright views on virtually all they had discussed reflected such a difference from what he had expected. The renewal of their mutual affection, declared so unambiguously by Ada, then the intimacy of her arm through his. It was perhaps the psychological moment which allowed his courage to overcome reticence, to tell her of his love for Alec. He expected her to respond differently, sympathetic but with misgivings. In the event she surpassed even his expectations. It was the manner in which she expressed herself that drew them so much closer together.

He experienced a few doubts about revealing his homosexuality in the way he had, but they occupied no permanence. "No", he said speaking aloud to himself. "I must never associate deviousness with Ada, ever."

In thinking on about their meeting he recalled again how straight Ada had been, pulling no punches yet being fair. He could but admit that that had always been a quality in Ada. 'A rarity today,' he thought. Once the ground had been swept clear of past misunderstandings, she had never once tinkered with the truth in order to obtain his confidence on other matters, though at the time he thought she might, which now, looking back, made him feel ashamed.

Moments of concern attached to whether she would keep his 'secret' to herself. That she would discuss it with Arthur he had no doubt at all, and somehow that pleased him. In a strange way he felt their new closeness would protect him. It was a funny sensation knowing that he had bared his soul in this way, but who better than to his sister Ada? Well, not exactly bared, but at least shown the skeleton! Ada, he instinctively knew would, from now on, provide an ally with whom to contain the family.

Maurice spent the rest of the afternoon in his office. A lot of the time was spent talking to his business colleagues, discussing and answering questions relating to the business of stocks and shares. Having made the necessary arrangements for a planned absence from his office, he caught the train west, to Clive country.

His departure from the City had been delayed and, unfortunately, he missed catching the earlier train.

It was late afternoon. As he slouched into the back of his seat in the first class carriage, he felt totally at peace with the world. It was a sensation, which had been absent for some time. With little effort he glanced out at the changing landscape.

At this time of the year the sky shook off the sun much earlier and darkness seemed to descend more quickly. He wished the train had wings to speed the journey; such was his eagerness to get to Alec. After only a short while he witnessed what seemed to be a rapid sunset. One moment he was admiring the circle of scarlet hovering just above the distant horizon, and then, as if a lantern slide had gone out of focus, it became worn and woolly, changing from one shade to another – gone now the vivid flame orange. Then the last segment disappeared. Nature's magic suddenly, or so it appeared, turned all to blackness, swiftly obliterating the dim outlines of the passing fields and trees.

Maurice cursed because it was a slow train. It stopped interminably, usually at semi-lit stations, which appeared to be completely deserted. Ghost stations, he reflected with a shudder. His impatience was ever invisible to the driver and his fireman as the train chugged along, ratity, ratity, ratity, over invisible joints of the endless rails. Maurice got up to stretch. Then he lowered the window to look out. Using a hand to shield his eyes from the black specks flying dangerously past, he glanced upward. There he observed a continuous plume of light grey smoke and steam, carrying red cinder sparks in its wraithlike shape. It floated past the moving train, as silent as the night. There in the distance he saw the lights of another station, not very bright but giving promise. He heard the rushing of steam as the brakes were applied and felt the train gradually reduce speed. To the sound of colliding buffers, the carriages eventually inclined to stop. He had arrived.

George had given him written directions to the cottage and he now prayed that the one cab, which served the village, would be available to carry him there.

He was the sole passenger on the platform. From beneath an oil fired lamp spluttering in the night air, a lone station attendant took his ticket. "Good night, Sir," he said.

"Good night," Maurice replied and walked through the booking hall and into the world outside which began with a cobbled lane. Moving from the dim yellow light of the station into the pitch darkness outside, made for momentary blindness. "Hell," he muttered to himself. There was no cab. All he could see was a horse and dray standing on the opposite side of the path.

A touch and at once Alec was breathing on his face. In the darkness they fell into an embrace.

"I've met every blooming train since five o'clock. I knew you would be along some time this evening but I got worried as I always do with you. Anyway, now you're here. Come on, Maurice, give me your bag and let's get off to George's."

Alec could not see the passenger beside him but the feel of his body close and the touch of his hand heightened Alec's sensitivity and the expectations he knew were assured. They drove through the night with the small carriage lights grumbling a tune in their rigid metal holders. The single experience of this quiet and lonely drive brought a realisation that this, yes, this, was the very watershed of their lives. Now they really were on their own, together as one, in a marriage both natural and unsullied by forged contrivances.

"Bloody bumpy, isn't it, Maurice? Still, don't worry, I'll be making it much bumpier for you later on." Alec grinned to himself for he had the future of the night before him and for the moment that meant all.

Maurice was hanging on to Alec both for safety and by choice. Alec handled the horse well. They were both laughing, intoxicated by the freedom that had descended upon them in their getaway chariot to the heavens.

"God, Alec. How did all this happen? It's beyond belief, it really is. To think you might be half way across the Atlantic on your way to some godforsaken spot in Argentina. And I, who knows? In sheer desperation and fear I might even have considered an alternative, not, I might add, matrimony – a la Clive. Perish the thought."

"Just as well I come along then."

Ahead of them a solitary light shone in isolation.

"That's George's place," said Alec brightly.

They drew up outside George and John's small cottage. Standing outside to welcome them was John, George's partner, lover, whatever, a tall handsome man whose dark hair, even in the dim light, showed highlights of grey at the temples. Light shining through the open door helped to illuminate the small courtyard. John moved quickly forward to take the case, which Alec handed down. Then, with a broad smile, turned to offer a helping as well as welcoming hand to Maurice.

"Welcome to our modest abode, Maurice. Not exactly San Moritz but in this climate it's cosy and warm. By the way, the name's John. That's the formalities bit over, now please do come inside where it's warmer. Alec has just taken the horse to the paddock round the back, he won't be more than a few minutes."

The ease with which John approached him, pleased Maurice no end and made him feel immediately relaxed. It was as if he had known him for a long time. The fire had been stoked up and the roaring flames, as they flickered towards the blackened chimney, added further charm to the room. The flames gleamed their reflections onto the beamed walls and ceiling. This added to the inviting homeliness of the whole room. Maurice felt he and Alec had finally come home.

George had taken Alec home earlier, after Maurice departed for the station. John had the responsibility of looking after him until the others returned. Although used to a more coordinated audience, John nevertheless found the experience of talking with Alec very rewarding. He spoke to Alec with perhaps a little more care, for in George's words, Alec needed coaxing into a universe somewhat foreign to him. The climate was totally relaxed, nothing pretentious, nothing forced.

During the next hour, after a prepared supper, Maurice learned that John and George had been together for some twenty years. It turned out that John was an archaeologist.

It was not a time for intensive debate on the subject of archaeology but Maurice saw its possibility for a later date. It surprised Maurice to learn that apart from his time abroad on fieldwork, John also spent part of his time lecturing at university, and by coincidence, Cambridge. He would have been there when Maurice and Clive were in residence.

"A turn up for the books, eh, Maurice?" said Alec.

Maurice looked puzzled.

"John and George," Alec continued, "within spitting distance of your dear ol' friend Durham." He laughed.

"You had better watch out, young Alec," said John, "or else dear ol' Durham might put old Borenius on your tail. Somehow, don't think he would approve of you two bucks wedded and bedded! Certainly stretch his imagination. A good subject for a sermon!" John grinned then turned to Maurice.

"I probably know more about you than you do me, but I assure you, Maurice, that is no disadvantage. I cannot tell you how pleased we are that you and Alec are staying with us for a while. The prospect of your company has made George and me very happy. Stay for as long as you will and come and go as you please. If we can oil the wheels of fortune to promote your progression in this hard world of ours, then that will be reward in itself. It may surprise you to learn, Maurice, that since you first arrived down here, and George became certain of your, er, orientation shall we say, we have followed your activities with some interest, albeit from afar. On the subject of one's sexuality I, like Alec here, had no difficulties."

"Worrying 'bout what other folk think? Never. When I first saw Maurice, I knew straight away. Yer calls it destiny, well, he was mine, make no bones about it. I didn't 'ave to think very 'ard about Maurice. It come natural, like."

John looked over at Alec. He marvelled at how naturally he turned to the situation, how naturally he tuned his mind to seemingly simplistic answers, to what is, after all, fundamentally natural. He considered Alec a thinker, certainly no Voltaire, but within his capacity of knowledge ran a strain of logic which might defeat some of his more educated brothers.

Addressing Maurice, John went on, "Apart from being discrete, life for us is not a problem. We have often thought about you, Maurice, the truth as George knew it. Thankfully the staff were clueless." John smiles. "Rightly, Alec didn't see his homosexuality as some God awful phenomenon. It takes a clear brain like Alec's to get the equation right. We have a real success story. You and Alec, here, safe and sound.

"Dear George, he went through a really bad patch before we met. All that's in the past," he said decisively. "Certainly, discretion is a consideration but otherwise life for us and others like us, shouldn't become a burden."

"Thank you, John. We are both terribly grateful and so fortunate," said Maurice.

"Certainly are," echoed Alec, "and tonight, Maurice, tonight, the both of us can lie abed and not worry about daybreak or the bloody clock striking five. Nor worry about Clive turning up and finding us there. If he'd seen us last night, Maurice, with you stretched damn near naked on top of me – Christ I'd have given a mighty lot to 'ave seen his face."

John gave a laugh.

"No doubt you would, Alec," said Maurice "but it wouldn't have suited me and thank goodness George came along."

Later on, both tired yet not wanting the day to end, the two young men finally climbed the stairs to their room.

Their bed was cool with fresh sweet smelling linen. Alec climbed into the bed then scurried like a crab until his body fused with his lover. With frenzied fervour Maurice stretched his arms beneath the naked body and drew Alec ever closer to him. Passion, unbridled, totally consumed them. They were frantic with unity of purpose. Maurice turned to whisper in Alec's ear.

"This is it, my love, this, pray God, forever and ever."

"They talk of virgins, don't they Maurice, well, I guess I'm one of 'em."

Maurice laughed as they huddled together. "Whatever you are, I love you."

"No more running away or hiding, Maurice. Able to touch your body when I wants and know 'tis alright. Yes, Maurice, though I can't use big words nor sound them right, I'm sure of one thing, you and me, and that's what matters. Like growing up really. The first bit was fine, or at least not bad. But this, this is what it's all been leading to, an' I ain't never gonner let it go."

Maurice shuddered at the touch of finesse behind Alec's words.

"Alec, what more can I say? If I had used a thousand words to describe it, or a thousand actions to confirm it, I could not have been any nearer the meaning than that."

And so throughout the night they lay in a union of peace and harmony.

Chapter Six

There was a knock on the door. Maurice woke with a start and sat bolt upright in panic. Then the now familiar surroundings came into focus and he relaxed and fell back heavily onto the bed. Alec rubbed his eyes, looked towards Maurice then closed his eyes again with a satisfied smirk or smile hanging from his lips.

John appeared through the door with a tray of tea. "Here you are, boys," he said as he placed the tray on the chest of drawers by Maurice's side of the bed.

Maurice levered himself up in the bed then shook Alec roughly who leaned over and kissed him. Maurice experienced a tinge of embarrassment but John's face reassured him.

"'Fraid the service doesn't extend to breakfast in bed. Downstairs in half an hour suit you?"

"Sure, John," said Alec slurping the hot tea. "Thanks," he added as his other hand suddenly disappeared under the sheet.

"Alec," Maurice blurted out, the cup in his hand tilting dangerously.

"Alec," he said again this time looking at John who obviously found the scene amusing. Alec was undeterred and continued his digital tour. Maurice shook his head in fake disapproval then a broad smile, and finally laughter as his body all at once became sensitive. He hastily put his cup down. As John walked away he heard the bed springs responding to their struggles and echoes of their laughter followed him down the stairs.

'What it is to be young,' he mused.

Maurice viewed the scene of breakfast as he entered the dining room. It was far removed from the middle class setting he was used to. On the wooden bench type table stood a large glazed earthenware teapot, bowl of brown sugar and glass jug filled with milk. Cups lay alongside waiting to be filled. Instead of the nicety of prepared toast arranged in silver-plated racks there was instead a large cottage loaf resting on an equally large wooden board. Several thick slices had been cut from it. Arranged around the table in each seated position had been placed the meal, which consisted of eggs, bacon and sausages. There were other things on offer but it was a question of help yourself. Not a single domestic servant in sight! Maurice was impressed with the breakfast John had prepared for he had never cooked anything in his life, unless you count the toasted muffins up at Cambridge.

"Smells delicious," Maurice remarked as he sat down. "We'll have to learn the art," he said looking seriously at Alec.

Alec laughed. "Learn the art as you calls it. I was only that 'igh," he said measuring up to his waist, "when I learnt to cook a breakfast. Nothing grand, mind you, like up at the house, but good enough for me Ma and Pa. You've got a long way to go, Maurice, but I'll show you. Or are you planning to have lots o' servants around the place? I don't really fancy that."

Alec reached over to fill his and Maurice's teacup.

"You'll manage, both of you," said John, "in all things, one will complement the other. I know it does with us, and the will and determination – which you both have in abundance – will see you through."

"What was your worst experience?" asked Alec, as he finished eating his breakfast.

"Don't be so inquisitive, Alec," Maurice broke in.

"It's alright, Maurice. When you find yourself in our situation, it's natural to want to know how others have managed. George and I had a few problems along the way; as of course do conventionally married couples. Ours seemed larger because there were fewer sympathetic ears. Mention homosexuality, in this island anyway, and the reaction is likely to be pretty uncomfortable. On the continent, sexuality, of whatever combination, is, generally speaking, taken as part of the nature of living. This objective approach may have something to do with their culture, perhaps. I often wonder what happened to ours. I have to say, however, that apart from that episode with George's school, we have not been burdened with any major problems. Maybe 'tis because of the company we keep."

"A bit of a blow for George wasn't it?" asked Alec.

"Yes, it was at first. Beastly business. I can still remember that day with George arriving home, obviously upset. The whole affair came as a bit of a shock, I can tell you, but not terminally so. Fortunately I was home at the time, which I like to imagine helped. George got over it soon enough but decided not to go back into teaching. We had resolved long, long before that, in fact from the very beginning of our relationship, never, ever, to allow ourselves to be diverted from each other, come what may. Our cardinal rule, selfish though it might seem, was that our relationship, our love for one another, must come before all else, and that is the way it has always been, and in my view should always be.

"So you see, Alec," John continued, lightly dismissing this one upset, and with a smile on his face, "when the local witch doctor comes to take you away, or that canine horror from up at the manse, complete with his dog collar, wants to force your obedience to his God, Maurice will be there to rescue you."

"Oh, I don't know about that, John," joked Maurice, "maybe he will get to like the sack-cloth and ashes bit." They both laughed.

"He can go shoot himself whoever that evil old bugger be. An' don't talk down to me, Maurice."

"Sorry, Alec, really sorry. Forgiven?" he said soothingly.

"I don't know what it is about you, Maurice. I keep thinking I am dreaming all this. Then, when I touch you – even when you say things what I don't understand – it's like, well, it's just blooming wonderful, that's all." Alec's voice now took on a strength, which surprised both John, and Maurice. "Yes," he said raising his voice, "right now I feel I want to be on an island, miles and miles from everywhere, just us two, you and me, Maurice, and to flaming hell with the rest o' the world. Of course, I don't mean you, John, or George – you could come with us!" Maurice walked around the table to where Alec was sitting. Overcome with emotion he stooped and kissed Alec lightly on his lips. Their excursion into the real yet romantic world, was born but a few weeks. Their love was as a chrysalis, which as it emerged took on ever increasing colours of beauty. John looked on at this incredulous display of affection. He instantly knew that the strength of their bond would overcome future problems. They were so committed. Neither Maurice, or Alec for that matter were totally unaware of the world outside, but for the moment they were swamped in a surfeit of love and passion which now had priority over all else.

"Forgive us John, we just have to express what this means to us as often as we can. God knows the chains have been on for far too long. I don't believe either of us wants to curb these feelings; love is such a precious commodity. Using the vernacular, it's taken a bloody long time getting here." Pointing to Alec he said, "There, as Wellington might have said, is my Waterloo. On reflection I rather think it would have been better if Napoleon had won."

"I wonder?" John said aloud, "Hmm," he pondered.

"What is it?" asked Maurice suddenly worried.

"Just an idea, that's all. Only shortly, we are going on holiday to Greece. Not digging, no, no, just a return visit to Athens, the Acropolis, a kind of busman's holiday really, but without driving the bus. George and I decided on this only last week, you might call it a Byronic urge. George does get a holiday you know. Now, why don't you two join us?"

"To Greece," said Alec, "that's miles away, isn't it, t'other side of Europe or somewhere, least from what I learned at school?"

"Tell him – tell him he'll love it, Maurice. Well, what do you think?"

"Well, to be quite honest, John, I was rather hoping that Alec and I could start planning what we are going to do, something together obviously. I've to decide what to do with my interests in town, then where to live. Oh, there are so many things to discuss with Alec that need to be done sooner than later."

"Do let me tempt you, Maurice," persisted John. "Just think what it will do for your state of mind, quite apart from your complexion," he said laughing.

"You will really be able to enjoy yourself in a relatively free society. To relax, and even if exhausted by whatever the climes of Greece encourage, it will still make a wonderful climax – if you'll pardon the expression – to events over the past month.

"I've already booked a beautiful villa which will accommodate all of us, comfortably. It's near to a small port called Zea. Can you swim, Alec? No! Well, we will soon teach you. It is as quiet as you want it to be. What better opportunity, and with glorious weather guaranteed, in which to contemplate the future?"

"I must say it's very tempting," said Maurice, warming to the idea. "What do you say, Alec?"

"Is it for me to say anything?" replied Alec. "It cost me more 'an I could afford meeting you in London that time, Maurice."

"I know, Alec," said Maurice softly and remembering with pride the occasion.

"John, I'm very grateful, and subject to me convincing Alec – we'll manage something between us – then we would love to join you and George. I forgot to ask. How long should we be away?"

"Just over six weeks."

"Oh!" said Maurice, somewhat surprised.

"Anyway, think it over and let me know later on today."

Later that morning John disappeared into Southampton, to attend a seminar.

Maurice and Alec walked into the village where they bought groceries from a small store. This was an activity unfamiliar to Maurice and although it was simple enough Alec took charge of the proceedings, dealing with a rather haughty Miss Martin who hardly looked at Alec's familiar face. Alec at once became irritated by her unfriendliness and took his revenge by insisting that she provide an additional bag for the fruit he had chosen and at the same time remarking that its quality was not as it should be. He achieved his objective, for the lady's face took on a thunderous scowl. As they left the store Alec burst out laughing and even Maurice, who had witnessed the scene, was forced to smile. Maurice located a Manchester Guardian at the local newsagents. On the way home they ambled slowly along a narrow lane, which was gradually being covered by falling leaves. Autumn was already in its stride and most of the trees were near naked and dancing less readily to the tune of a northerly wind.

Their steps were near silent as they trod on the multi-tinted carpet, Alec occasionally kicking mounds of the leaves into the air where they tried to take flight when caught in the breeze.

"What are we going to do, Maurice?" Alec suddenly asked. "I mean, I have to work soon and what money I have won't take us very far, you know. I've saved a bit, believe it or not, near fifty pounds!"

"That is quite remarkable," replied Maurice with evident sincerity.

"By the way, Maurice, you ought 'o know that I keep it in an old red tobacco tin. It's wrapped up in the foot of an old sock which is 'idden at the bottom of my canvas bag – just in case you ever need it."

"Heavens alive!" exclaimed Maurice.

"Now what's I said wrong?" cried Alec.

"Alec, Alec my love, you've said nothing wrong." With great feeling Maurice continued. "All you say is so right, so perfect. Now this! It's just incredible. You offer to share with me, all the money you have in the world. Fifty pounds is a bloody fortune to you. To me, Alec, it is worth infinitely more. Your words, once again, give proof of your love." Maurice shakes his head, amazed. "If I live to be a hundred I'll never, no never," he said, his voice gathering strength, "meet anyone who will measure up to you." He paused for breath. "Let me tell you this, Alec. I'm what's called a broker. I deal in stocks and shares. It's the punters who gamble, not me, and I make a lot of money from it." Maurice sounded very pleased with himself as he continued. "We now have a common currency, Alec, you and I, common in that we own each other and it follows, all we possess. So there can be no problem with affording a holiday in Greece anymore.

Agreed?" Maurice gives a laugh.

"You're a tricky fellow, Maurice," said Alec smiling.

"I have to be, after all, you're the most valuable possession I'll ever have. We'll tell George and John after dinner."

Increasingly, Maurice gave thought to the very short time he and Alec had been together and marvelled at the incredible pace at which their relationship was developing. This is not to say that he was blind to all else. He accepted, yet put on hold, other realities he would have to face in the future. For the moment he unashamedly welcomed all the sensations his body and mind could garner. To Alec, all this was new, all was come afresh, whereas Maurice had previously been touched lightly by it. Previous experience did not compare with this. Here there was consistency. Alec's innocence allowed Maurice to weigh the differences and accept the conclusion that all was complete and sealed forever.

It was evening and beyond the cottage's leaded windows all was shrouded in darkness. The spread of yellow light from a hanging oil lamp contrasted them against the background of beamed whitewashed walls, their shadows lightly painted. They sat around the table, complete and leaning relaxed in historic oak Windsor chairs.

"I'll never believe you cooked this meal, Alec," George exclaimed.

"I can vouch that he did. Though I peeled the onions," John said, smiling at George, "I was crying all afternoon."

"Mrs. Brent would be quite surprised, Alec," said George

"She weren't such a bad old stick," said Alec. "I used to watch her sometimes when I were cleaning the guns. Couldn't better her pastry. Nor her puddings. 'Specially her suet dumplings. Think she only made them for the staff.

They don't know what they missed upstairs, do they, George?"

"I still think she would be proud of you, Alec," he replied.

"I'm so glad that you and Alec have decided to come on holiday with us," said John. "It's unusual for us to have company – and what company. The classic spirits of the old Greek philosophers will be sure to come down if only for old times' sake."

"We leave a week today, on the fifth."

"I shall hate the Channel crossing," said George. "Pray for calm seas, Maurice. The journey over is short, thank the Lord. I am certain that Alec will enjoy it as much as I did on my first visit to Europe."

"I've told him as much as I can remember," said Maurice.

"There will be many long train journeys, Alec," said George. "Remember, we shall be travelling through a lot of different countries. You can expect a feast of beautiful and ever changing landscapes. Sheer poetry in motion," he enthused.

"It shall be our 'oneymoon, Maurice," remarked Alec. "One to look back on in our old age," he said laughing.

George and John exchanged glances, which reflected their happiness at being present and somewhat involved in the continuing expansion of love between Maurice and Alec.

George walked over to the bookcase and taking out a large map of Europe spread it out over the table. "Come over here, young Alec," he said. The enthusiasm of one infected the other. They bubbled over with excitement. John and Maurice joined them at the table stretching to follow George's pointing finger.

Tracing a line on the map, George pointed first to Dover. "From here, Alec, it's across the Channel by ferry then a train through to Paris. Unfortunately, we shall not be stopping there, which is a pity," he sighed.

"Why the sigh, George?" interrupted Maurice.

"It is where we first met," said John. "On the steps of the famous opera house. We had individually booked seats for Faust, for the Sunday afternoon performance. Luck, fate or whatever, what matters is that at that precious moment in time we two individual spirits were drawn, as if by compulsion, into one. I remember," he said chuckling, "just how shy and self-conscious we both were as we took tea in the Café de la Paix. Of course there was no need to be. We will always remember it as our city of freedom. A city that, even now, is a haven for the romantic. No penal laws against homosexuals there," he continued, then,

"Sorry, I interrupted."

"You needn't apologise, John," said Maurice, "for such pointers give strength to others, including Alec and me."

George smiled. "Anyway, where was I? Oh, yes. From there it is a wonderful journey through eastern France to Strasbourg."

"I've lost the place, George," said Alec.

George gently took Alec's hand and retraced the journey so far.

"Across here, Alec, to the right, across eastern France. Down through the lower part of Germany – near the famous Black Forest – and into Austria where the train terminates at Vienna."

"My god," said Alec, with enthusiasm, "seems a bloody long way to me."

"'Tis," agreed Maurice, "but well worth it. It can't be long enough for me. Our honeymoon, you first said, Alec. Well, I want it to last as long as possible." he said holding Alec's arm affectionately.

George turned briefly towards Maurice. "According to Bradshaw's Guide we can catch the sleeper which leaves Vienna at twenty past ten in the evening and arrives at Budapest – here Alec," he said turning back to the map and moving their hands down to the spot, "at just before half past six the following morning."

The next hour was taken up with describing the journey through Yugoslavia and into Greece. The rafters of the cottage shook with their laughter, sometimes occasioned by the odd quaint remark from Alec.

"Heavens alive, George, I don't think I've looked so forward to a holiday like this in years. Oh, Maurice, we are both so pleased that you and Alec agreed to come along."

When the time came to retire for the night they were all well and truly imbued with the holiday spirit.

"George, Alec and I will be away tomorrow. There are one or two matters I have to attend to and also I have to pick up some clothes from home, where, God willing – and Alec more particularly – we shall spend the night."

"That's fine. I shall be staying over at Penge tomorrow night but John will be here when you get back."

Chapter Seven

"Hurry, Alec," called Maurice as he watched the train heave its way into the station. Alec had borrowed a small case from George into which he had piled a few clothes. He had on a brown peaked cap, which was pushed to the back of his head. His hair, hanging from one side of his forehead, flopped from one side to the other as he ran from the booking hall. Maurice noticed the appreciative glance Alec got from a young female passenger waiting on the platform. Yes, he concluded, Alec does look damned attractive. He was simply oozing with sexual, as well as sensual, charm. Maurice smiled to himself. The lady in question could not know the cause of Alec's disinterest.

"Here, Alec, quick," cried Maurice as he held open the door of the carriage.

Breathing heavily Alec clambered up dragging his luggage with him. Leaning out he took Maurice's bag, which although large, and heavy, he flipped through the air and into the compartment as if it contained feathers. With the guard's whistle sounding urgent, Maurice, helped by Alec's strong arms, virtually jumped up into the compartment. Sighing with relief he quickly slammed the door shut. With barely seconds to spare they heard steam escaping from the engine as it strained to begin the journey. They felt it shudder, followed by jolting, as the carriages began cannoning into one another. As the labouring engine relaxed, a degree of smoothness returned and the train moved faster and further away from the station.

The train had no corridors and they were the sole occupants of their carriage. Maurice prayed for good fortune to keep it that way for the rest of the journey. There would be two other stops before they reached London.

"Well, old chap," said Maurice looking longingly over at Alec, "our first 'foreign' trip together. How does it feel? Don't answer, just give us a kiss."

"What here?" laughed Alec with a touch of embarrassment.

"Yes, why not?" he said grabbing Alec and making sure their lips met, and not without passion.

"Blimey, what if someone sees us doing this, Maurice?"

"A bit unlikely, Alec, now that the train's moving. What's more we're not 'royalty' so it's unlikely that anyone will chase after us! Mind you, I would, knowing that you're on board, Alec. As far as I'm concerned your star ranks brighter than that of any royal," he said gazing into Alec's face.

Speeding past a field of grazing sheep and lambs, Maurice urgently pointed to them. "Look there, Alec, see the sheep don't seem to care. For all I know they do the same – with each other! I'll bet there's some stupid law, ecclesiastical one I shouldn't doubt, which would criminalize rams romping with rams!"

A grin spread over Alec's face. "Maurice, you look so good right now, good enough to eat," he said laughing.

Alec's face glowed, not only because of his shorn bristles but with a benevolence upon a world, which at this moment, at least, reciprocated. He grabbed Maurice's hand.

"I hope your mum won't mind."

"Of course not, why should she? You will be a guest in my house. I contacted my sister Ada earlier. She wants to meet you. That will be really something," he said with a chuckle. "Sounds formidable I know, but remember, Alec, you owe them nothing and to me you are more important than anyone else on this earth."

"I know, Maurice, I know." Alec was quiet for a few seconds, then remarked.

"Funny you know, Maurice, but your lot…"

"Our lot!" interrupted Maurice, frowning.

"Yes, your lot, Maurice. They never bats an eyelid when dealing with the likes of our class. They'd never attempt to touch us o' course! 'Perish the thought' I once heard one of 'em say, cheeky sod. If it weren't that we do all the bloody work for 'em, then they'd probably never ever speak to us." He said with a touch of bitterness.

"And just what do we do about it, eh?" continued Alec giving voice to feelings, which, to him, were important. "Most of the time damn all. We grind on, and bow, and say yes Sir, and yes bloody Madam, and feel great when some toffee nosed blighter, like Clive Durham, moves down to our 'level', usually with a sniff in their nose like we was muck from Gawd knows where, and says, 'well done, old chap', or some such soppy thing."

Maurice was quite shocked by this outburst. He wanted Alec to feel free to express how he felt and now here was a sample. It may not be elegant prose but its content was clear enough. In a way it frightened Maurice. It was not the political content that worried him. No, it was the thought that if Alec pursued a personal vendetta against Maurice's family then it might cause problems. He hoped this could be avoided. He vowed, however, that his relationship with Alec would take precedence over all else. It was untouchable.

"Alec," Maurice shouted, "stop this nonsense. Maybe you're right, but for Christ's sake don't undermine the only thing we have of value, namely each other. We shall work things out to suit ourselves, which means just that, you and me, Alec, not anyone else. Not my mother or sisters or yours for that matter."

"No, Alec," said Maurice. "The substance of what you say matters, of course, but there is often a danger in expressing such views too freely. There are a few who, given half a chance, would fetter you with their hates and dislikes. And we, of all people, should know where hatred leads. Others must work out their own salvation. And that, Alec my dear, is an observation relating to all bloody classes," he said slightly annoyed.

"Just give a moment's thought to our language, Alec? Listen to all its shades and distortions. They all come with accompanying trappings often representing our prejudices."

"Alright, alright, Maurice," said Alec, smiling. "Keep you 'air on. Just poke me in the ribs when you fancy I'm wrong. When I'm right, which I'll be most of the time, then…" Alec grinned then gave a laugh. "'Ere" he said, "Give us a kiss, providing there ain't no sheep looking." On a more serious note, Alec went on.

"No, you're right, Maurice, we mustn't let other things or people bother us. Come on, Maurice, just take 'old of me hand, then I'll know you want me."

"You needn't worry, my lad, you're mine as if my life depended on it, which from now on it does, Alec. Metaphorically speaking, my hand will always be in yours, for its strength, and yours, my dear Alec, in mine. Poetic don't you think?"

Alec made a face then gave a smile, which stretched from east to west or thereabouts. "Big words but I think I know what you're meaning, Maurice."

"Anyway, back to Ada. I am so sure that you will like her, Alec."

They arrived at Piccadilly Circus and began walking down Piccadilly until they reached a rather imposing building which appeared supported by two large marble

Corinthian columns. Stationed in the centre and by a door stood a commissionaire in what to Alec was a comic uniform – 'guarding' the entrance to the building.

"Does he have to stand there all day?" asked Alec.

"I imagine so," answered Maurice.

"Bloody daft," said Alec.

"Come on, Alec, stop worrying about things like that." Followed by Alec, Maurice made to move towards the door, which the commissionaire in the comic uniform had already opened for him. When he saw Alec following behind he put up a hand to stop him.

"Eh, where the 'eck do you think you're going?" he said roughly. "We don't let the likes o' you in 'ere. Go on, sling yer 'ook and take yer clawth cap wi' yer."

"You damn well get out of the way before I sling you one," said Alec belligerently and adopting a pose which supported his threat.

"Alec," called Maurice. He turned to the other man, "that young man is with me so kindly make room for him." Recognising the authority in Maurice's voice the 'other man' stood promptly aside without saying another word. Maurice heard Alec muttering under his breath so quickly led him into the tearoom.

The tearoom was very large. Alec reckoned there to be about fifty tables. From what he could see it catered for people in very expensive clothes who had nothing to do but just lounge around for hours stuffing themselves full of rich looking cakes and sandwiches. Mostly women he observed.

Alec was impressed with the room's rich decorations. He spotted a small quartet of men on a raised dais playing music. He found it disturbing that no one seemed to be listening. To Alec this was unfair and confirmed his belief that the seated babbling women were spoilt and certainly not of his world. His judgement was quick in coming.

"What a useless and stupid lot of women in here."

Maurice watched Alec for a few seconds, amused at his reactions and just slightly apprehensive that he might suddenly embark on another of his judgemental bouts, and within earshot of some of the clients. Alec, with cloth cap in hand, was a character unfamiliar to this setting. There were already one or two covered heads, which had turned to look decidedly in his direction. Alec responded with the most defiant of looks, which found its mark on their retreating faces.

"There she is," said Maurice excitedly, pointing to a table at the end of the restaurant. To Alec all that was visible was a body, side view, and a hat that supported a quill.

He laughed. "Gawd, what a hat!" he said as he followed Maurice towards her table.

"Bit of a corker isn't it?" Maurice responded. As they neared the table Ada rose to meet them, a grinning smile portending well.

"Maurice," she said and they kissed.

"Ada, let me introduce Alec," he said proudly.

Alec pushed his hand forward and felt hers, soft and delicate, open into his. Then to his surprise she kissed him lightly on the cheek. For the moment he was transfixed with awkwardness and embarrassment. Reality dawned quickly and he was suddenly aware that he was seated next to Maurice and opposite Ada. He looked up as Ada began pouring tea from an ornate china teapot into ornate china cups.

"Milk, Alec?" she asked pleasantly.

"Thanks."

Ada was anxious to make a good impression on Alec. Previously informed as to his situation she decided to make great efforts to put him at his ease. She immediately noted the handsome features, then, with a sense of guilt, stopped herself from being caught taking an inventory. She liked what she saw and had no difficulty in beginning a conversation.

"Don't mind me, Alec." She continued smiling at him with as much disarming endeavour as she could muster. "I'm much like Maurice if that's any consolation, except his temper is more violent."

"'Haven't seen it yet," said Alec grinning, "then he knows 'e's met his match in me." They all laughed.

"Well that at least has broken the ice. I don't know about you, Alec, but I was terrified at meeting you. You know, first impressions and all that. I always get that way when I am to meet a perfect stranger – though you're not exactly a total stranger, for Maurice told me a little, very little I hasten add, when we spoke on the telephone this morning."

"I liked you as soon as I saw you," said Alec looking directly at her.

"Well, Alec, that's straight to the point I must say," laughed Ada, "and it goes without saying that I am nearly jealous of Maurice's very excellent choice, and so very attractive."

"When you two have finished with the mutual admiration bit, I'll have another cup of tea, please, Ada," Maurice said grinning.

"And how is Mother?" asked Maurice.

"Very well, Maurice. I explained that you would be staying the night with your friend – I said friend, as I thought companion, colleague, partner, all sounded rather impersonal. The truth, as I know it," she said with a sly laugh, "would have sounded rather strange to her Victorian ears."

"Yes," said Maurice, "we must let her down gradually, though how to achieve that is anyone's guess."

"By the way your trunk left yesterday."

"Oh good, thanks Ada. There are a number of books from the library that I would like to take. If I pack them perhaps you could arrange for them to be sent on as well."

"Of course," Ada answered.

"Has the venerable doctor been around with any ideas of abasement for the errant son?"

Ada laughed. "I really think you are enjoying this. You know it is on the fifth?"

"That's the day we're going," said Alec.

"Going, going where?" asked Ada inquisitively.

"I was going to tell you, Ada," Maurice replied quickly. "The friends we're staying with are off to Athens next week and have invited us to go along with them."

"Lord!" said Ada.

"Why Lord, what's he to do with this?"

She shook her head in mock anger. "Alec, you've got a big job on your hands there."

"And don't I know it," mocked Alec.

"What I meant, Maurice, is that that's where we are going for our honeymoon, or at least part of it. We go first to Paris."

"Well I'll be damned," said Alec grinning wickedly and knowing that his next remark would cause a few eyebrows to lift. "It's me and Maurice's honeymoon as well."

"Alec, hush," cautioned Maurice as a long beribboned wrinkled neck from the next table appeared to stretch in their direction.

Ada shrieked with laughter. It was like a breath of fresh air in that it removed any cautiousness, which one might expect on first meetings. Alec quickly decided to value Ada as a friend, a mate. She was, in a way, so like Maurice, he thought, straightforward, no airs and graces to put him to shame. He liked that.

The originality of Alec's remark or its direct comparison with Ada's situation had caused the outburst. It was either sheer audaciousness or more likely an innocent observation. Maurice thought it a bit of both. The look on Ada's face – a stretch of glorious amusement and understanding, shed any doubt as to the nature of her feelings towards them.

"Did I say something wrong?" Alec said looking directly at Maurice. Maurice stuck his tongue out at him. Not to be outdone Alec pulled a face and using a finger to displace his nose made it more grotesque, then with eyes bulging, or so he thought, gave a long searing look at the owner of that intruding neck which still reached in their direction. On seeing the direction of Alec's clown-like display, the neck swiftly retracted and its owner's gaze averted.

"Gracious," joked Ada, "that look was enough to paralyse the soul of the devil."

"Ada, he doesn't need encouragement from you," Maurice remarked desperately trying to keep a straight face. "And," he whispered at Alec, "you dare throw me a kiss and I'll, I'll squash your nose in that plate of cream doughnuts."

Alec beamed a smile that could have melted the heart of every chaste maiden in the restaurant, well those that were maidens and, if any, chaste!

As if reading Alec's mind, or his venturesome thoughts, Ada turned to her brother.

"Oh, Maurice," said Ada drying her eyes. "Alec's such a dear." She then became more serious. "I do wish you both so much happiness. Maurice, my dear, you have suffered so much. I wish I had understood earlier; it would have made such a difference." She leaned across the table. "Give me your hand Alec – and yours, Maurice." Maurice with some reluctance, complied. Alec had no such reservations. "Darlings Maurice and Alec, good fortune continues to follow me, for now I have two brothers." For a moment she was silent, then, as if to sanctify their relationship she deliberately placed their hands together.

It all happened so quickly that Maurice was taken by surprise. She looked at them and her blue thoughtful eyes told them all that they could wish to know. A tiny droplet, like clear wine, ran down her upturned cheek.

"Thank you, Ada," said Alec, now suddenly experiencing a growth in their intimacy.

"You have made me so happy, Ada," said Maurice, "and now we are completely *en famille* again, be it an enlarged one." Maurice leaned over and kissed her.

Chapter Eight

They arrived at Maurice's home late that afternoon. Having spent such a happy hour with Ada, Alec was not too perturbed at the prospect of meeting other members of the family. There were certain reservations he retained about Maurice's mother. He had originally imagined someone in the style of Clive's mother, the 'old bitch' as he called her.

Ada reassured him that Mother was not someone from the dark ages standing ready to chop off his head. As it turned out, Mother gave the appearance of being far less forbidding than he had expected.

Maurice was naturally very fond of his mother. His manner and attitude, however, offered her little scope for changing his pattern of behaviour. Like his father before him he believed in making his own decisions regarding the life he intended to lead. As she looked across at Alec, Mrs. Hall had, as yet, no idea where he featured in Maurice's scheme of things.

It was during dinner that the fabric of behaviour – peculiar to certain groups in society – began to wear a trifle thin. Maybe it was Alec's utilisation of a piece of bread to fetch the remaining soup from his plate, that first caused a mild disturbance in Mrs. Hall's manner. Evidence of her reaction was decidedly visual, including the sudden movement of her ample bosom occasioned by a larger than normal intake of air.

Ada was quick to notice but only found it amusing. Luckily she was alone in this observation, or so she imagined.

As Alec was unfamiliar with a number of the so-called 'niceties of the table', he could not be held responsible to those who were. His concern was more on what was on offer, and a strong appetite, which had to be satisfied. He had now become accustomed to eating with Maurice, John and George and had, unconsciously, adopted a few of their refinements along the way. None had ever uttered a hint of criticism.

This was not a problem as far as Alec was concerned. His standards, however, were not those of Mrs. Hall, and he did not escape her sharp eye. Mrs. Hall made a serious effort to disguise her – well – distaste. He was, after all, a guest and more important, a friend of Maurice. A little eccentric perhaps? Items of class, grammar, breeding, and the usual decorative elements of her society, had little option but to be recorded in her mental diary as decidedly lacking. That she should put voice to such thoughts or utter advice on the subject, would, she knew, immediately invoke the wrath of her son. She was sad. Where was the bride Clive had spoken of earlier? Now they were talking of going to Greece. A spark of hope crossed her brow. Isn't Greece where Clive met his wife?

After dinner Mrs. Hall retired to her room early, feigning rheumatic pains to which she claimed she was a martyr.

Maurice was pleased. Dinner had been excellent. He had had a quick talk with his mother in the library. Later, in the drawing room, Ada and Arthur joined them. Arthur had obviously been fully briefed about Alec. He and Alec had a discussion on the effect of placing players too long off the batsman or something of that sort. Alec became quite animated and his coloured dialogue was something, if not an acquired taste! In any event it appeared to give Arthur immense pleasure. Arthur's behaviour was immaculate and, on the face of it, quite genuine, though Ada's influence no doubt had something to do with it.

When they had drunk their coffee, Ada and Arthur went into the garden leaving Maurice and Alec alone in the drawing room.

"Your room is next to mine, Alec," said Maurice slyly as they sat together on the settee.

"Oh, it is, is it? Why can't I be with you?"

Maurice laughed. "Because it would not seem proper," he teased. "Imagine if the maid walked in and we were in bed together and... we would be the talk of the kitchen for weeks."

"I don't care. It didn't worry you down at Clive's that time, did it? Come on, Maurice, I got used to being with you," he pleaded.

"I was only joking, Alec," he said at the forlorn face. Instinctively he pulled him towards him.

"Not worried about the maid now, are you? You old hypocrite."

They lay for some time facing each other, arms, legs, hands and feet constantly searching, seeking to rest where passion demanded. At this time, heaven and hell, those manmade devices, were as far away as was their validity. Maurice could feel a light breeze on his neck from Alec's steady breathing. The heat between their naked bodies was without loss. Their proximity immediate. Maurice felt the sudden climax, violent in its intensity, just as Alec's body shook with a raging fire, which gradually became becalmed. Although now sexually replete they remained entangled, arms allowing hands to stretch for palms, to stroke lips, legs moving restlessly along lines of thighs, bodies pressing urgently against one another. This was a display of their absolute harmony together.

"Well, my prince of the night," said Maurice finally surfacing, "what price happiness?"

"Price?" queried Alec. "Happiness don't have no price, unless you count the bloody misery on the way." Alec thought more about it.

"Luck, that's what it is – no, not only luck, you have to grab what you want when you see it. Like I did." Alec further tightened his grip on Maurice.

"We wouldn't be lying here like this if I hadn't gone after you and grabbed you, Maurice. I was determined, Maurice, even if it had meant me climbing some bloody great mountain – or ladder," he said with a laugh. "I knew you needed me alright even if you didn't – well, perhaps you did after all. Anyway, you was lucky I came along."

Maurice shuddered, He now dreaded to imagine, even for a moment, that the ghost of a possibility may have deprived him of this. He clung more tightly to the body beside him. He knew that he was finally secure but there always remained the need for constant re-assurance. He blew lightly at the lock of Alec's hair, which tangled with his lips. This was his idea of paradise, something beyond his wildest dreams. It was a situation that met everything he desired in life.

"You can't be cold, Maurice," Alec said as Maurice forced his body even closer.

"No, far from it."

"Do you love me then, Maurice? Say you love me as I love you."

A chuckle. "Love you, well, perhaps, just a little. Enough to kill for! God! The word love was never invented until I met you. So you see, Alec, there is nothing over. All my love is here, for you, forever. Is that enough for you?"

Alec's face lifted as he whispered, "I wonder if Clive is as happy as we are. He didn't look like it when I saw him last. Poor devil, and married to that mare."

"Don't be unkind," said Maurice, "Just be thankful that we've got each other."

"You're alright, Maurice. More kind-hearted than me, you are." Alec said in a whisper.

"I can't always say things as pretty as you do, Maurice, but what you see here in this package called Alec, you got for as long as I live." Words such as these meant so much to Alec and suddenly he was crying. Moisture, yielding and dropping cool, fell between them. Maurice heard a sob and felt as if his own heart would break with the very seriousness of it all.

"Alec, my dear boy," Maurice murmured softly. He rolled away drawing Alec with him to lie protected in his arms. They were together in the seclusion of the night and finally were swept into that universe called slumber.

Maurice and Alec arrived a little late. The others were already seated and had nearly finished their breakfast. Alec waited, and then with a nod from Maurice, followed him over to the sideboard to collect breakfast. They were all still seated at the table. Alec and Maurice were waiting for the maid to bring in more tea.

Looking directly toward her son Mrs. Hall said, "You know, Maurice, that I bitterly disapprove of you being away during Ada's wedding." She looked across at Ada who was obviously enjoying the situation. Now she was actually smiling. It was quite outrageous of her, thought Mrs. Hall.

"Ada!" called Mrs. Hall. "Well I must say you are treating it all very casually. I knew that you and Maurice were, for a time, awf song. But now, I gather, all lies well between you – in fact I have noticed a very marked change in both of you – surely we can now do things the proper way."

Ada shook her head. "I do not accept that there is a proper way. Shaw once wrote that 'The golden rule is that there are no golden rules'. That expresses my sentiments exactly. It is only important that Arthur and I are wed. No. The arrangements are to remain as they are. Maurice? Yes of course I shall miss him, but then I shall look forward to seeing him during our honeymoon."

She paused when she saw a fiendish grin spread across Alec's face. "Alec! Don't you dare echo that sentiment hovering on your lips," she said with a giggle.

Mrs. Hall looked first at Alec – who struggled to maintain a straight face then her gaze shifted to Ada.

"In my day," Mrs. Hall started, "such behaviour would have been unheard of. Dr Barry agreed. He has been so sympathetic and understanding."

"Of course he would be," remarked Maurice sharply, "though he is not exactly a paragon of virtue himself nor an habitual client of the parish church, is he?" said Maurice with sarcasm. "He will do you proud, though, Ada. It will make him feel important, a real fillip to his ego. Maybe he will unburden his wallet a trifle more."

"Maurice! I do not like this conversation at all. I feel as if I am being shunned by my own son."

"It is Ada's wedding, after all, Mother. She has made it clear that she is happy with things remaining as they are. That should be good enough," he said, clearly meaning that he would not change his mind.

"In any event I shall be away, as you already know."

"Yes, of course, Greece. Well maybe something will come of that," she said, her manner changing slightly as if to signify her expectations.

In traditional fashion she returned to her duties as hostess and directed her next question at Alec. "And what, young man, will you do whilst Maurice is away? You are working I presume?"

Alec, somewhat taken aback by this sudden attention was momentarily lost for words and before he could answer Maurice spoke for him.

"Alec is coming to Greece with me."

"Oh!" exclaimed Mrs. Hall suddenly tilting her nose towards the ceiling as if some unpleasant odour had drifted in through the window. The movement, though sudden, was made with such deliberation that Maurice could not fail to notice. He felt angry at the thought that Alec may also have seen this ill-mannered gesture by his mother. Alec had and his reaction was to follow very quickly.

"Have you a pain, Mother?" Maurice said sharply.

Ada, also witness to this critical behaviour of her mother also worried that the gesture may have found its mark. Ada thought it ungracious and unfair. While contemplating on the effect it may have had on Alec the maid entered the room with a tray of tea.

In the beginning Alec had felt uncomfortable with Mrs. Hall. Now, following her display of obvious dislike he was greatly disturbed. He found it bad enough trying to keep up with their upper class habits and behaviour, something he had not been conscious of at John and George's, but now the oppressive nature of recent events made him angry and depressed. Without offering any explanation whatsoever he jumped up from the table, overturning his cup in the process, and rushed out through the French doors into the garden.

"Alec," cried Maurice, rushing to join him.

"OK, Maurice," began Alec as Maurice reached him, "'Tis all over. I am just another piece of shit to them. You belong to them not me", he said, his anger rising. "They can treat me like shit in their house, but I don't have to stay, and I won't. I cannot go along with you and your family, Maurice. 'Tis over, you and me. I don't belong 'ere."

Maurice was beside himself with anger and now fear. "Alec, Alec, stop it, you don't know what you're saying."

"Oh yes I damn well do, Maurice. You saw what happened back there. 'Twas the same last night over dinner.

I should never have come 'ere. I love you, Maurice, but I'll never be able to fit in with your lot. The future, what hope have we got, eh? It will be the same over and over again. I also 'ave my pride, Maurice, and will not be treated like some ignorant, fucking..." Alec paused for a moment, "It's no use, Maurice. Don't ever want to come 'ere again. 'Tis over for us. I should have gone to Argentina." At this point his anger had subsided, now he was near to tears. "What a mess I've made of it all. Go back to your Clive, he's your sort. Your mum wouldn't treat him like that."

Maurice felt utterly wretched at what was happening, he had done nothing to cause it, it was his mother's ill-mannered behaviour. His heart sank in despair and the depression he now felt was reminiscent of the past.

"I'll get my bag from the room. I'll need my train ticket." Alec's face reflected all too clearly the emotional state he was in.

All this while Maurice had been trying to interrupt. He wanted to take him in his arms but with the others staring at them through the open doors could not do so.

"Christ Almighty, Alec," Maurice cried, now utterly distraught. "Come Alec, please, come back inside, to our room, you mustn't let this happen, I mustn't let it happen, I bloody well won't let it happen. Come on Alec, my love, come on." With great reluctance Alec allowed himself to be virtually dragged back into the house, back past staring eyes, and finally up the stairs to their bedroom. Once there Maurice slammed the door shut.

"I'm still going, Maurice. Can you not see, Maurice" he said shaking his head, "your family. I know what they think. Working class is beneath 'em. I've 'eard them. I hate them too."

"Then if you do, so will I. Anyway, Alec, my dear, dear, love, that is simply not true of everyone. What of Ada, of John and George, do you hate them? I know you don't."

"But, Maurice," began Alec, "can't you see the..."

"No, Alec, I see only what is right for us, you and me, and if the rest of the fucking world doesn't like it, we'll go to that island you mentioned earlier."

"Oh, Maurice," cried Alec, "what is to become of us?"

"Whatever it is it will be us, not me, not you, but us, displayed as big as you like and for all to see if it helps dispel your doubts."

Alec smiled slightly at this, which gave Maurice the opening he was waiting for.

"That's the Alec I know," Maurice said as he put his hands around Alec's waist, then rested his head on Alec's shoulder, their faces touching. "Oh God, Alec, you must know that I can't live without you, nor you without me. We've known all along that there would be problems, but we are two pretty healthy men with pretty healthy appetites, so no problem is insurmountable."

For a while they remained clutching each other, both somewhat exhausted by the trial they had passed through.

"Well, my love, remind me that you love me, will never leave me."

Alec lifted his face, turned and kissed Maurice on the lips. "Is that enough proof for you?"

"Yes, Alec, it is. Remember, we are always first to each other, nothing, no-one will ever change that."

"Now, Alec, we had better go downstairs. Would you go into the garden with Ada while I have a talk with mother?"

"Yes, all right Maurice. One thing though, don't go on at her too much, after all, she don't know no better."

They both smiled which gave evidence of their return to their world.

"No, alright, Alec, I'll be gentle." Maurice was not quite sure how he would approach his mother but equally determined not to allow her to damage his relationship with Alec.

When they returned and the maid had gone from the room, Maurice walked slowly over to Ada.

"Be a dear," he said giving her a conspiratorial wink, "as you have finished breakfast would you show Alec the garden?"

"Of course, Maurice. Come on Alec, my dear," she said taking his arm and walking with him out through the garden doors.

Once on their own Maurice swiftly turned to face his mother. With all humour in his voice gone, he began.

"A moment ago, by an action of unmistakable contempt, you managed to insult our guest and my dearest friend. This saddens me considerably, Mother, because you are forcing me to make certain choices. I have set my priorities, and the one of prime importance is Alec," he said with firmness. "I recognise that that may seem strange to you. Class, I remember you once saying, divides so many of us in this country. That is so true. Well, here is an opportunity for us to overturn the maxim that different classes cannot mix. During the last war we were very anxious that they should otherwise it might well have been lost.

"I think it best that you be aware that my relationship with Alec is of special importance to me. Whether it pleases or offends, you may as well know that I am taking him on as a partner. We have yet to decide what type of business will suit us both, but that can wait until we return from Greece."

His mother, in somewhat belligerent mood, began to rise from her chair.

"No, Mother, I have not finished. Stay for just a little longer," he demanded.

Breathing heavily, she sat down again.

Continuing, he said,

"I shall, at some time in the near future, be buying a house from which Alec and I can operate and control our future."

"Good God, Maurice, you make it sound like a marriage!"

"In a way it is."

"Don't be disgusting, Maurice!"

Maurice began to feel the edge of anger creeping into his voice.

"God help us! I really expected better of you than that, mother. I have in the past listened to you recounting your own experiences in Europe after the war, where misery and depravation prevailed on a grand scale. I've heard you severely criticise those in your circle of friends whose views you consider pernicious in the extreme. Narrow minded, selfish and lacking true morality, I've heard you say. A few, I have no doubt, would deem my behaviour heresy, and if burning at the stake were still popular, would eagerly will it on me. I pray for enlightenment in my life time. I do hope that we are not far apart in our thinking," At this point his mother tried to protest.

"First hear me out," he insisted.

The thoughts going through his mother's mind right then oscillated from conventionality to a passion for compromise. She could also detect something about which she was not entirely knowledgeable or had merely or purposely forgotten. Deep from within her memory she now struggled with recollections of events past, particularly those from her time abroad, the reasons and causes for much of man's behaviour, the violence created through greed, ignorance and intolerance, both personal and national. So where did this leave her? She heard Maurice's voice again.

"I have to tell you that should my friend Alec be unwelcome here, then my visits will be rare indeed."

"Maurice," she cried, "what are you saying?"

"Good gracious, Mother, surely I make myself perfectly clear. There is plenty of pious cant around, I have lived amongst it for too long, but no more. I now have a real purpose for living," Maurice went on, "and it carries one name, Alec." Before Mrs. Hall had a chance to speak, Maurice went on, "I do not seek your approval, Mother, and by the same token, I will not tolerate the evident disapproval you show."

"Oh, Maurice, what can I say?" she started to weep.

"If you start at the beginning by accepting me for what I am and not for what you would like me to be, then, maybe, you will get to understand me better."

She dried her eyes. "I think I understand you, Maurice, but be also tolerant with me, give me time, Maurice. I can't just suddenly divorce myself from the culture I have lived with for so long. I probably have a lot of re-appraising to do, some things remain foreign to me, and new ideas take time. But I am willing to try, if only for your sake, I promise, Maurice my dear," she pleaded.

He went to her. "I'm sure you will, my dearest mother and we will talk about it another time. In the meantime, try to be pleasant to Alec for you now know of his importance to me." He spoke kindly, all passion spent. Taking her by the arm they walked slowly out into the garden to join the others. As was to be expected there was a feeling of great affection between them, which Maurice knew instinctively would provide a linchpin to their future relationship as mother and son.

Chapter Nine

On the return journey, sitting back relaxed in his seat, Maurice had given much thought to the encounter with his mother. They had had a further discussion before he left the house. She was quite tearful yet rational as she told of her worries and concern. He really did appreciate and understand that – he was a son whose identity now gave her great anxiety. She feared what it all signified, yet instinctively knew that its full identity would unquestionably be made clear to her eventually. To her it was a dismal prospect. His future worried her too, for his situation, as she was slowly if reluctantly beginning to appreciate, would require a lot of courage, care and understanding. As for Alec, she had to accept what little Maurice had told her about their relationship. His involvement did not altogether please her. She viewed his integration – if that was what it was to be – in Maurice's life as posing great problems. Her only consolation was in the knowledge that he seemed to offer peace and tranquillity to her son. After considering the options, she accepted that that was more important to her than anything else. All else must juggle its own way into the jigsaw Maurice and Alec had created.

"How did it go?" asked George when they met later that evening.

"Amazingly well, at least after a rather bumpy start," began Maurice. "Ada has taken it all so calmly, and, remarkable though it may seem, accepts the situation without hint of disapproval of any kind. Mind you, she had already set her pitch the last time we met so I didn't have to concern myself there. As for Alec, well, I shall certainly have to put a ball and chain on him when Ada's lurking around," he said smiling. "Seriously though, George, they really got on terribly well, as in fact did Arthur – her husband to be. At least that's one member of the family – soon to be two – I shall not be losing."

"I am so glad," said George.

"And your mother?" asked George.

"Mother, ah, that was a problem to begin with, for she managed to upset poor Alec, needless to say. It began when she knew he was coming to Greece with us. She no doubt thought I would end up as Clive has, God forbid. She made her disapproval of him very evident, so much so that Alec walked out on us. Bloody nearly lost him, well, not really, but he was terribly upset, and I don't blame him. Explanations were more of a problem to begin with though. I think, nevertheless, that she is a good mother in that she was prepared to listen. Mind you she didn't get much option. Without dotting and crossing all the digits, I managed to convey to her the situation vis-à-vis Alec and me. When I say convey, well, I left her with sufficient leaders to provide an answer to the questions she will now begin asking herself. Put in her position I doubt if I would have been as generous as she. I am fortunate in having a mother who has witnessed the other side of life, its misery, unhappiness, war torn countries with their human derelicts, and so on. She has a starting point where ignorance cannot claim any priority. As I said before, although she is my mother I think she is unique in understanding. She will come to terms with the 'me and Alec' situation, probably without bothering with the detail." Maurice gave a slight laugh, which did not under-play the seriousness of what he had been saying.

"Ada was smashing," interrupted Alec, "and Maurice's mum? Well she turned out better in the end." Alec may not have been so generous had he been privy to her thoughts.

"I am really pleased for you, Maurice. That really is splendid. A super send-off."

"Thank you, George, I am pleased as well."

"Now boys, are you all geared up for the holiday?" Thankful for this lighter subject, Maurice was encouraged to say:

"Believe it or not, George, but I even managed to drag Alec into Moss Brothers."

"Spent a hell of a lot of money, he did," said Alec.

"We did," corrected Maurice. "I shall have to watch when we are in Greece. I tell you, George, that is some body when clad in a swim suit."

"Maurice, you toad," said an embarrassed yet delighted Alec.

The following morning Maurice caught an early train to the city. As George was working, Alec and John were left on their own.

"I feel like walking into the village. How about it, Alec? The sun is out; the air is fresh. Do us both good."

"Yes, alright, John. Just 'ope, er, hope," he said, proudly correcting himself, which made John smile to himself, "that I don't bump into any of the staff from up at the h-house."

"Does it really matter?"

"I suppose not, though they might wonder what I be doing around 'ere."

"If they ask, tell them that you're visiting relations, or," he said with a grin "that you have just got married and are on your honeymoon."

Alec laughed. "Yes, that would do it for sure, and they'd believe it too. Mrs. Brent would be bound to tell the young Mrs. Hall and," here Alec gave another chuckle "what would Durham have to say when his missus mentioned it to 'im, eh!? What could he say? Not the truth that's for sure. You know, John, sometimes I feel right sorry for him. Poor fellow, and saddled with that silly cow."

It was a warm day with not a cloud in the sky. They took a short cut through the woods on a rough path, which led to the village square. John bought stamps from the post office and Alec some tobacco for Maurice.

"How about a drink, John?" suggested Alec. "The Coach is only round the corner."

John had never previously been inside the Coach and Horses. Public houses to him always seemed to be half lit and lacking certain elements of hygiene. They both chose to sit at a table near to the open door. Alec fetched two halves of the best draught beer. For the next ten minutes or so they talked mostly about Alec's interests, and about his family. John was pleasantly surprised at Alec's general alertness. This, together with his avid and enquiring mind gave John confidence in the ongoing relationship between Alec and Maurice.

Suddenly there came a strange voice, at least strange to John's ears. The voice was attached to a short individual wearing a squashed hat, and face to match, boots with leggings, and carrying a small sack tied at the top with rope

"Ullo, young Alec," the voice called," 'ow yer doing? 'eard yer was gorn to foreign parts with yer brother."

Alec turned. It was Frank Minnis the local poacher. He was always up at the house, usually scrounging from the cook, a very friendly and buxom lady to be sure, who, everyone knew, was hoping to provide Frank with more than the odd tit bit! She was a spinster who, although starting late was apparently willing to make up for lost time! As under gamekeeper, Alec had run Frank off the estate many times. Often he had turned a blind eye to the rabbits and pheasants that Frank had already bagged. Live an' let live he used to think.

"No, Frank, I changed me mind."

"Gonner work fer Durham agin?"

Alec shook his head.

"Pity," he said by way of a compliment. "Well, cheerio ole son. Sorry can't 'ang around. Jest in fer a quick 'alf. Look after yerself."

Frank quickly disappeared into the darkness of the public bar. Not long after that Alec and John left the Coach and Horses.

About the time that Alec and John were turning the corner away from the Coach and Horses and onto a public footpath which led to the cottage, Clive and his wife were coming to rest after a fast canter across a field which formed part of his estate. It would be a journey from which neither would return the same as when they set out.

Clive had battled against his homosexuality and now he was battling to sustain his assumed role of heterosexual. This battle had already caused a good measure of stress. Orchestrated by his original decision to acquire a wife, the choice, right from the very beginning, had been fraught with difficulties, both physical and intellectual. It was he who had cast the first dice and hence was mainly responsible for subsequent events, events that were now striving towards some sort of ending. With his decision to marry came untold problems that he could not have foretold, but then his imagination in this field had not been trained! Nor did his wife Anne carry the enthusiasm that he imagined would transform his life into some sort of normality. She was nearly as restrained in heterosexual matters as Clive. It is conceivable that she was lesbian for her inclinations were more towards her girl friends in London than to Clive or other men for that matter. He was unaware of anything specific in that direction though the thought did once cross his mind, more than once in fact.

Perhaps it might have resolved a lot of the problems if the truth about their sexual inclination had been shared. 'Nice' people, Clive and Anne possibly fell into that category, would not discuss it, therefore lack of understanding prevailed. Such was left to the psychiatrist.

"Anne," Clive called over, moving his horse closer to her, "now that we are on our own I think we should have a talk."

He had been dreading this moment all morning. He was as sensitive about it as she. Yet he knew it had to be faced.

"What about?" she replied offhandedly.

"About us, about our relationship, about the future."

"Now, Clive, don't start that all over again," Anne, said defiantly.

"But, Anne, we are supposed to be married, or have you forgotten?" he added, in a tone which he immediately regretted. "Marriage," he went on, "brings certain commitments and er... obligations."

"I know exactly what you are on about" she said, reining in her horse which was becoming restless. "And, as I have repeatedly said, I will not allow you near me if you have any intention of attempting any of that disgusting business."

"Disgusting business? For God's sake, Anne," cried Clive angrily, "we haven't yet consummated our relationship. You surely didn't enter marriage not understanding that part of it. Don't you want a family?" he said growing even angrier. "Are there to be no children? What, might I ask, is the damn point of having got married at all?"

"Don't you dare to shout at me, Clive Durham," she said haughtily.

Then in a more composed manner she continued.

"I really believed that marriage was about two people just being good friends, going out together, sharing things –

but not that," she said sniffing with disapproval. "I find it disgusting," she said again. "Very simply, I do not want to see you re... removing your clothes with," here she hesitated finding it difficult to find the right words, "with such vulgar intentions," she finally managed. "Since we have been married you have tried several times to get me to, er, entertain those nasty ideas. I will just not have it," she said with determination.

Clive looked at her as she sat rigidly on the horse without looking directly at him.

"I have been very patient, Anne, and now I demand that you act like a wife, like a woman. Mother must think..."

Anne's normal flawless face changed so rapidly as to deceive the eye, and was now screwed up in temper, teeth bared like that of a wild animal.

Screeching it out loud, she cried, "I don't give a damn what your blasted mother thinks. Whether you, or your mother," she added for good measure, "like it or not, I was not brought up to think about such things and what's more the very idea of what you are suggesting makes me feel quite sick. No, no, no, no," she ended angrily.

"It seems to me that you don't give a tuppenny damn about anyone except yourself," Clive remarked scornfully.

Anne, recovering from her outburst, turned slowly towards Clive.

"I am quite happy as I am. I did love you, or rather the idea appealed to me. What is love, anyway, Clive?" Clive did not reply.

"If it existed, love that is, then it has turned to dross. I can tell you now, Clive, that if I had known the depths of degradation to which I would be subjected then I would never have married you, or any other man for that matter. My mother is also partly to blame. She must have known what I was letting myself in for. It was mainly her idea anyway. Some of my friends have since told me what has happened to them. I hate men." She spoke with venom in her voice.

Said with such force it frightened Clive, though it came as no great surprise. He considered that possibly his approach, from a physical point of view, was not all it might have been. Nevertheless, on the few occasions when he had attempted such closeness, Anne had persistently and defiantly refused to cooperate. This impasse had not been a developing one, but one that had prevailed since the day they were married. Clive recollected minimal sexual flurry during their honeymoon and, in retrospect, now understood Anne's lack of purpose.

"So, Anne," Clive asked "where does that leave me?"

"I neither know, nor do I care, Clive. And what is more I am not interested in discussing it further. But whilst we are on this distasteful subject, let me say that it is high time that you moved into another room. I find sharing an apartment with you extremely disagreeable and, from my point of view, totally unnecessary."

Clive felt considerably hurt by this onslaught. The background to his getting married in the first place had been difficult enough, and now this. God, he thought to himself, what a mess. During this clash with Anne, he had continuously tried to disassociate himself from a frightening thought. A thought he didn't want to identify. He shuffled it around, backwards and forwards, but ended up identifying its meaning, namely a feeling of great relief! A relief from something that he dared not put a name to. Because of the sheer momentum of their passionate anger, however, both were propelled into pursuing further what was now a futile and utterly unnecessary dialogue.

"You realise, Anne, that denying me my conjugal rights," he said pompously, "could be grounds for divorce."

"Go ahead then, see if I care." Then with a giggle, added, "Perhaps you had better wait until after you are elected to parliament before you do anything like that."

Clive felt he should be angry but even he had to smile inwardly at this remark. He moved his horse slowly forward. Anne followed. They were still near enough to converse.

To Clive their marriage was now nothing more than a couple of signatures on a certificate. The true reality of their situation now began to open out with clarity. Their union – union, that's a joke mused Clive – was dead. Clive admitted to himself that he had entered it with a leaden heart, with the knowledge that it was an enforced second best, well, not even that, for escape and fear had been his predominant reason. He could remember agonising over the decision he had taken and the doubts he had entertained at the time. Perhaps if Anne had been the complete wife it may have worked, he said to himself. He did not dare consider addressing the obvious question of whether he was capable of being the complete husband. Anne would now never know, and neither would he.

All this time they had been virtually shouting across at each other.

"Maurice", the name formed on his lips without intention, then again, "Maurice," he heard himself saying, then, "Oh dear God! What have I done, what on earth would Maurice have to say if he were here now?"

"What did you say, Clive?" called Anne.

Clive reflected on the recent past. It was not long since he was recommending the same matrimonial farce to his best friend, as a device for salvaging his life! 'It will provide stability to your life, Maurice' he remembered saying. It was as dishonest then as it was now, he concluded.

Clive was frightened of the developing situation and of the future. Why had he purposely snubbed and violated the only thing he had ever cared for – Maurice. And now this!

"Anne," he said pitifully, "can we not try? A fresh start maybe. Imagine the joy children would bring to us and the household!" He neither believed this nor had any great desire for it.

Anne shuddered with exaggeration in order to make sure that Clive was left in no doubt about her feelings.

"Clive!" she said, now exasperated with him. Then, speaking slowly at first and emphasising every word, she began. "We have been over this old ground so many times. I shall never, never, change my mind. I should not have got married to you. Mother's idea, though I went along with it. Why can't parents mind their own blasted business? Yes, Clive, I accept my share of the blame and would like to remain your friend, for I am truly quite fond of you. But I will not, under any circumstances, accept the role of Wife in the horrid manner in which you clearly see it. The very idea revolts me. Do I make myself clear?"

"And what, might I ask, if I become a Member of Parliament?" he said, suddenly realising the problems that would bring.

"If I can help, then, of course, I will," she said shrugging her shoulders. "But don't expect me to act out all the wifely stuff; playing host to a bunch of gossiping women and the like. Never! Anyway from what I hear, most of the husbands are whooping it up in town whilst their wives sit at home entertaining boring old matrons or vicars."

"Is that a reference to Mother?" he said sharply.

"No, not exactly, though she is a trifle overpowering, is she not? I have said all I have to say on the subject, Clive, and refuse ever to discuss it again. Is that clear?"

At that moment Clive horse seemed to stumble.

"Hell, what's wrong now?" he said dismounting.

Anne watched as Clive dismounted and began to inspect one of the hoofs. The horse was a reluctant patient. Clive had to force it up and in the process caught the palm of his hand on one of the remaining nails in the hoof. The shoe was missing. His hand started to bleed.

"Blast and damn," he said, his annoyance directed at the hoof, his damaged hand, and more particularly Anne, but not in that order.

"You had better ride on, Anne," he said angrily.

She did not reply. Suddenly she slapped the horse with the reins causing it to gallop off at great speed towards the house.

The sun was still warm. Alec and John had earlier decided to take the longer and more scenic route back to the cottage. This meant walking along a public footpath, which skirted part of Clive's property.

After they had walked for about half a mile they caught the dull sounds of horses' hoofs pounding the soft turf. It was still some distance from them. Neither of them turned until it was obvious that the riders were getting closer. Alec was inquisitive to find out who they were. About a couple of hundred yards away they saw two riders, a man and a woman, following a route parallel to their own. The common land on which they were now walking and that belonging to the Durham estate was separated only by a gravel path and a thin barrier of shrubs.

The steady sound of the horses changed to a slower pace. Within minutes it was obliterated by loud voices. The riders had obviously stopped and were having a very noisy argument. Then they were shouting at each other. Alec and John stopped. They saw the man dismount. That something was wrong with the horse was evident. He was attempting to lift one of his horse's hind legs.

"Expect his horse has shed a shoe," said Alec, "that means they'll have to walk him home."

They saw the woman rider suddenly career ahead, head high. She swept past them at quite a gallop never for a moment looking towards them, whipping the horse viciously as she went.

"Well, well," said Alec with a grin, "that was Clive's wife, young Mrs. Durham, not bad looking is she? Spoiled to 'ell. Doesn't treat the horse too well. It's what she needs. A bit of the whip and on her arse."

John laughed. "I can't say that I saw her clearly enough, Alec, to pass an opinion. Just a petite bundle on a nag. Good heavens, Alec!" cried John, "how on earth did I get into this sort of conversation?"

Alec laughed. "The other's catching us up," he said turning to look back.

"Alec, is his horse hurt do you think? It doesn't seem too willing"

"No, it should be all right, don't forget it's got its own hoof though if a horse walks far like that 'twill become sore and possibly lame," he said. John was noticeably impressed. "It ain't very willing right now because the silly sod is trying to pull it along too quickly."

"Of course," agreed John, though on this subject he was out of his depth.

The other rider was nearly abreast of them but still hidden from them by the horse. Suddenly he moved forward in front of the horse. Almost immediately he recognised Alec.

"Good God! Scudder!" he said, utterly surprised at meeting him. His mood and temper had deteriorated considerably after Anne had ridden off so abruptly.

Alec was also quick of temper and replied quickly and as offensively as he could.

"My, my, 'tis Durham! It's Mr. Scudder to you."

"Watch your manners, Scudder."

"Go to hell. I suppose you lost yours in the mud back there," Alec answered as insolently as possible.

"I'm not usually given to violence," Clive Durham said angrily, "but for two pins I'd lay into you with this horsewhip," he said slapping the side of his riding boot with his crop as if to emphasise his meaning. He knew immediately that he had spoken out of turn, but the damage was done.

"That's fucking wishful thinking," sneered Alec. "Just you try. And the way you're dragging that 'orse along you'll make it lame. Ought to bloody well know better."

This fracas was not of John's liking. He could sense danger and intervened.

"Come Alec," he said, "this is not of our choosing." He turned to Clive and remarked. "Kindly keep your horse and yourself to your side of the fence. And if you attempted to carry out your threat, which is probably unlikely, your electioneering campaign would hardly be enhanced by such a public spectacle," said John, recalling that Clive was a candidate.

"Who the devil are you?" asked Clive rudely.

"Dear, oh dear," commented John, "at least I know who the devil you are," he said in a commanding tone. "I vaguely remember hearing about you. Up at Cambridge with Maurice Hall wasn't it? For your information the name is Jenkins, Professor Jenkins, though why you should be so informed I'm not precisely sure."

Clive forgot completely what he had intended saying. The entry of a tutor from Cambridge complicated still further the thoughts that had been racing through his head. Why would a Cambridge professor be out walking with Scudder?

He paced the horse with the walkers. He knew that he should go on but felt an invisible restraining hand holding him back. Alec looked at John, and then shrugged.

John was the first to speak. "We gather your horse has thrown a shoe."

With embarrassment Clive managed a reply. "Yes, as a matter of fact it has." There was a further pause.

Clive's attitude to those of a lower order was of tolerance only. Now he was confronted with a university professor and his ex under gamekeeper. Also, both were obviously aware of his previous 'friendship' with Maurice and to make matters worse, the under gamekeeper was in a relationship with him. As they were not on his land Clive recognised that he had no right to quarrel with them. He felt rather foolish. In an attempt to alleviate the situation, he was prompted to apologise for his behaviour towards Alec.

"I am sorry, Alec Scudder. There was no reason for my outburst," Clive managed. He was disinclined to say any more.

"That's alright then," came a begrudging response.

Clive was finally stopped by the horse's reluctance to go further. Alec and John moved slowly ahead. Moments later the horse agreed to move forward again.

"Thank God he's gone. Damn, he's still following us. Come on John, hurry before he catches us up. I don't want no more of his bloody cheek. Scudder indeed," he mumbled.

They set off at a faster pace. But before long Clive had caught up with them again. They could hear his heavy breathing as he stumbled along pulling what appeared to be a very unwilling horse.

"Just look at the silly bugger. Doesn't look so high and mighty now, does he?"

"Alec, don't be uncharitable," said John, and added, "the poor chap has just had a row with his wife."

Alec, followed by John, began walking at a faster pace, determined to distance himself from Clive.

"I don't give a damn. He's a nuisance. All right when all goes well. Scudder this and Scudder that. Well I don't work for him no more, so he can go to hell."

"Wait, please wait," they heard Clive cry out.

They turned. John stopped. After walking a few yards ahead Alec turned back to join him.

Clive addressed Alec again, this time in a more tempered voice. "Could you possibly hold the horse for a short while? I cut my hand on a nail when I lifted his foot and the pull of his bridle is making it very sore."

Subdued anger still registered on Alec's face. The decision was slow in coming.

"Alright then," he said without enthusiasm.

He walked over and took the reins from Clive. John smiled at the irony of the situation – to watch these two young men, proud and defensive of their independence, becoming companions on the common land. Clive allowed Alec to set the pace as he led the horse slowly forward.

The silence which followed was utter misery to Clive. He knew he was going to ask the question but found great difficulty in forming the words.

"How is Maurice?" he said at last, addressing John, yet knowing the answer had to come from Scudder.

"Do you really care?" said Alec, still with anger in his voice.

"I imagine that I shouldn't, but yes, I do care."

"Well, in that case, if you mind about him then you have to mind about me, and Alec's the name."

Clive did not immediately reply. He was beginning to feel wretched, what with Anne, the horse and now this.

Finally, he managed to say, "Yes, I am aware that you and Maurice are friends."

In short staccato bursts, Alec, in a manner of speech and voice, which his own ears could hardly believe, heard himself saying.

"No, Mr. Durham, we are lovers. Make what you like of that."

For a moment Clive was at a loss for words. Alec's choice of the very absolute had brought him up with a start. The old love which had carried him once very high and which he had thrown needlessly away now appeared to mock him. He edged nearer to Alec as if to draw from him some imaginary part of Maurice. Lost in thought and time, his heart sang an unusual beat which highlighted emotions that he thought had gone forever.

They walked in silence. Their direction was towards where Alec and Maurice had recently been 'found' by George.

"You know we are near the boathouse – er, Alec," there, at last, Clive had said the word which came out with great difficulty. "Would you and Professor…"

"John" came the voice on his other side.

"John, walk with me as far as that."

"We have the time, certainly. All right with you, Alec?"

With a move away from his previous determination to remain stubborn, Alec nodded his agreement.

It was but a short distance to the boathouse, a part of Clive's estate that Alec used to regard as his own. Alec expected Clive to take over the horse.

"Tie it to that stanchion," Clive said then immediately sensed the danger in what had sounded like an order and hastened to add, "If you would, please, Alec." With this afterthought came relief and his voice now calmed, its earlier hostility rapidly subsiding.

A situation prevailed, as if frozen in time, where no one appeared willing to be the first to speak or to make the first move. There was no question of those old chestnuts, etiquette or decorum, coming into it, just a question of obstinacy or embarrassment, or perhaps a bit of both. The situation was not of John's making or to his particular liking. He waited for what seemed like an eternity for Alec to suggest moving on. Alec was reluctant to relinquish a fleeting desire to stay. He had a certain attachment to this boathouse; it was synonymous with that of homesickness.

Clive also went through painful recollections. He wanted to extend this encounter. Strange though it may seem, he desperately wanted their company, just for a little longer. They stood, somewhat awkwardly, waiting for a lead. John, unused to this sort of behaviour and realising that they were getting nowhere finally suggested that they should move on.

"Please," came the charged, somewhat pleading, voice of Clive, "Perhaps you would consider staying for a while? The boathouse is not the most comfortable, I know, but I can at least offer you some sort of refreshment, a beer or a lemonade perhaps."

The invitation came as a relief to Alec but he was disinclined to show it and continued with his display of defiance. John was unimpressed with the visitor so far and the whole thing was an inconvenience. John saw that Alec showed some inclination to hang around but was disinclined to say so. The ugly face of pride once again. Oh, well, he thought to himself there seemed little harm in accepting Clive's hospitality. They still had quite a distance to walk back to the cottage.

"Not for long," said Alec once John had accepted the invitation. He could not hide his eagerness, however.

Clive studied Alec as they walked down the path. "You know the boathouse better than I, er, Alec." The name came no easier.

"You'd better let me 'ave a look at that hand, it's still bleeding," Alec said.

Clive looked down as if to study his injury. "It will be alright, thank you."

Alec took out a handkerchief, which was clean and unspoiled. He tore it in two. Then he walked over to Clive and ignoring his protestations firmly took his hand. Clive abandoned himself to Alec's ministrations. John watched with hidden amusement.

The angel blew and now the chest of fire was no more, for the coarse and the smooth have met on equal terms.

That is how John saw them, with their creeks of smiles and doubts.

"Alec," said a less wooden voice, "At the top of the cupboard, in the corner, is a flagon of beer. Do you think you can reach it? I know the glasses are in the chest."

Clive was beset with the fear that he had out-reached his hospitality, and particularly to a former employee. It jerked into focus his sense of what might be considered proper for a former employer. At the back of his mind, however, was the fear that they might leave and he currently needed a psychological boost. He looked over at Alec and, in a way, admired his refusal to give way to his, Clive's, superior approach. It was one of those few occasions when Clive was not in control and simply gave in to what was happening.

He watched as Alec lifted the stone jar by its two ear shaped handles and place it on the table. Alec's dignity had been hurt but his help had been needed and begrudgingly accepted. The subconscious weight of one against the other resulted in a more tolerant humour.

The sun shone through a solitary window. An oak table stood in the centre of the room around which they now sat. A most unlikely situation, John thought to himself. Had he anticipated this he would have suggested the ordinary route back to their cottage.

As Clive turned the sun flooded his face but he still kept his eyes on Alec. He raised his glass. "Your very good health," he proposed.

John and Alec responded, Alec in a muffled voice.

There prevailed at this time a tacit armistice between Alec and Clive, which the situation demanded. It could not have been otherwise, particularly as Clive had invited them to the boathouse. Clive was intrigued to learn what the origin of John and Alec's relationship might be. He knew of course that it involved Maurice.

"Might I ask what brings you to this part of the country, John?" Clive asked.

"This is where I live. I regret to say that I'm away far too often. Our cottage is t'other side of the field."

"Excellent," said Clive. He was still puzzled over what part Alec played in all of this.

"It is isolated," said John "but we like our solitude. That is what appeals."

"Does not your wife find it a trifle lonely?"

John glanced at Alec who gave a huge smile at the question, daring John to give an honest answer.

Speaking directly to Clive yet with a glint of mischief in his eyes, John said,

"Alec, my young friend here, finds your question amusing, which, given the circumstances it is. The ancient Greeks had a name for it," They waited for him to continue. "My relationship, unconventional today, would have appeared quite normal to them."

"Oh!" Clive stammered.

"To recall the name Ganymede, one I believe, with which you are probably familiar, will concentrate the mind."

Clive was silent. Alec wondered who the deuce Ganymede was.

John went on: "I understand from Maurice that you were in Greece a year or two ago. A beautiful country. Being an archaeologist the country naturally attracts me, though there are fewer opportunities these days for new excavations. Still, look what we have above ground! The edifice of Pericles with its Doric columns is a landscape gem. In a way it's a pity that the Parthenon attracts so many tourists — too many souvenir hunters, past and present. Alec, my dear boy, I am sure you will be entranced." John was forgetting his audience. At least he was forgetting Alec's current limitations.

John went on. "Lord Byron lived and died there, of course. Apart from being a writer and poet he sponsored a number of uprisings against the Turks. Bisexual, you know. Small wonder that it became his home."

All this time Clive was worrying about the theme of the conversation, and its direction.

"At the time the Parthenon was built," John continued, "love between two men would have been considered the finest. So you're in good company there, Alec."

'What sort of man is this,' thought Clive. 'It is obvious that he knows of my affair with Maurice.'

"I think you are stretching it somewhat," said Clive, intent on making some contribution.

"Not at all," replied John calmly. "Liaisons in the conventional sense, arranged or otherwise, did nothing to upset the quite common, and by Greek standards, normal practice of homosexual love. Alexander The Great, whose sexuality was never in doubt — there was no need for secrecy then — formed several powerful male relationships. Plato, in his Symposium talks of the general acceptance (to which Socrates as well as Aristophanes subscribed) of homosexual love's capacity for satisfying a man's highest and noblest aspirations. But then, of course, male bonding had not been denigrated to the gutter by the Christians. It was once deemed a natural act in the human order of things. Is that not so, Clive?"

"Historically, certainly. Circumstances today, however, are quite different as I am sure you well know." As Clive said this a shadow of the old fear intruded for just a moment.

"The very mention of the word homosexual," Clive went on, "can invite some pretty dangerous and damaging reactions."

"Yes, unfortunately that is so," sighed John, "at least in this part of the world. Must have something to do with the diet and lack of sunshine," he said somewhat jokingly.

For the first time in a long time Clive could now take comfort in the knowledge that the confidences they now shared, neutralized any abiding fears.

"Might I ask, Clive, what took you off to Greece?" John asked.

Clive had known that John was bound to ask this question sometime or other, and here it was.

"I had been unwell," he started. Then, "Also, I had to be on my own. My life was in a state of flux and nothing was simple anymore."

"Was it because of Maurice?" asked Alec with marked innocence.

Clive looked at Alec and marvelled at his naive yet natural approach. He smiled, perhaps for the first time since they had met.

"Yes, Alec, it is fair to say that it was," he said sadly.

This was the very first time that Clive had mentioned it to another living soul. And now his audience was a complete stranger and his ex-gamekeeper. Somehow it didn't seem to matter anymore. There was in fact some relief in sharing this knowledge.

Clive continued. "In all honesty I was frightened. Frightened sick of the way things were going. I am sure you understand what I mean, John. I can't begin to describe the problems I faced at that time. To me they seemed formidable. Events," here he paused, "events, one after the other got me to a point where I could hardly think straight.

Then on one fateful day, in June I think it was, I went through sheer hell. It did not concern me directly but instead a close friend. The consequences for him were horrifying and it struck terror in me as well. Living with it was more than I could take."

John searched his memory and could vaguely remember George mentioning the Risley case.

"It is a tragedy," Clive continued, "that we allow ourselves to be exploited in war for what is termed freedom, then, when we want the freedom to choose who to love, a harmless yet essential human endeavour, we cannot, under penalty of imprisonment, choose our own sex. So fighting for freedom seems a bloody waste of time. You can become severely crippled with or without fighting. I suppose you're wondering, John, why, with views like these, I would want to stand for parliament. The answer at this moment is, I don't know." There was a silence. A trinity in mourning.

"So," said John breaking the spell, "it was from the ruins of Greece that you sought solace, sought answers. Old Athens does have magic, but in finding it one needs to swim in its atmospherics."

"Fine, John, wonderful," said Clive, somewhat impatiently, "providing the atmosphere one has to return to is not laundered by plagues of vultures ravenous for the flesh of men like me."

Alec and John sadly watched Clive's gradual deterioration into melancholy.

"I met my wife, Anne, there. No doubt Maurice mentioned her?"

John shook his head.

"She was on holiday with her mother. She was young and very pretty, in fact still is. In retrospect, now it is too bloody late, I recognise that she was out there, being paraded around by her mother, with the sole object of finding a husband."

Seeing the look of shock on Alec's face made Clive consider him more thoughtfully.

"A common pursuit by mothers of her class, I can assure you, Alec," he said, smiling as he saw amusement spread over John's face.

"It was all so simple, really," he commented, acknowledging that he had been easy prey.

"We were both staying at the same hotel. She, with a mother acting as chaperon and for all practical purposes, as manager, agent, call it what you like," he said sounding bitter.

"It was all very business-like, but then I expected it to be. She was very attractive, witty and amusing, and I, susceptible and looking for an escape route. She provided such an opportunity – or so I reasoned – and there it was, presented to me, you might say, on a platter.

"Up until then I had not settled on any particular course of action. My reasoning was not very reliable at that time, but such had been the pressures over recent months that reason seemed to provide no faculty for resolution. I wanted to accept that escaping from all the problems of the past lay within the scope of conventional marriage. I grasped with both hands this fiction of an idea."

"Has it worked?" remarked John.

"How I wish to God it had," Clive moaned.

"As Maurice will confirm, I did all I could to hurry up the wedding. I wanted so fervently to get the matter settled, to get my life going again. I attempted to smother all the love I still felt for Maurice, not with a great deal of success. I no doubt caused him to suffer very considerably which is to my eternal regret. There, I have at last said it. We, or rather I, believed one could trade our 'friendship' in exchange for a type of fruitless or platonic sort, which of course was less than honest. And recently I was dishonest enough to try and persuade my dear friend Maurice that marriage was a sensible course for him. Heaven forgive me, I am totally ashamed."

"Was there no room for compromise?" asked John

"Unfortunately, no. Right from the beginning with Anne, I've had to bludgeon my mind into drawing a mental blind over my homosexual past. Believe me, that's practically impossible. The past would simply not go away. I suppose the very fact of being married created some diversion. Small comfort as it turned out. There seems little hope of salvaging anything from the chaos."

This unburdening came as a relief, his audience seemed miles away as he continued to unwind.

"She is still a child at heart," Clive said sadly, "never really grown up. To her I am like a surrogate father, one to whom she is quite affectionate. She pretends no physical inclinations towards me, or men for that matter. If you heard our conversation you will have judged that."

"Hopeless," Clive remarked in despair.

"To be honest my own feelings are suspect," he said with a sigh, "the opportunity for them to be exercised might have helped. Now I shall never know," Clive said.

Suddenly he remembered his guests. "Oh God, why am I telling you all this?" He considered whether he was behaving badly, breaching confidentiality between him and Anne – his wife. Wife! He concluded there was no contest. "The answer I suppose is simple, Maurice is no longer available for me to talk to, but you are his friends and, thankfully, I am here with you.

"Anne, strange girl," he said thoughtfully and once again forgetting his audience. "The very thought of sex, especially with me, horrifies her. She has strong views on this. In fact, the subject is now taboo following our row this afternoon. The term couple will not apply to us any more, not that it ever did. We shared a bed, but nothing of a physical nature ever occurred."

Clive seemed lost in thought for a few moments. His brow furrowed.

Alec adequately followed the outline of what Clive had been saying. Christ, Alec thought to himself, it don't pay to be so intelligent, for in the end they don't seem able to know what they damn well want, or how to go about it. I know what I want and there weren't no problems thinking about it.

"So, there you have it. I've not only made my bed but dug my grave." Clive visibly trembled.

"Good God!" said John, appalled at what he was hearing, "You really shouldn't talk that way. There are, I am sure, many positive steps you could take. Some of them will be drastic, of course that is obvious. But in trying to maintain the situation you have described to us, well it's unfair to yourself and, I would suggest, to your wife." Suddenly John felt that he had no right to comment.

"Sorry, Clive, I have no right to talk to you this way, please forgive me."

"You do go on, John," said Alec.

"Yes, I know. I guess you want to go?"

Addressing Clive, Alec asked, "Is it still Scudder?"

"Spare me that, Alec. For we have both changed. Your courage and determination is what I lacked. I envy you, I really do. I have created a quagmire for myself, one proving disastrous for there is no escape that I can see," said Clive kindly. "I am not trying to belittle what you have, for I know from what Maurice told me the other night how vital your relationship is, and in all honesty I am jealous of your happiness.

"I met Maurice up at Cambridge, and after emerging through a maze of inhibitions, fell in love. A moment I'll never forget and I imagine neither will Maurice – once we got over the shock of realisation." Clive gives a slight laugh. "Look at me now. Married, playing country squire, politics and so on. Whatever I try, I know that nothing will ever erase my Athenian inclinations, why should it. I shall no longer try."

"You've got more problems than you started with," suggested Alec.

"Yes, Alec, admitting the truth often creates more problems," Clive said with a sigh.

"The other evening, for instance, when Maurice and I last met, my head ached, not so much from what Maurice had told me, surprising though it was, but at my worry over what was to become of me. I had confided in no one. Maurice, though only in the background, had at least provided me with some kind of balance or anchor. Now that has gone. I am lost, for all directions lead to melancholy and despair.

"I can tell you now, Alec, your name rings funny on my lips, but I am slowly getting there. The other night I stood by the hedge long after Maurice had left, looking out into the darkness. My wife called out, I made no reply. I still carried my speech notes. Then, at last, the blow fell, for now I realised the true value of what I had lost forever." Clive sat quiet for several moments.

"Oh, yes, John, I cried; I'm not ashamed of that. In fact, I was proud of at last doing something that had meaning. I cried out for the eternal ghost of that which had disappeared into the night. And the tears which stained my speech might just as well have been drops of blood coming from a heart spiritually torn from me." Clive's face sank into his arms on the table.

"Clive, my dear fellow, is this why we are here? To help ameliorate your distress," asked John in a voice softened by his pity for Clive.

Clive slowly sat up.

"You happened along, John, that's all, as if sent by Providence, at the very moment that Anne abdicated from our marriage. Does it surprise you, John that I look for sympathy? If I had a problem before it is nothing compared to my situation now. Where, in God's name, do I turn?" he said, looking towards them both.

"But please, let Maurice know that I grieve in parting the way we did. That my words to him that night were a crumbling defence of my own inadequate self. Tell him, if you will, of this visit, of what you see before you. But, I beg you, tell him also that I am sincere in wishing him, with all the love I can bring to bear, eternal happiness." Clive stumbled on those last words. "Eternal happiness," he repeated, "it could have been mine."

With emotions still high, Clive addressed Alec. "Your chance meeting, Alec, will, I now realise all too clearly, bring Maurice the happiness he has always looked for and, rightly, deserves, as in fact do you. I, to my everlasting regret and shame, allowed it to slip away. Entreat him to forgive me, for all the torment I have caused him."

Clive by now had reached a new low. For a while he just sat there, then speaking to them both, asked. "Can we perhaps remain friends? I have to retain some link with the past, an escape route from madness, if you like. Without it I shall be lost and in this wilderness there is but one solution. Sometimes I have prayed that it may come all too soon."

Alec had listened carefully. Some of the conversation was obscure to him, but the vision before him, a Clive he had never really known, was a tragic one. Alec had not been privy to feelings of homosexual love until meeting Maurice. In his working class environment, he had not encountered such elements of emotion. He was maturing fast. Rather like the fluffy chick emerging from the shell proclaiming its freedom.

Those so-called normal instincts some of his contemporaries enjoyed were not marked down for Alec.

The language of his love had been hidden and it was only now, as if by accident, that he was beginning to understand. Maurice, on the other hand, did not have quite the same excuse for lack of understanding. He had been intellectually careless and as a result could have ended up in the same tragic circumstance as Clive.

"Why not come an' see Maurice at the cottage? Have to be before next week though," said Alec.

"We are away then," said John. "Initiating Alec into the joys of travel. Our destination is where you went for inspiration."

"Greece! Oh my God. It had to be an idea of Maurice's. Like returning to the seat of my crime."

"No Clive, in fact it was mine," said John.

"John, we'd better be moving."

Clive looked over toward Alec. Now he saw him differently – no longer the scruffy servant with the insolent scowl. Here he observed another human creature, delighting in his new environment. He was dressed casually, as suited him, with clothes that could not fail to subscribe to a physique of good proportions. There was charm in those well-set eyes, which shone from beneath a cascade of dark hair. His masculinity was immediate. Clive shuddered when confronted with his thoughts. He continued staring at Alec, willing him to speak.

To Clive's relief Alec finally remarked,

"You'll be coming to the house then? 'tis cottage edge of ol' Simon's field."

"Yes," Clive replied. Hesitating for a moment, he then asked. "Will Thursday morning be convenient?"

"Sounds alright to me. I'll tell Maurice you're coming. Come on, John, gets dark soon. You be alright now with the horse or shall we ..."

"Thanks for your help, Alec. I am more than alright, now."

Chapter Ten

"Alec, Alec, John, I'm home," Maurice shouted, entering the front door. There was no reply. He searched the house but they were nowhere to be seen. "Where the devil are they?" he muttered to himself.

He looked at his watch. Gone five. He started a search of the garden, even as far as the shed, which lay at the end. As he was returning he saw them coming from the lane.

He quickly slipped his arm through Alec's, marching him hurriedly into the cottage. Once inside he turned and they hugged each other.

"My God, John, I'm beginning to become obsessive about him. Just a few hours away and it's as if I've been to the other end of the world. And what mischief did you get up to today?"

"Before I tell you anything," said Alec, "we both need a rest. Upstairs!" he demanded, eyes set with purpose.

"Gracious, is this a portent of the future?" laughed Maurice as Alec began pulling him towards the stairs.

"Whatever that means, it'll have to wait for what I've got in mind right now. So, come on, Maurice, can't spend all day talking."

They both re-appeared just before dinner, looking, according to George, "flushed, guilty and with a devilish grin of contentment on your faces."

"It just has to be," Maurice claimed.

"Just look at them, John, two perfect blooms on a single stem, all colour and energy."

"The roots are also of importance," said John, turning toward them, smiling, "tend them carefully, boys, and they will see you through a lifetime of happiness."

"Well said," said George.

"How about a drink before dinner, Alec?" queried John.

"I'll get them," said Maurice going over to the sideboard.

"Guess who we met today, Maurice?" Alec said mysteriously.

"Who?"

"Guess."

"How can I guess, you idiot, I know no one in the village. Come on, Alec, don't be so dramatic."

"I said guess."

Maurice pretended to attack Alec, holding him gently by the arm in a wrestler's grip.

"Tell me you scamp."

Alec turned in Maurice's arms and tried to escape but Maurice's grip held firm.

"I'm curious to know as well," said George.

"I give in – just this once," Alec said laughing, as Maurice released him.

"Well, we bumped into your old friend Clive Durham."

"Hell," exclaimed Maurice, "did he see you?"

"Rather more than that, I'm afraid," said John. Isn't that so, Alec?"

"It's alright, Maurice, don't look so worried, after all, I didn't get into a fight with 'im," Alec said, meaningfully, as if that was a possibility. He put his arm protectively through Maurice's.

"Ol' Durham was out riding with that wife of his. John and me, er... I, were walking back from the village. No, we weren't on 'is blasted land, Maurice," he said hastily. Maurice looked from Alec to John wondering what was coming next as Alec continued.

"I tell you, Maurice, you could hear the pair of 'em, real angry they were, voices would 'ave carried for miles, well at least a couple of 'undred yards or so anyway. The first we knew anything was wrong was when we saw 'is wife suddenly shoot off like the ruddy wind. She was whacking the poor old horse something rotten – got a bit of a temper 'as that one. It's what she needs, as I told John, a good whacking, and on 'er backside." Here Alec laughed aloud. "Durham's horse was in trouble and he'd had to dismount. It had thrown a shoe. Fancy his wife just leaving 'im to it, the bitch!"

"Did he see you, Alec?" repeated Maurice, fearful of what might have happened.

"You tell him, John."

John then began to tell the whole story, right from the very beginning, from the time they first heard horses pounding along the path, to the time they left the boathouse. There were some details he missed, but, as often as not, Alec would joyfully interrupt to provide them. It took some time for John to complete the story, especially with Maurice and George constantly urging him on. Eventually he got down to the tears, the remorse, and finally the proposed visit on Thursday.

"I haven't left anything out have I, Alec?"

"No, that's it, more or less. But I can tell you, Maurice, I wasn't going to talk to him. He spoke first – and bloody rude he was too. So I was bloody rude back. We wasn't even on his land. Tried to leave him behind but the quicker we walked the faster pace 'e made to keep up with us. When we reached the boathouse his hand was still bleeding, and awkward bugger though he was, I made him let me wrap it with my handkerchief." Maurice shook his head in disbelief, amazed at what he was hearing.

"Somehow we all finished up in the boathouse. Seemed funny being there without you, Maurice."

"Heavens alive!" cried Maurice somewhat alarmed, "he invited you into the boathouse and actually let you tend to his hand? Hard to believe. And coming here! Decidedly odd. Oh God! I'd rather hoped that we had seen the last of Clive and his problems. Coming here?" he repeated, "Well, well," he said, then as an afterthought added, "there's one thing you both seem to have forgotten, and that is George. Bit of a dilemma for him don't you see?"

It suddenly struck Maurice that there was something very bizarre about this situation, which, to him, had a very funny side to it. It suddenly made him burst into laughter.

"How about that, eh! Meeting my ex-lover in the house of his butler! No offence, George, but the position you have to admit is rather quaint. Ha, ha, ha," he chuckled. "Please forgive me, George," he said his face still creased with laughter "it just struck me as funny, that's all," he said wiping a tear from his face with the back of his hand.

"Oh dear, what have we done, Alec?" said John.

"It's very simple," said George, "You just do not mention me to him at all. I'll keep away from the cottage during his visit."

This annoyed Alec considerably. He would not be party to such behaviour. He thought it unnecessary and would have none of it.

"Why do you all make it so bloody difficult?" he said angrily. "This is George's home, and he comes first. I was also one of his workers in case you 'ave forgotten, and compared to George a lowly one at that. As I said then I say now, if he can't accept us as we are then to hell with him," he said, his voice rising.

"Though I promise you'll find him different now, Maurice," Alec said, his voice dropping. "The poor sod needs a bit of help – but," he said shaking his head and raising his voice again, "not if it means leaving George out in the cold if you sees what I mean. No, that definitely won't do. And he knows by now that I don't give a fig for his airs and graces." At this point Alec paused, the fire in his voice partially quelled.

"Seems to me," he went on, "trouble with folk starts when they cares so much about what others think, or what others might be saying about 'em. Not me, not likely," he said, speaking his thoughts clearly. "What I now cares about is you, Maurice. I cares that much for you, Maurice, that I say, to hell with anyone who doesn't. And if they would hurt you by so much as a hair of your 'ead," he said recalling having heard the expression somewhere before, "then, by God, they'd have a lot to worry about. And if the going gets really rough, alright, we'll bugger off to some other place."

"Well, Maurice," said George, "you couldn't get anything more blunt and to the point than that. He's right, of course. Well said, well said, young Alec," he congratulated. "Of course if, once he is informed of my relationship with John and indicates that he is uncomfortable with the situation, as well he might be, then I will be out of a job, for I would simply leave. The dilemma would be his, not mine. I am sure that he will also realise that his security is not under threat, for, as they say, we all swim together."

"George is right. Clive should have no fear of us. I also have to agree with Alec." remarked John. "We do behave in an odd way, sometimes. Erecting fences to deceive others and fool ourselves. True friendship never got far that way. What's the point of adopting disguises? That way no one ever gets to know you, or you them."

"I've only one disguise, George," interrupted Alec, "and that's me, Alec. Not much changes with me except my temper.

"Let Clive come. What's it to us? He can either take us as we are or clear off. He'll want to stay alright if I read the old signs correctly."

"George, what do you say?" questioned John.

"I think it is really up to Maurice. He is his friend after all. I have no objections."

"I am not feeling particularly benevolent towards him right now," said Maurice, "but as you have arranged the visit, then of course, with George's permission, he must come."

"In that case" said George, "I feel it right to let Clive know the situation, apropos John and me, before he comes here. When he is on his own, I'll tell him. It is quite possibly, of course, that with me in the equation he will find it all too embarrassing or just too difficult to cope with. Whatever his response may be, I agree that we should at least give him the opportunity of coming over if he wishes."

"It will be his last, as far as I'm concerned," said Maurice decidedly. "I'm finished with all his vacillation."

It is fair to say that in his emotional frame of mind Clive had allowed himself to forget the difficulties that might arise if he followed up the invitation to visit the cottage where Maurice was staying. The old recurring fears concerning his relationship with him did cause concern, if only minimal, and now he began to reflect on his conversation with John and Alec. His irrationality began to rise again and he imagined all sorts of ill-founded consequences following his openness with them. He even let the spectre of being publicly reviled appear and, with a shudder, recalled the ghost of Risley. It was nonsense, of course, but it would take a saner moment to realise it. His bitter discourse with Anne had relaxed his hold on the guard which protected him from himself. So he continued on this blind course, holding to the irrational idea than it would be better keeping things as they were and not, as he imagined, tempting fate.

He knew that he shared, with Maurice and the others, knowledge which held potential danger. But now he entered one of his saner moments, and was able to recognise the common factor they all shared which provided the safeguard he looked for. The relief this gave permitted his gloom to settle.

He admired the degree of freedom that John had demonstrated, his openness pleased him. It consoled him that John's awareness of his and Maurice's 'relationship' had permitted him to indulge in such a degree of intimacy. Then there was Scudder. Clive took on a frown, which further altered his mood. Clive's present position in the community gave some satisfaction, even with its pride and prejudices. His future was not settled; he was now less enthusiastic about his campaign for parliament than when it began.

Clive tried vigorously to shake off the depression, with fortunately some success, and set about attending to other matters. At about nine o'clock the following evening, an hour after serving dinner, George managed to attract Clive's attention, as he was about to enter his study.

"Yes, Simcox?" Clive asked pleasantly.

"It is of a very personal nature, Mr. Durham," began George. Even at this stage he felt unsure of how exactly to proceed.

"Do go on," remarked Clive.

"It concerns a conversation you had recently with a friend of mine, his name is John."

"John?" exclaimed Clive with a frown.

"Yes, John Jenkins."

"Good God. He is a friend of yours?" Clive asked incredulously, all the fears he thought he had overcome beginning to crowd in again. His mind raced ahead.

"How's this?" he asked in a surly manner, yet anxiety blended with his voice.

George did not like the way the conversation was going, and Clive's attitude did not encourage more. George had no intention of offering excuses of any kind and certainly not of apologising. From Clive's reaction to the little he had said, George realised the futility of proceeding further and decided to end it abruptly.

"I am sorry, Mr. Durham if the subject disturbs you. I will pursue it no further. The circumstances surrounding my life would certainly not interest you nor are they, for that matter, any business of yours." George said abruptly. This drew an abrupt gasp from Clive, which George ignored. "I regret that my position here is now untenable."

Clive made to speak, but George was determined to finish.

"Do not concern yourself on my part, Mr. Durham, for I am sure that you will be more than happy that I offer you my notice of leaving your service. It is the only thing under the circumstances. At the end of the month will suit me, if that is convenient, or sooner if you prefer."

With the full implication of George's revelations finally sinking in, Clive's mind became a tempest of utter confusion and fear. It took little imagination for him to glean the relationship between them. Even more intolerable was the involvement of Alec. And now he was leaving.

Clive, yet again, was at a loss. He was overcome with all manner of disturbing thoughts. He looked at George and took in the solemn creature that stood before him. He had always behaved impeccably and Clive admired his honesty and integrity. He now believed that here was another situation similar to that of Maurice and Alec. He realised at once that escape from their shared knowledge was impossible, yet Simcox displayed a degree of trust, which even Clive recognised. This judgement greatly ameliorated Clive's fears.

"Oh dear, oh dear," was all Clive managed.

Their exchange had been brief. There was a noticeable change to Clive's normally placid face indicating the distress he felt. He managed, rather stiltedly, to thank George for telling him and was about to speak further but the sudden appearance of his wife quickly terminated their conversation.

About an hour later Clive asked George to come to his study. He was again polite and courteous, but there was no hint of intimacy in his voice. He stated, quite simply, that 'of the matter we discussed I am of the opinion that it best be forgotten'. It was uttered, as might be some badly rehearsed part in a play. George noticed the total lack of variety of tone normally associated with the man. Clive made no mention of him leaving and George decided to send a note of resignation the following day.

Clive's somewhat terse and brief statement did not appear to demand or require any reply from George and after a brief and silent interval George ended the interview with Clive by making his exit from the room in total silence. The manner of Clive's reply still bothered George a little, having regard to the account given by John and Alec.

"It is of no great consequence," he said when he reached home later that evening.

"The whole thing is a bore," remarked Maurice "and what is more quite absurd. Clive must have had an aberration. Are you sure he didn't fall off the blasted horse, Alec?"

"I expect George's exposé tipped the balance. In his present state of mind his values probably oscillate. Currently he probably feels, 'should I with the devil sup'." John offered.

"I really have no further interest in the matter," reflected Maurice, "Let's discuss the arrangements for next Thursday, much more interesting."

"Don't you think it would be a good idea," suggested John "if we stayed at the Victoria Hotel on the Wednesday night? We have to get down to Dover before midday on the following day. I've checked the connections, and the train for Dover leaves Victoria at eight thirty. By the way, Maurice, has Alec got a passport?"

"Yes," answered Alec, "and what a game that was. Wanted me birth certificate they did."

"And what a job to find it," exclaimed Maurice laughing, "took some searching in the archives of Somerset House I can tell you. Began to wonder if he'd ever been born."

Alec lunged towards him. "You're lucky I was."

"Yes, Alec, I am the luckiest man in the world that you were conceived. My eternal thanks to your parents."

"What'd they have to do with it?" The others all rocked with laughter. "Ask them next time you see them, Alec," teased Maurice.

"You're bloody sure of yourself, Maurice." The aggrieved tone in Alec's voice alerted Maurice.

"I had bloody well better be, my love. Forgive me Alec if I go too far sometimes. I really mean well, for you occupy my mind all of the time, and my life, even longer."

They talked well into the night, Alec getting more excited by the hour. Later, as he lay facing Maurice he asked, "Do we really go to bed on the train?"

"Of course."

"What about, well, you know, Maurice."

"No, Alec, I don't know." Maurice grinned to himself in the dark.

"Come off it, Maurice, you know what I'm on about." Silence.

"Alright then, for a start, where do we piss?"

Maurice pressed closer as he whispered,

"Out of the window." Alec took Maurice's face and kissed him on the cheek then worked down to his lips.

"'Course you're lying," he said.

"You know I am. It's alright, love, they have all the facilities."

Later, Alec repeated this to John who commented, "Not having experienced travel in this way, Alec, you were sensible to enquire. Ask Maurice to comment on managing a game reserve and he would be lost and would have to go to you for help. It is refreshing to come across innocence anyway."

Alec enjoyed the complement and looked over at Maurice, grinning and daring him to disagree.

"Innocence!" exclaimed Maurice, "I can tell you, John, that that youth knows more tricks than a court jester."

"That's fine coming from you, Maurice. If my dad knew the tricks you showed me, he'd have got his strap out. Mind you, Maurice," Alec said laughing, "I did teach you a thing or two."

"There, John, I told you, is he not incorrigible?"

"Such happiness," John said with a sigh, nodding his head at the same time. "I've not seen such a show of it in a very long time. The pair of you rightly deserve an award - for effort alone."

Chapter Eleven

On the Thursday morning the weather was overcast, but as the morning developed, patches of blue broke out from the dull grey mask that had covered the sky. As the sun moved into the expanding region of blue, it pitched its rays to warm the earth, making away with many of the dismal and depressing shadows. The advancing signs of autumn seemed also to fade from sight.

George had the day off and was busy preparing dinner. John and Alec, somewhat prematurely, were checking their holiday luggage. For Alec, the trip to Greece was an adventure, which began on the very day that they had agreed to go. Packing new clothes into new suitcases was part of the fun and Maurice was overjoyed to see him so happy and excited.

Maurice decided to take a walk into the village.

With the sun shining brilliantly outside, Maurice ignored John's advice to wear a jacket. The route he took was not familiar to him, and then neither was the area. He began crossing a field following a well-trodden route. Around him were a number of sheep grazing continuously on the grass. There were also one or two lambs that had been kept back for purposes of breeding, or so Alec had told him.

Behind him lay George's cottage and ahead he could see the steeple of the village church. 'It would be impossible to get lost around here' he thought to himself.

The flat of the land made the church visible for several miles around. At the end of the field he could just make out the boundary of part of Clive's estate.

Maurice was sure that he could see Clive's house.

Although partially hidden by a line of conifers it still loomed large even from where Maurice was walking. He decided to take no chances and to keep strictly to the public footpath.

As is often the case in an environment such as this, everything peaceful and relatively quiet, and with the sun providing luxuriant warmth to the body, one begins to relax, to unwind, sufficiently, one might hope, to begin to appreciate the beauty of the countryside. Details of its fauna and flora, such as there were, are facets of life not normally noticed. Maurice was trying not to concentrate on anything in particular, but he did notice two young rabbits scamper past him barely ten feet away, and saw them disappear into one of the many burrows that pitted the field.

In a short while he saw, by a wire fence at the end of the field, an old wooden bench. It had been placed adjacent to a stile. He reached the stile and began climbing over it, then came the idea of lying in the sun for a while. He turned around and, vaulting over the stile, moved back into the field once again. He walked slowly over to the bench seat, which he noticed was quite dry and well maintained.

After removing his shirt, he folded it into a small bundle, which he placed at one end of the seat. He then stretched himself out on the wooden slats that had already become quite warm. Almost immediately he began to enjoy the heat of the sun on his face and felt its warmth gathering on the upper part of his body. The sun was by now quite high and strong enough to force Maurice to close his eyes.

This was a time when he could afford to reflect on events of the past. Apart from the effort of getting his brain into a selective mood, there were no other distractions which could bother him. His mind inevitably dwelt upon the successes of the last few days. Their new friends George and John had been a godsend. Then came the surprise reconciliation with Ada and the 'sorting out' of his mother. All of this contributed to his present happiness and peace of mind. The past and its problems was no longer worth thinking about. They remained in the past, where they belonged, and Maurice had skirted clear of them and moved on. His mind concentrated on Alec, now to the forefront in everything he did. He tried to intellectualise on the subject of love. Do emotions cloud one's mind? Is there any logic in love?

He remembered once attempting to write down the distinction. Clive had laughed at his 'poetical' offering. It went something like this.

Logic is a path of clear definitions orientated to make appreciations global, to provide a vista from high up where the air is purified and unsullied by imperfections, inhibitions, prejudices, and cant. Love, however, seems to defy logic in that there is a chemistry of undefined formulae that exists between two bodies.

Maurice thought it not bad. Whether it was or not, the latter, love, was something he intended never to let slip from his grasp for as long as he lived.

He must have fallen asleep, some might claim with mental exertion, but in truth it was just the soothing balm provided by the heat of the sun.

Clive had spent many unhappy moments since George had approached him on the previous day. Their conversation may have been brief but its impact, on Clive at least, had been considerable. His pride had been somewhat bruised. His resolution to continue with the life he had chosen had been undermined, not because of his butler's intervention – though that, as far as Clive was concerned, had been dramatic enough. No, it was Anne's ultimatum, final and without further conference. He had agonised over what he should now do. There was his constant pride in conflict with the fear of an unresolved situation. Despite all the options which now swept before him, that single element which had attracted him to Maurice in the first place, brought more powerfully to the fore by his wife's recent action, crashed repeatedly to the front of his mind. Such was the nature of his problem that he knew of no one to whom he could turn. He hated the situation and could not see hope of any resolution.

He now moved out of the house and began walking aimlessly towards a meadow, which lay alongside his own estate. By this he hoped to shake off the melancholy or at least restrict its increasing force. There was also an alternative motive. He shook his head as if other ideas might suddenly appear and claim some validity. He had more or less convinced himself that his future carried no substance. He was dangerously close to the very edge of the precipice to oblivion. He now seriously dwelt on a swift and final solution. His eyes followed a young rabbit, which raced towards the stile at the edge of the field. At the same time he saw the body which lay stretched on the bench. His heart took a leap, a near somersault would be more accurate. It was Maurice.

"Hello, Maurice," came a voice.

He heard the familiar sound. In the beginning it seemed far away.

"Maurice!"

In opening his eyes, the sun made him blink, then a shadow covered him. He looked up and began to recognise the voice.

"Maurice," said the voice more urgently this time. A hand lightly touched his naked shoulder.

"Well, I'll be damned! Clive!"

"Yes, Maurice, 'tis me," Clive said awkwardly.

Maurice drew himself up, reached for his shirt, which he pulled over his head. He then swung round on the bench to face Clive.

"Don't tell me you just happened to be passing," Maurice said bluntly. "I thought we had had our final conversation. Ought you not to be out canvassing, or speech making? Our association was terminated – remember? You have found your peace and I, thank the Lord, have found mine. Now why don't we just leave it at that?"

Maurice was angry that he had been disturbed. He got up to go.

"Maurice," pleaded Clive, "you really must talk to me."

"Look, Clive, as far as I am concerned all the talking has been done. Alec – does that name make you wince …"

"Maurice, please."

"John and Alec told me about their encounter with you the other day. They also mentioned that you were invited to the cottage – this morning, wasn't it?" He said with sarcasm in his voice. "That was before Simcox – George – entered the scene. Following that revelation, you chucked the idea. Under the circumstances perhaps you might be excused, for, after all, the suggestion that you call at the cottage was Alec's – or perhaps you prefer Scudder – dear thing that he is. Frankly I am amazed that you accepted his invitation in the first place. Now, Clive," he said keeping his voice under control, "I suggest that you bloody well get on with your own life!"

"You hate me so?" asked Clive sadly.

"No, Clive, I do not hate you. In the name of God how could I?" he said with some force. "I unreservedly worshipped you for a couple of long, trouble-filled, years, often bearing the anguish of frustration through your constant fear of our love affair. Believe it or not, but I would have given my life for you. No, Clive, I do not hate you but I have a new life. I believe I am one of the luckiest persons on this planet to find someone who really loves me."

"With that abundance of happiness will you not spare me a little?" asked Clive looking even more forlorn.

"Oh, Clive, you prevaricate so much. How can one possibly help you? You have your so-called intrinsic values and these provide the standards by which you wish or have decided to live. Your marital problems come as no surprise. You were a bloody fool in the first place and I nearly fell for your idea that all was sweet and light in that enterprise. You left me in a state of near suicide, which took all of my will power, and the help of an American doctor, to sort out. It was with the best will in the world that I tried to compromise. Alec, dear Alec, he provided all the balm that was needed to cure me of my idiocy, to bring me to my senses, to give meaning to my life, to give me uninhibited love, that which previously I had desperately sought from you and which you so easily pushed aside. Why? Well I think we know the answer to that."

Maurice was determined to let Clive know how much harm he had caused in his life.

"No, no," cried Clive, "your situation never developed as mine, Maurice. I never got over that dreadful time in court, when they virtually crucified poor Risley. You cannot imagine what it was like to hear the putrid morality issuing from the lips of that judge. Then to see the poor bastard wilt as they sentenced him. I tell you, Maurice, when they sent him down, part of me felt as if it had been excised. The right thing, the right thing, I kept repeating until I began to convince myself that I must go away from you, away in fact from myself. For what purpose? I have since asked myself. Now, when it is too late, we all know. To satisfy the bigots, of which Borenius – and, to some extent, I regret to admit, my own mother."

"You did not mention all of this to me at the time, Clive. Of course I remember you going to Risley's trial. But right from the beginning did we not commit ourselves to discussing with each other anything that might affect our relationship?"

Shaking his head, Maurice continued, "Oh, yes, I remember the case well enough. June, I believe. Yes, come to think of it, it was the time when you began to question our future together. The time when you began talking in platonic terms. Of how marvellous such a close bond between us would be providing that the normal conventions were observed. For God's sake, Clive, how could I possibly ever forget?"

Clive sat down on the seat next to Maurice, hoping to get closer as Maurice went on.

"Oh, yes, Clive, I remember the beginning of the hell I went through as you began gradually to destroy the framework of our bond, the trust, the love. Oh, yes, my memory is quite clear on that. Of course I knew that you also suffered – first your breakdown at my home, then your trip to Greece. But you cannot possibly imagine the agony I went through. Waiting for you to return home yet knowing that you would never return for me. I, like the idiot I am, just would not accept what my instincts told me.

"I was like a ship at sea heading for the rocks, hoping for survival yet knowing the wind would never change. Then the final blow, like an iron fist knocking me down for six. The news, not from you, oh no, but coming second hand from my mother, of your decision to marry. In my heart I was near dead. Perhaps you can imagine. You made bloody sure, Clive, once and for all, that it was all over between us.

"Survival meant little or nothing to me. You offered me open house at Penge as if I were some poor relative over whom you had a slight conscience."

"Maurice, that is unfair," cried Clive.

Maurice purposely ignored the interruption. He went on: "I tried to re-arrange my life around a variety of activities. But there always remained my homosexuality. Yes, Clive, my homosexuality. I went to the trouble of seeing a psychiatrist in London. He was practical, sympathetic, and even suggested I live in a more civilised country. At the end of the day I was, thank God, saved from humiliation, I met Alec."

"Maurice, Maurice," Clive moaned, "I've made such a mess of my life."

He leaned towards Maurice until finally resting on his shoulder.

"You have a wife," Maurice said abruptly and with malice in his voice. "You made the choice. You will have to live with that. It should please your idea of status in the world, of your so called superiority, twist your values to some form of conventionality to suit those insufferable acquaintances of yours. Those who if they knew more about you would string you up like some common criminal. It is they who should be punished." The voice had an edge which cut Clive to the quick. Its tone was unmistakable. Clive's hope's sank and with it his ability to care anymore. This was the bitter reward that he knew he deserved.

The echo of Maurice's words rang in Clive ears like a death knell. He imagined his world to have collapsed and any purpose in living now seemed meaningless. Slowly, he lifted his face and looked directly at Maurice. The friendliness, which he had always managed to identify, was gone. There was no vestige of it to be seen.

"You are right, Maurice, I do have a wife, or rather a companion," he said bitterly. "You know all about that of course." He looked away, defeated, anxious not to betray his feelings. "For the past I owe you a debt of gratitude I can never repay, Maurice. I should not have come here like this. I know that I am now the very pestilence of your past, a cancerous growth which you hoped had gone away."

Here he paused, fearing a break in his voice. He moved away from the comfort of Maurice's shoulder.

"I am truly very sorry, Maurice. I have caused you so much sorrow. I shall not concern you with my problems ever again." He stood up, weary yet determined. "I shall miss you, my dear, dear friend. Within the next week I shall settle my affairs, then I shall be free, and forever. Happiness no longer counts when the soul departs."

He bent down and suddenly kissed Maurice lightly on the cheek. "Forgive me," he said with a choke in his voice.

Clive moved away and with bowed head, shoulders dejected, began to walk hurriedly across the field.

Maurice looked after him. Emotions swelled to painful dimensions. Compassion raised him to a new consciousness. "Come back, come back, you fool," Maurice shouted.

There was no answer. Maurice saw the bent figure break into a run.

"Clive, for Christ's sake come back."

Maurice raced after the disappearing figure. He was stronger and faster than Clive. When finally running alongside him he called, "Clive, you must stop, stop I say."

Clive ignored him and changed direction as if to evade him, heading towards the boundary fence.

Maurice caught up with him again and grabbed him by the arm. Clive struggled free but Maurice took him more firmly.

They began to struggle.

"Maurice, leave me alone, let me be," Clive muttered between sobs of despair. "Please," he begged once more.

Clive was now actually fighting and in the struggle they both fell onto the grass. Maurice sat astride him pinning his arms to the ground. Clive continued to resist for a while then of a sudden, relaxed, defeated.

"I am both a better wrestler and boxer than you," Maurice reminded Clive. "I will not let you go until you agree to act sensibly."

Clive's resistance was gone. They were both covered in grass and mud when they eventually rose from the ground.

Maurice put his arm around Clive's shoulders.

"Christ, what a mess we are in. Well, one thing is now certain, you cannot possibly go home in your present state of mind."

Raising a tear stained face, his hair totally askew, Clive gave a final sob then quickly buried his face in his hands.

"Maurice, Maurice, what is to become of me?" he cried between sobs. "At your home it was the same. I just cannot seem to get anything right."

"I want you to come to the cottage as was previously arranged," Maurice said, experiencing a great surge of pity for his friend.

With Maurice guiding, his arm still around Clive's shoulder, they both walked slowly across the field.

"Let's head toward the bench," said Maurice in a voice filled with tenderness.

"It is only natural that I should be concerned about you, Clive, after what we have both been through. So, yes, Clive. I really want you to come back with me."

Neither spoke for several moments. Maurice suddenly thought of another possible problem.

"Just one thing, Clive, call it a minor question of adjustment if you like. Are you ready, do you think you are in a fit state, to be able to cope with treating George, George Simcox, as an ordinary human being?"

"George Simcox?" queried Clive, slightly recovering.

"Yes, the same one, John's lover, in whose house Alec and I are staying."

"Yes, yes of course," Clive spoke slowly. The recollection of his brief interview with George the previous evening came slowly back to him.

"Does it make a difference?" Maurice asked gently.

Clive looked over at him, and then with a slight trace of a smile, shook his head. In the state he was in, emotional and somewhat confused, there was no hope, or inclination on Clive's part, to re arrange the cards to satisfy propriety or the demands of society. Without any need of prompting, Clive knew instinctively that Maurice's support was more important than anything else at this time.

They walked in silence for a while then Clive heard himself saying, "Why, Maurice, why did you stop me?"

"Because, my dear old friend, despite what we both may think, that link which our maturity promoted is luckily still partly there. I say this in all honesty, and without regrets. It may not have remained that way, but now it will, and I am glad. I believe you feel the same."

"Oh yes, Maurice, yes, I do," Clive replied quickly fearful least the moment be lost. "There is no doubt in my mind, none. I still retain much affection for you, Maurice but I promise that it won't intrude." He continued looking sideways towards Maurice.

"What you were saying earlier, Clive is just too horrible to contemplate. Not that anyone is immune from thoughts of that kind, given the right state of mind. And, yes, Clive, the ultimate solution of suicide did once cross my mind. But it was never a serious contender for my life. You must accept that I, with Alec of course, am with you from now on. Does that alter your attraction for life, to being around, and to a friendship which offers you sustained support, providing you do not go off at a tangent again?"

"Yes, Maurice, it does. That is why I had to see you. You were my last chance. I can understand your anger. I really thought it was the end. Can I..." here Clive broke down completely and began to sob.

Maurice was physically upset by Clive's behaviour. He pulled Clive towards him, an arm resting over his shoulder. Speaking softly, he said,

"Well Clive, from now on you will always be able to count on me and also Alec – remember the scruffy under game keeper?"

"Maurice, please," he said sadly wiping his eyes.

"I was joking, at least now I am joking. The big question is... can I count on you? Do you want me to be involved in your life?"

"Is it not obvious, Maurice?"

"Well, let it be so. No more acts of desperation, agreed?"

Clive gives a deep sigh. "Agreed," he said with a voice still unsteady.

They got back to the bench where their conversation had first begun.

They both sat in silence, Maurice with a leg propped up and leaning back against the wooden slats, Clive sitting close but bent slightly forward.

"I suppose," Clive began quietly "the reality of the situation is that my life is being forced to come into focus."

"It has chosen an unfortunate time to start doing so," said Maurice calmly.

"It was your blatant admission and bloody determination, Maurice, which really did it – your crazy excitement the other night. And to cap it all, with Alec Scudder!" Here Clive raised a defending hand as if to ward off an attack. "It's alright Maurice, Alec, the name, rolls readily off my tongue now.

"Since then of course everything has changed or rather I have changed. Not really changed but forced to accept the self that I have been avoiding for so long. That moment in the garden was the catalyst, for truth and honesty."

"Now that you are calm and talking as the Clive I once used to know, perhaps we can talk with honestly and with utter frankness. As friends, we are together again, for as long as openness is our byword."

"Together again, yes, friends. That is all I ask, Maurice."

"As you rightly said a while ago, Maurice, I still have a wife." He paused. "In name at least. I have to tell you, Maurice, that since my marriage to Anne the transformation that I had expected, foolishly perhaps, has not happened. The situation, in fact, deteriorates each day. All I can say is that yesterday Anne and I reached some sort of an understanding – or so I believe. What a pathetic creature you see before you, Maurice," he said sadly. He found it difficult to continue.

"Consummation of marriage? What a sick joke that turned out to be, Maurice," Clive finally blurted out. "Maybe the consolation is in not having to put to the test my own willingness." He gave a short nervous laugh then began to sob.

Maurice again placed an arm around Clive's shoulders causing him to sigh deeply as the weight of his depression grew lighter.

Within the comfort of Maurice's protective arm, Clive calmed and his eyes cleared. He had not wept in vain.

"Marriage for Anne," he continued slowly, "is just 'great fun'. Last week, and again yesterday, she demanded separate rooms. Her nervousness with me at night makes me feel like an intruder. It is all so unreal. You will find this hard to believe, Maurice, but I suffered a huge sense of guilt when I agreed, this very morning, to move into a separate room. Our lives have to run separately but together, if you see what I mean."

"I think so," said Maurice, sad at the knowledge of Clive's disastrous marital experiment.

"Maybe this will help you to understand why I am so wretched, Maurice. Yesterday my world, such as it was, began really to fall apart. Had I not been out riding with Anne, had not the horse lost a shoe, had not I recovered my temper when I first met your friends, then, dear Maurice, I should not have been able to clutch at my last hope, my only hope, and that as you know, Maurice, is you."

Maurice felt Clive's body tremble with emotions. He now knew that he had some responsible for this sad creature.

"I am now of a mind for change, Maurice," Clive said after a while. He now appeared brighter, the burden of his admission of failure now shared. "Your friendship I know is the only means of retaining my sanity."

"Well, Clive, you have that."

Clive moved closer. "Maurice," he said, as if it were some sacred word.

Pausing just briefly Clive went on.

"A week or so ago, Maurice, I had decided that mother and Anne would remain at Penge and I would move to the dower house in Sellinge. I had intended asking George Simcox to come with me."

"Have you mentioned it to George yet?"

"No," he said sadly, then looked questioningly towards Maurice. He paused then said.

"Obviously he hasn't told you that he gave me notice of leaving, only this morning."

"Oh," said Maurice, "No, I had no idea."

"Then, today, well I knew that I was nearing the end of my options, of what I could cope with, of the futility of the future, of, in fact, the point of going on. Then I saw you. It was not a coincidence really, Maurice for I decided earlier to head towards your cottage in the hope of meeting you.

"Perhaps when I see George Simcox and can explain, he will change his mind about leaving," suggested Clive.

"Perhaps," agreed Maurice. "Anyway you will be able to ask him shortly. Come on Clive, enough confessions for one morning."

"Maurice, you're a brick, and..."

"Enough, Clive. You're pretty good yourself. I speak after considerable experience of the beast," he said with a laugh.

They joined arms and walked slowly back across the field.

"Did George tell you he was leaving?" asked John.

"Leaving, what, leaving here, George?" queried Alec.

"No, Alec, leaving Penge. About time I had a change. Told Mr. Durham last evening." Said George.

"Bit sudden wasn't it? What did old Clive say?"

"Rather embarrassing really," George answered.

"Although I said little, what I did say would have sparked off a trail of understanding of the situation between John and me and therefore our association with you and Maurice. Later, he called me to his study. He looked quite sad and said he was very sorry that I felt I had to leave. His manner was most strange. He looked vacantly towards the window as if half expecting someone to appear. Then I noticed his hands were shaking. I began to wonder if he was ill. Something is decidedly wrong with that young man. When I mentioned that I would like to leave at the end of this month he looked at me as if in a trance. I repeated it. He just smiled then walked away. Most peculiar."

"Got himself into one frightful mess if you ask me," offered John.

"Maybe," said George sadly, "maybe you are right."

"Well, well! I don't believe it, just look who's here!" said Alec suddenly spotting Maurice with Clive through the window. They were walking towards the front gate.

"Who?" queried John who had just walked into the room. "Why Maurice, and with Clive!"

"Gracious!" said George.

This was one of those occasions when George felt unable to cope. Being confronted with a situation such as this, and without any warning, disturbed him considerably.

Up until now, contact between Clive and George within the confines of Penge had been straightforward as employer and employee. Neither of them had had occasion nor, for that matter, desire to share the other's interests outside of Penge. It is true that George probably knew more about Clive than Clive did about him but only to the extent of Clive's earlier relationship with Maurice. Now, here he was, stepping over his doorstep, about to enter his house and as a guest. Shaking his head George muttered to himself, "tis a queer, unpredictable world, to be sure."

He was none too convinced that he liked the idea of meeting Clive under these circumstances. Clive's invitation to George's house had once been rejected, so why had he suddenly changed his mind? George thought also of the problems this might create. He was concerned for both Alec and Maurice.

"Alec," he said "and you as well, John. You both started all this so you can jolly well help me out of this embarrassing situation."

"My dear George, he's only human and a very unhappy one at that," said John.

"If he calls you, Simcox, George, I'll slay him alive," exclaimed Alec.

As they approached the front door of the cottage Clive hesitated. Maurice pulled on his arm. "No backing out now, Clive." Clive nodded agreement.

"Well," said Maurice as they entered the open doorway, "at least introductions won't be necessary. Come on in, Clive, and meet the villains of the peace. Good thing they haven't made a magistrate of you yet, Clive," he joked.

Clive quietly and secretly took in the surroundings. He did not attempt to make comparisons. He couldn't have anyway for the ambience which now surrounded him was entirely different. There was a freshness which was immediate. Nothing was on parade, or false. Freedom, that magical word, seemed the order here. The faces of Maurice and his friends looked on him with kindness in their eyes that soon turned to welcoming smiles.

He was entering their lives and it made him nervous. But the relief at just being there, although strange, somehow gave him a sense of confidence and belonging. He had had to get used to Maurice's Alec, who, remarkably enough, now provided him with considerable comfort with his easy and direct ways. John he knew. Maurice, well of course. Simcox, now George, produced another adjustment he knew he had to make.

John sensed his difficulty.

"Well, Clive," John began, "at least we've already met. Now that was stupid of me, Clive, for of course so has everyone else," and gave a laugh which provided an excuse for everyone to unwind. Continuing, John said, as casually as he could, "As George is leaving Penge perhaps that will make it less difficult for you."

They all waited for Clive to answer.

Clive hesitated before answering.

"Please," he said nervously, "do not make excuses for me, John. I have made so many for myself already. So many changes, unexpected ones, forgive me, George, but if I offended you the other night, please believe me, it was not my intention."

When George smiled Clive relaxed and was more at ease.

"Up to a few years ago," Clive went on "my problems were few, or so I thought. Look at me now. I suppose I am a coward." Maurice made as if to move towards him.

In a voice strengthening by the moment, Clive went on. "Yes, Maurice, that's exactly what I am, a coward. I should have fought that much harder. But now at last, pray God, I can live with myself and my conscience, and hopefully my friends," he said encompassing them all.

"You needn't worry on my account," said George kindly. "I think you are much too harsh on yourself. When one tries to compromise in this life it more often than not goes wrong. I have experienced some grisly moments, myself. You will no doubt get to know a bit about my past, the truth that is." Here he gave a slight laugh. "John can vouch that I am really a bit of a fraud. He will no doubt tell you about it sometime."

George did not consider there was any need to make excuses, for to have done so would have been to admit to some failure where there was none.

George felt pleased at having got this far with Clive. Initially he had had reservations about saying anything at all. He bore no malice towards Clive, quite the contrary in fact. It was just that the nature of their previous relationship had been on an entirely different basis.

"Go on, John," said Alec, "Tell him, tell him what happened to poor old George at that posh school where he teached."

"Taught, Alec," corrected Maurice.

"Tell him about the row over, what's his name, Oscar Wilde, tell him what it's like to be kicked out of your job 'cause you're like us."

"Alec," intervened Maurice "calm down. George is quite capable of defending himself."

"Bloody unfair," continued Alec.

"Of course it is, my love," said Maurice, his arm around him.

Just before Maurice and Clive had arrived, John had been pouring drinks.

"Maurice," he said offering him a glass.

"Can I offer you a drink, Clive?"

"Thank you. Yes, sherry will be fine."

As time sped by there was a noticeable change in the acceptance of Clive by the others and equally of them by Clive. Soon, tentativeness gave way to an easy freedom in their approach to one another. Laughter punctuated their conversation, and it was evident that Clive had once again found a milieu to his liking. At one time Clive whispered to Maurice.

"You have one doting creature in Alec, you lucky devil. He is also fortunate, and I should know!"

"Thanks for that, Clive. Our happiness will be even greater with your friendship."

Looking at the clock on the wall Clive announced.

"I made an appointment to see the game keeper at three o'clock so I really think that I should be leaving."

He shook hands, first with John and then with George, saying,

"Will you think about my offer, George?"

"Perhaps after we come back, Clive," insisted John.

Maurice and Alec walked with him to the end of the lane.

"Well, Clive," said Maurice, "this is as far as we go. I will write to you during the holiday to keep you up to date. Now, my friend, I have your word that you have rid yourself of those macabre notions."

Clive smiled then nodding his head affirmatively, said, "Yes, dear Maurice, of that you can be sure. I have a lot of things to organise and think about now. Thanks to you I've recovered a purpose for carrying on. The campaign is still demanding a hell of a lot of my time. Still, that will be over in a few weeks from now. You will obviously not be voting. Nor Alec for that matter – not even for me! I shall miss you both; still the thought of your return will be enough. The future, whatever it holds in store for me, will at least be manageable, no longer all enemy. You have all done something rather remarkable. I, who not long ago prayed for some type of conclusion to my life, no, Maurice, it is true, but now I will not live a lie any more. I, with all my learning, botched most everything, simply because I would not identify with the person I really am. Well, that is done with. Bless you, Maurice for saving my life."

"Nonsense."

"No, Maurice, believe me, it is not nonsense. But I can now, for the first time, see a new dawn and with it a great deal of hope. Christ, I could hug you both."

"Be quick about it then before the neighbours see," said Alec with a daring look in his eyes.

Clive paused for just a moment, then, taking up Alec's challenge, performed this show of affection without further ado. Maurice peered furtively around while Alec had no such reservations. Maurice was pleased at the unrestrained way in which Clive behaved. It augured well for their future friendship.

Clive laughed. "My God, Maurice, you've got a handful there. And, Alec, let me thank you also. I am envious of you, of course, then, come to think about it, I am envious of you too, Maurice."

Alec grinned at this remark.

Chapter Twelve

As they waited for the taxi Maurice had time to contemplate on just how amazing it was that he should be setting off on a holiday with someone he had known but a short time.

Fate had first dealt Maurice a hand with new and exciting promise, one that brought to the fore feelings of the most remarkable kind, feelings that would define his sexuality forever. He remembered his difficulty in accepting it. One might consider it the arrival of manhood, at least Maurice's, albeit somewhat late. Clive had kindled the flame and then, subsequently, had nearly extinguished it. Luckily time then moved on and a relenting hand of fate moved with it. Melancholy thoughts such as these Maurice quickly banished and at the moment gave a great sigh.

"Old Jack and his taxi's 'ere," yelled Alec from the front door.

"Bring some of the bags, Alec," cried Maurice struggling with a heavy case.

Jack Boughton had indeed arrived. His taxi stood, highly polished, beyond the gate. "Mornin, Zer," he said to Maurice as he took charge of one of the cases. With Alec's help he loaded the rest of the baggage onto the grid at the rear of the car.

John sat in the front while George got into a rear seat.

"You get in first, Maurice," said Alec holding the door and resting one foot on the running board.

"Bit of a squeeze," Alec muttered as he eased his way into the space beside Maurice and the door.

With the glass thermometer on the bonnet leading the way the car moved slowly down the gravelled lane and out onto the road.

Putting his lips to Alec's ear, Maurice whispered, "Just for this once keep your ardour under control. I don't want Boughton alarmed by your behaviour."

A hand met his, then a finger snaked out.

Maurice suppressed a smile. Alec grinned in open defiance. George viewed the scene with satisfaction.

"Pity Clive couldn't come," said Alec. "Because of the bloody election. He won't win anyway."

"Such faith in our friend is really touching, Alec."

"I didn't mean it like that, Maurice. It will be real good if he loses. He has difficulty enough sorting out his own life, let alone that of other people."

Alec really believed this for he had seen Clive at his very lowest, had seen and understood how delicate affairs of the heart were, had seen how carelessly people dealt with their emotions. Alec, despite not having the eloquence education provides, was able to express himself quite adequately. He was quite honest in his behaviour. He saw no point in adopting poses or a false identity, or having false pride for that matter. These he believed resulted in ultimate chaos and unhappiness, such, he believed, had been Clive's misfortune. His erudition was not of the finest but its purpose was crystal clear.

"Maybe you are right, Alec, though if he is going to lose I would like to have been there, to hold his hand you might say. God knows he's had enough drama to be getting on with."

The journey to London was in a first class carriage. Such luxury was still a novelty to Alec. He noticed that John and George slept most of the way which he ascribed to being 'old'! When Maurice tried to do the same, if only for a short nap, Alec gave him a nudge or kept on talking to him.

It was beginning to rain as they approached London and the damp windows attracted atoms of black particles from the engine as it raced through one tunnel after another. Eventually they emerged into daylight as the train began its final run into Paddington station where a welcoming pair of buffers beckoned it in. Porters descended and luggage was quickly whisked away.

"Last time I come," began Alec.

"Came," corrected Maurice.

"Last time I come to London," Alec persisted, "I carried my own bag. Why don't everyone do that?"

"Because Alec, everyone doesn't choose to. If we did everything for ourselves these men would be out of work."

"Other things to do 'part from acting as bloody nurse maids to lazy sods like you lot. Different if you're old and too stiff to move."

"You're a dear old thing, Alec," he said ruffling his hair.

Another taxi ride before they alighted onto the front elegant steps of the Victoria Hotel. Again there was a flurry of porters opening doors and swishing the luggage up steps and into the foyer. Alec experienced a new sensation when the metal crisscross folding doors of the lift clanged shut and they sped quickly to the third floor. Their particular 'boy', a man in his fifties – bloody silly calling him a boy, thought Alec – preceded them. He first led George and John into their room. Alec followed Maurice as they were shown into an adjoining room.

Alec watched as money was exchanged.

"Thank you, Sir," said the man, gratefully.

"You gave him half a crown!" said Alec incredulously, after the man had left, "half a crown just for carrying our bags. And they are doing that all day! Don't seem fair them earning all that. I only got seven and sixpence when I was working at Penge, and that for a week – a whole week!"

"I offered you a tip once and you refused it, remember?" said Maurice with a grin.

"Course I did. Take your money? Knowing 'ow I feel about you, Maurice, 'ow could I do that?"

Maurice was contented, more than he dare admit. Alec reacted by falling onto the bed in a heap and dragging Maurice with him.

"Last time we were in London had our first real night together. And what a night! Didn't sleep much did we?"

"No we didn't and the mattress was damned uncomfortable."

Maurice had cause to remember that day. Alec's sudden appearance at his offices in the city, dressed in his best clothes and cloth cap. He was conspicuous amongst others milling around the entrance hall and who tended to stare at this stranger. Even Maurice felt a tinge of embarrassment. Alec's unreal blackmail threat, said in the heat of the moment, exposed Alec's injured heart. All misunderstandings were resolved, however, and they ended up spending the night together. Despite this, Alec remained unsure of Maurice's true feelings and was persuaded to join his brother in emigrating to Argentina. It was a careless decision which at the time shattered Maurice's hope for a life with Alec. Love will out, as they say, for Alec could not sustain the idea of being parted from Maurice.

Daring to retrace that treacherous time made Maurice momentarily shudder. Each of these negative thoughts made him cherish even more their love for each other.

"You look so darn good, Maurice. Nearly left it too late you know. Still, here we are and I'm so blooming excited. Do you like me as much as you did Clive?"

"I love you, not like you, you ass. I couldn't help loving you more. Oh, so much more, you have no idea, Alec."

"Good then," replied Alec simply, roughly wrestling them into a greater tangle on the bed.

The sun had re-appeared and with time on their hands George suggested that they walk to Hyde Park. Maurice greatly enthused over the idea for, not only would they skirt the Palace gardens, but the enormity of the park was sure to impress Alec.

As they strolled aimlessly along, endless motor cabs, trams and other vehicles including a couple of horse drawn carts passed them. Pedestrians became more numerous as they neared the Palace. To Alec it seemed as if the whole of the human race was being compressed into just one very small part of London. Maurice, meanwhile, wanted Alec to share in the excitement of London's history. As they walked slowly along, he felt both a desire and obligation to now talk to Alec about part of it, that relating to Hyde Park.

He touched on the famed Victorian exhibition of 1851 and the speed at which the grand Crystal Palace had been erected. He dwelt briefly on the part Hyde Park had played in politics at that time, of the crowds attending the speakers who stood on boxes on the green near Marble Arch, propounding on every subject under the sun. The beginning of proletarian enlightenment – he laughed as he explained it's meaning to Alec – an event that coincided with expanding railroads.

"Yes, Alec, trains were just beginning to provide affordable travel for the masses. Socialism, Alec. I must introduce you to its ethics, and the Trade Unions you already know about if you listened to Sam Horler when he came to the village. Their humanitarian philosophies frightened the living daylights out of Queen Victoria and her German relations. Even now 'royalty' still guard the portals of privilege with tremendous determination." Alec asked and questioned Maurice on everything and anything. Never once did Maurice become exasperated with him, even when the questioning became prolonged.

Of Boswell – Alec had certainly never heard of him before who had regularly trod the turf in the Regency days. "Boswell," Maurice told Alec, "refers to it frequently in his diaries – yes, yes, Alec, he wrote a diary – 'to its dark walks, especially at night. Bright lights, music and picnics'," quoted Maurice.

"It was a place of entertainment, Alec, and became a favourite parade ground for fashionable society in more ways than one," Maurice said with a laugh. "In the late eighteenth century it was most favoured by the 'elite' of society." Maurice stopped to explain who the elite society were, causing Alec to make some unfavourable remarks about their origin.

"The gentlemen, or as they were often called, fops" another explanation from Maurice – "could be seen promenading around in powdered wigs." A great guffaw from Alec. "You laugh, Alec, but 'twas the fashion then or a little earlier."

"You're making all this up," said Alec.

"Of course I'm not." Maurice said with laugh. "Mind you, Alec, there were also some pretty seedy old things going on in those days – not that that has changed very much. You got the high class damsels who strutted around here like decorated peahens looking for husbands, and then, of course, in greater abundance, were the more obvious professionals plying their trade, often for only a copper or two."

Alec listened, fascinated, as Maurice continued to paint a glimpse of 18th and 19th century London.

"Maybe it was around here that Boswell caught the pox!" Maurice suggested with a grin.

Alec laughed and laughed. Although right now he was in great awe of Maurice's knowledge and marvelled at the unfolding story which Maurice told so vividly, Alec was cautious in believing it entirely, for embellishment was the property of everyone.

It took them about thirty minutes to walk the half-mile or so to Hyde Park.

Alec's first impression was immediate as he gazed at the vast area of fields stretching a long way ahead of them. Nearer the centre, yet some distance away, he could hear music. It was some time before he spotted the ornate bandstand from which came the glazed shine of brass instruments as the military band with its standing conductor came into view. With the sun now having avoided the clouds it grew warmer and people were beginning to gather in haphazard groups to listen to the musicians.

John led them further on, between tall trees. Suddenly opening out in front of them was a large expanse of sparkling water. "This, Alec, is the Serpentine."

Alec's interest was now turned towards the hordes of people, young and old, who ambled leisurely along. To him, the whole of London seemed to be on holiday.

There were children romping in the grass, young heads in pigtails chased toy hoops. Maids (maybe also mothers) manoeuvred prams as they glanced and tittered at the attention of some prospective beau or admirer. Lovers walked jauntily arm in arm and from what Alec could see were totally unaware of the critical (or otherwise) gaze of other visitors to the park. Soldiers in red and blue uniforms, possibly from the Chelsea barracks, added highlights to this snapshot of late summer. In fact, everyone, with one or two exceptions, was taking advantage of the freshness of the park after the light early morning rain.

They walked slowly on for some time, talking and joking together, often with Alec observing and remarking on the strangeness of this or that. It was a world far removed from his own country surroundings. They trailed the edge of the Serpentine, watching several very regal white swans. Occasionally the swans would paddle madly towards the bank, there to extend their long necks to collect, in formidable black beaks, a biscuit or a piece of bread offered by some nervous hand.

The relaxing nature of the park affected many of the visitors including Maurice and the others and it was not long before they had joined with them in resting or lying stretched out on the grass. They lazed for a while, enjoying the heat of the sun and the vista of the world around them. George closed his eyes and allowed the sun full access to his face.

"You'll end up with a red beak, like the ducks, George," said Alec laughing.

Eventually, and with considerable reluctance, they got up and moved on. After walking for a short time they entered an area, which had very little to commend it, just bushes, untended shrubs and trees. The path which divided it was narrow and restrictive.

"I think we must be nearly at the other end. Near Marble Arch," said John.

"God! Have we walked that far?" exclaimed George. "Don't you think we should go back?"

It was agreed and they all turned and began walking slowly back along the same path.

They had gone but a few yards when suddenly ahead of them came what seemed to Maurice's keen ears a single cry for help. They hurried forward until, ahead of them, they could see the cause of the disturbance. There, standing near the edge of the path, was a policeman. He seemed to be having difficulty pulling or dragging something, or maybe someone, from behind the bushes. As if from nowhere a soldier in a blue uniform miraculously appeared. He gave support to the policeman and the cause of their joint endeavours came tumbling and falling towards them. Maurice noticed that it was a young man in his late teens.

The soldier was talking quickly and pointed an accusing finger at the boy. The boy was protesting violently.

The policeman suddenly raised his truncheon and there seemed every possibility that he would strike the boy. Maurice looked quickly at Alec, which served as a signal, and together they raced forward towards what appeared to be a very belligerent member of the metropolitan police, leaving George and John to follow.

With the sudden appearance of a 'gentleman' the policeman, who was in fact about to strike the boy, hesitated, then, with obvious reluctance, lowered the truncheon to his side. His thoughts at that moment were more with this well dressed stranger. The freedom of action which he preferred, including the use of violence when he felt like it, might not necessarily be appreciated by this member of the upper class. He had had some bad experiences in the past. There had been a few public-spirited members amongst the visitors who had actually complained about his behaviour to his superiors. On a couple of occasions, he had been severely reprimanded which had significantly retarded his prospects of promotion. He now remembered this.

"That gen'lemun," he said pointing to the soldier with his truncheon, and addressing his remarks to Maurice, "'as made a seri-serious complaint against this man. 'E says that 'e made an indecent... made to touch 'im."

Maurice had summed up the situation immediately. He did not like what he now saw, and his memory of the Risley affair quickly came into focus. He saw this as a challenge.

"Really, constable, and did you see him do this?" he asked in his haughtiest and most demeaning of tones.

"Well, no Sir, not exactly, though I might 'ave done."

"Well," said the soldier, in a voice hinting great dislike for this interfering busybody, "well," he repeated in a loud and coarse voice, "if he didn't, I did, an' I intend to make a complaint."

"That should be most interesting," exclaimed Maurice, intending to intimidate the man now facing him. "Just precisely what were you doing in the shrubs?" asked Maurice ignoring the policeman and assuming the role of interrogator.

"What damned business o' yours, is it?" said the soldier insolently, now very angry at their intrusion. Maurice raised his eyes and quizzically looked the soldier directly in the face. He then moved his gaze slowly up and down, and with obvious deliberation. He hoped by this to make the soldier feel uncomfortable, which in fact it did. Then he studied the uniform, and by sheer coincidence was rewarded.

"Well, I'll be damned!" he suddenly exploded, causing all eyes to focus on him. "You're from Capt. Benson's regiment, aren't you?" he said in a whoop of triumph at the discovery, suddenly remembering his old school friend. "I'd recognise that insignia anywhere. Well, well, well!" Maurice spoke with emphasis and meaning as he had every reason to do at this opportunistic bit of luck.

The soldier at once looked startled and began backing away.

"Oh, for Gawd's sake, Sir," said the soldier, with a swiftness and sudden change of manner which, in his case, cowardice had long since tutored. It now dawned on him very quickly that somehow, the person facing him was a danger and might well be able cause him some real trouble.

"'E 'as made a complaint," continued the constable, as if to reassert his authority, "and it is my duty to report it," he said pompously.

George and John had now joined them.

"Were you witness to this, Sir?" said the constable appealing to John as a newcomer to the scene.

John had overhead most of the conversation and realised Maurice's purpose.

"What the devil are you talking about, man? Have you been drinking?" asked John.

The constable was getting very confused as well he might. The situation was turning against him and he, like the soldier, began to worry as to its outcome.

Turning to the soldier Maurice twisted the screw further. "I think, my man," he began, adopting a commanding tone to which obedience was the considered military reaction, "that you had better give me your name and number."

"Trubshore," the soldier immediately responded, acting out of military habit. Suddenly realising all too late, the utter folly of providing any information to Maurice, he fell silent. This carelessness set his thought processes racing, flashes of impending disaster and unknown consequences triggered a reaction, both physical and mental. The soldier become extremely agitated which in turn led to panic. It was a panic of such magnitude that it resulted in the blue coated fusilier turning on his heels and running as fast as he could, his aim being to distance himself from the others as quickly as he could.

Maurice turned back to face the policeman whose countenance had undergone a significant change on seeing the soldier, his only witness, and possibly collaborator, disappearing into the distance.

The policeman was about thirty-five, short and stocky and a face not renowned for its looks. At that moment the colour of his cheeks was changing from pasty white to an unhealthy looking puce. A sure sign, thought Maurice, of his confusion and uncertainty of how things would develop.

For the moment Maurice seemed to have control of the situation.

"'E's still committed an offence," the policeman persisted, though by this time it was said with far less conviction.

"Has he, indeed!" Said Maurice empirically. "And with whom might I ask?"

"You were a witness, Sir," the constable went on.

"No constable. I most certainly was not," said Maurice angrily.

"Eh!"

"To put it simply, constable, your only witness has run off, scarpered. In my view, the guilty party in this affair is different from the one you have in mind," he said pointing in the direction of the departing soldier, "and your part in it is very suspect. I suggest that you would look rather foolish under the circumstances to make accusations against this young man. Incidentally," said Maurice looking directly at the constable, "why are you patrolling this particular area in the company of a soldier, and, what is more, behind shrubs and bushes. That must be very unusual, surely? It all looks terribly suspicious to me, constable," said Maurice.

The constable now looked extremely agitated.

"Conspiracy – No doubt about it," said Maurice to John, loud enough for the constable to hear.

All this while the policeman had been holding the slightly built boy tightly by the collar of his jacket. The boy looked deathly pale and the fear and terror in his eyes cried out for help.

"Alright then," he said roughly to the boy, "catch yer 'ere agin and yore for it." The constable then released his grip and pushed the lad from him. The boy simply fell to the ground in a sort of faint before anyone could stop him.

"Gawd," cried the constable "what, what now?" he stammered.

The boy lay prone on the pavement. Blood trickled slowly down his forehead from a cut he received on hitting the ground. Maurice bent down to help him. He quickly loosened the tie, which had been pulled tightly against his throat. Alec cradled the boy's head on one arm. John passed Maurice a handkerchief, which he used in an attempt to stop the bleeding.

Satisfied that he had suffered little damage, Maurice finally stood up, his anger, very evident. As he towered over the constable he had difficulty in suppressing an urgent desire to strike him.

"You blithering imbecile," he said slowly and with passion, "not only did you nearly choke him to death but caused him more injury by pushing him to the ground, and these gentlemen" he said pointing to the others, "are witness to this," he said menacingly. The constable seemed to shrink "I have made a note of your number, and I give you warning, constable, that if ever I see you in circumstances as suspicious as these, or hear of it for that matter, I will take every step within my power and influence to give you cause to rue the day."

"I have to agree" interrupted John, "the matter is very serious. I consider it an unprovoked attack on the young man." The constable shuffled nervously from one foot to the other.

Maurice went on. "You have not necessarily heard the last of this, anyway. If this young man's injury caused by your brutal assault requires medical attention then I will personally see to it that he seeks redress, through the courts if necessary. Do I make myself clear, constable?"

"Yes, Sir," spoke a nervous and now very worried member of the Force. He looked hurriedly around seeking an escape route.

"I think it would be better" Maurice went on, "if you left before I consider changing my mind about making a formal complaint to your superiors." With that Maurice dismissed him with the wave of a hand.

The constable took this as a signal of dismissal and was grateful that he could absolve himself, at least temporarily, from a rather tricky and potentially dangerous situation. With precision he produced an accentuated salute, and with practised ingratiation seemed to perform a kind of bow towards Maurice. His departure was as fast as the soldier's. Unfortunately, the constable's legs were that much shorter and he offered a rather comical silhouette.

"My, you're a cool one, Maurice," said Alec as the constable disappeared out of sight. "Then of course I should know that, shouldn't I?"

"I was bloody determined that those wretches wouldn't get away with this one. Remember the Risley case, George?"

"Oh, yes, I most certainly do. Similar situation if I remember. Very sad business."

George was kneeling beside the fair-haired lad who was coming to life again. With Alec's help they lifted him up. He looked first at George, then at Alec, and then saw the others. The culmination of all that had happened to him during this scuffle with the law produced a natural reaction and he began to openly weep.

George was noticeably distressed. "You are alright now," he said kindly, "they are both gone, you have nothing to fear any more. We are friends. Please," he said taking the bloodstained handkerchief from him and offering a clean one.

Maurice looked at the forlorn and tragic figure. About Alec's age he thought – a year or two younger than me. Gracious, that was his nearest thing to hell. Hard Labour – the thought made his flesh creep.

The boy's clothes were well tailored, though his shoes were down at the heels. Flaxen coloured hair which fell slightly onto his shoulders. There was a smear of blood near his right temple. Face, hard to tell right now, clear but tear stained. A flush had now been introduced to its paleness. Slim, and shorter than Maurice by a couple of inches.

"Well" said Maurice, quietly, "Do you feel up to telling us what happened?"

"Let's go back to the 'otel first," said Alec, "I'm dying for a cup of tea and I'm sure he is."

The boy, who up until then had remained silent, nodded his head. Together they walked slowly out of the park.

John hailed a taxi and with some difficulty the five of them climbed in. Almost immediately the driver expressed his displeasure at the thought of carrying so many passengers.

"I'm only supposed to carry four," he grumbled, "There'll be an extra charge," he said unpleasantly. There was nothing cheerful about his face at all. He looked decidedly unhappy and disgruntled and, as if to show his disapproval moved the taxi forward before the door was properly closed.

"Right," murmured Maurice, irritated by the man's behaviour, 'there'll be no damn tip for you, my man," he muttered under his breath.

For one fleeting moment Maurice pondered on the merit of what they were doing.

The journey to the hotel was of short duration. Within the crowded cab they tried to converse but the noise outside of the cab made it difficult. Maurice was very relieved when they arrived back at the hotel. The unhappy driver became quite abusive when there was no offering of the customary piece of silver. He departed quickly enough once Alec began moving aggressively towards him. During the journey their new acquaintance had offered little or no information about himself.

They avoided the hotel lift preferring to use the stairs. John led the way down the corridor and into his and George's room. Tea had been mentioned and John promptly ordered a tray to be sent up.

The young man, now much recovered from his ordeal, was standing uneasily near the door. They could not know that his unease was in not knowing just how to express his gratitude and to whom. He felt his position here comparable to that of a stranger walking into a party without an invitation.

John, sensing his difficulty introduced himself. "The name is John," he said offering his hand. The others in turn walked across and shook his hand.

Not used to standing on ceremony, at any rate not for very long, Alec asked, "What's your name?" and continued staring into the boy's face.

Maurice smiled at this directness of Alec's.

"Robert," he said shyly.

"Mine's Alec. Well, Robert, you needn't be shy of us lot," returned Alec without hesitation. "We go on holiday tomorrow; Greece," he said proudly. Then without hesitation asked,

"where you from?"

"Highgate," came the quiet voice.

"Come and sit down, Robert," said Maurice pushing a chair towards him. "You've been to hell and back. Dreadful experience, but the danger is now gone, Robert. You can relax again."

The tea arrived at last. George poured. He handed Robert the first cup.

"He needs it more than we do. Sugar?"

"Isn't he quiet?" Alec whispered to Maurice.

"We are not all extroverts like you."

"Extroverts?"

"Noisy, then." Maurice had to smile.

"Robert," said John gently, "I have a pretty shrewd idea of what happened back there in the park. Obviously that area is policed, but then you weren't to know that." Here John hesitated, allowing time for his meaning to become clear.

"They use agents provocateurs," he went on, "it is quite common. Absolutely despicable, a shabby lot of people but there, Robert, it goes on just the same. In your case it would seem that our friend from the Guards had an arrangement with the constable."

"I... I didn't know," said Robert. He put his hand to his forehead.

"Is it sore?" asked Alec.

"Just a little," he said his voice sounding stronger.

"You were terribly unlucky to get caught up in their vicious scheme of things, Robert." said Maurice, "thank heavens we came along and spoilt it for 'em. What happened is, I imagine, exactly as John described it. I wish the pair of 'em in hell. Could have caused enormous trouble. The soldier I shall probably deal with. As for the constable, well, let's just hope that this will frighten him off," said Maurice bitterly. "They can harm you no more, Robert."

Robert looked up. "Yes," he began, "it... it was just as you described. The soldier began it and I, well, I... just followed him. Why would he do such a wicked thing? What had he to gain?"

"Money, Robert, money," interrupted John. "Provocateurs are paid by the police, that's for sure, why else would they do it? As a guardsman he probably earns very little."

There were signs that Robert was beginning to recover. The drawn lines on his face were beginning to clear, as was the fear in his eyes. George was pleased to notice this change.

Robert took a deep breath. Speaking slowly, he said.

"Yes, I believe I now understand."

There was pause as they waited for him to continue.

"What can I say, how can I ever thank you enough?"

Another pause as if he were deciding what to say, another deep breath, then he continued.

"If you hadn't been there, hadn't intervened, I should now be in…" he hesitated, "in a jail somewhere." He shuddered. Signs of fear temporarily returning were evident. "To suffer the fate of other…" a pause, "other men like me." He trembled again as images of the recent drama and his lucky escape flashed vividly before him. "I still feel afraid just thinking about what the consequences might have been."

His body shook ever so slightly causing the cup he was holding rattle in its saucer.

"At least now, Robert, you are safe, no danger around here," said John, quietly.

"Thankfully, yes," Robert replied. "So stupid of me to go there. I really didn't believe there to be a risk." He closed his eyes for a few seconds as if reliving the frightful event. "I dare not think of it. It is like some horrible nightmare. I cannot believe it really happened," he said, his voice trailing with emotion.

Maurice and the others waited for Robert to continue.

"You see," he said sadly, "there is no one with whom to share my, er… pro… problem. No one that I know who would understand. At the theatre someone had mentioned to me that Hyde Park was the place to make a contact – if you understand what I mean."

"Yes, so I have heard," said John. "It is also, unfortunately, a fact of life in this country, that homosexuality," he said deliberately, "is a term relegated by some to sit alongside that of outlaws and criminals. Well, Robert, thankfully you are alright, and it may be of some comfort to know that you have just met some fellow travellers."

"I can hardly believe it."

"How old are you, Robert?" John asked.

"Nearly twenty-one."

"Are you living at home?" Maurice asked suddenly.

"No. Just a room, in lodgings."

"What about your parents?"

There was no immediate answer from Robert. Finally when he did speak it was as if he had been dredging up a treasured memory from deep within his soul.

"Mother... my mother, is, is no longer with us," he finally managed. Evidence of the pain in his voice encouraged deepening sympathy from his listeners, one moment steady then hesitant then threatening to break before the sentence was completed. In a voice drifting into melancholy he continued. "She... she died over three years ago." Robert's sadness at this point, brought on by his clear recollection of her, overwhelmed him, demanding a further delay in his explanation. Maurice and the others waited in silence, waited patiently for him to continue. Alec made to speak, probably to encourage Robert to go on, but a glance from Maurice stopped him. Robert, looking quickly at the others, went on.

"I feel with mother dying, part of me died as well." Even allowing for the emotions of it all, Robert was becoming more assured and his voice lifted to a steadier plane. "Even now I find it hard to totally accept that I am on my own. There have been many, many occasions, still are, when I have suffered great remorse over her dying as she did. For she was so very young an..." Here Robert paused to suppress a sob, "and so beautiful. It was so unfair. She would have understood, I know."

"I am so sorry," said Maurice with sympathy in his voice.

"Your dad, what about your dad?" asked Alec.

"My father?" Robert spoke as if frightened at the question. "My father is the reason why I am living in London. He has completely disowned me. He is of the church, you see. In fact, he is the vicar of the church where I lived with my parents. Now, of course, I am banned from his house." He saw the look of surprise on George's face.

Maurice spoke quietly into George ear. They agreed that after Robert's recent traumatic experience it was probably unfair to press him further. Even the brief disclosures about his family had been harrowing enough.

"Robert," said George, kindly, "don't talk about it anymore for it obviously distresses you. Maybe later when you are calmed from that frightening experience."

Robert looked around him, at the strangers who had befriended him. The coincidence of their appearance in his life had saved him from a calamity beyond believe. To keep silent at this stage might appear ungrateful, he thought. To tell them just what had happened between him and his father was not something he relished revisiting. It was like a scar, in more ways than one. At the time it had been very damaging and still remained so. All of this went through his mind until finally he decided that they were entitled to the truth about his recent past. He believed that by sharing its knowledge with these four friends, as he now regarded them, it would somehow ameliorate or diminish the pain.

"No, no," he began, "you have all been so terribly kind and even if I show some reluctance I feel I owe it to you to tell you of the unfortunate sequence of events that led me here. Yes, yes, you must know it all," he said.

While Maurice and the others waited, Robert sipped his tea. He then placed the saucer on the table. After shifting his chair slightly, he sat holding the cup in both hands.

"The truth is I was expelled from school. I was eighteen at the time. It was to have been my last term before going up to Cambridge. I mucked it all up." Dejectedly he went on.

"Suffice it to say that I was caught kissing another boy, kissing, that's all. Arguing with the headmaster was my mistake, if somewhat rewarding" he said with a slight laugh. "He expelled me immediately. He telephoned my father and gave a false account of my so called crime. After mother died, father and I drifted apart. He seemed to turn inwards, to isolate himself, and has become very quick tempered. When I arrived home he called me into the library. Almost immediately he began shouting and soon lost his temper completely. According to him I was a filthy sodomite and a lot of other things besides. Suddenly, without warning, he smashed his fist into my face knocking me down."

"Oh, my God!" exclaimed George putting his hand to his face, obviously alarmed.

"Monstrous, absolutely monstrous!" remarked John.

"Robert," said Maurice quietly, "you really mustn't upset yourself like this"

"No, I'm OK, really," insisted Robert, "it's good to be able to talk to someone about it at last.

"My parents had been very close, therefore I was surprised and very angry when he suggested I'd inherited evil traits from her." Robert paused, shook his head then, "I had borne his brutality, his scorn, his hate, but insulting the memory of my dear mother, was the last straw. In retrospect I believe he spoke in anger. My reaction was to punch him as hard as I could, twice. God, he looked so startled. His nose bled. Wrongly, perhaps, I felt satisfaction in seeing that look of sheer disbelief on his face. I felt avenged yet angry with myself. Soon after that he stormed into my room and ordered me out of the house."

"How absolutely dreadful!" said George

"What did you do then?" asked Maurice.

"Well," continued Robert, "I had to quickly decide where to go. London seemed my best bet. Within the hour I was on the train. Fortunately, I still had money from my allowance. I found a room in Highgate. Getting a job was difficult. I'd neither references nor anyone to recommend me. Despite that I got a job as a stage hand at the Royalty Theatre in Islington. Everyone's dogsbody in the theatrical sense of the word, but I did enjoy it. There were perks, such as seeing all of the shows for free. I worked until a month ago when the manager had to let me go. Attendances had been bad lately. I guess that brings me up to date."

"So, what will you do now?" queried Maurice

"I don't know," he said dejectedly. "Life has had so little purpose over the last couple of years. I don't really know," he repeated.

"Do you have any money?"

"Why do you ask?" queried Robert, frowning.

"Do you?" persisted Maurice.

"About fifteen shillings I believe," Robert replied with embarrassment.

"How much is your rent?"

"Twelve shillings a week. And yes." he said, anticipating the next question, "I do owe a few weeks, about three pounds I believe. Luckily Mrs. Stone, the landlady, is a gem, very kind. I shall get something very soon.

"But I say," Robert said suddenly, concerned at the direction of the questions, "I know that I am rather poor company at the moment, but this makes me feel as if I were begging. I would hate you to believe that I am capable of that.

Please, please, forgive me, if I gave that impression. I honestly had no idea. You have been generous enough as it is. My gratitude is, well, what can I say, beyond all measure."

"Robert, my dear fellow," said Maurice quickly, "I would not suggest that for a moment. No, no, my interest is in your safety. There is also this germ of an idea fermenting in my mind which you may find of help."

"I'm sorry, I'm really sorry," Robert replied nervously. "You have all done so much, more than I can ever repay. And now I feel that I should start looking for work and allow you to continue with your holiday."

Robert got up from his chair, intending to leave. He was intent, however, on thanking them all once again.

Maurice stopped him. "Now, Robert, just bide your time for a while, for I have an idea."

"Really I should go," began Robert.

"No, no," insisted Maurice, "please, Robert."

Maurice then took George to one side and they conversed briefly. Then he turned to Robert.

"Robert, stay with the others for just a little longer, will you? I want to 'phone a friend of mine."

Alec, ever inquisitive, followed Maurice into their room. Maurice gave a sigh of relief when he heard the voice of Clive on the line.

"Clive. Thank goodness you are at home."

"Maurice, this is a surprise!" exclaimed an excited Clive, "everything OK?"

"Yes" said Maurice, "fine, and before you ask, Alec is blooming! But I need your help, Clive." So as not to alarm Clive, Maurice spoke softly yet confidently. "We rescued a young man, Alec's age, in Hyde Park, who came bloody close to a fate a la Risley"

Maurice heard an intake of air, then a, "Good God!"

"Don't worry, Clive, everything's perfectly OK. Intelligent chap, problems at home, father a blasted vicar of all things," Maurice laughs. "We've talked it over and decided to help him as far as we can, but initially, Clive, can you look after him down at Penge whilst we're away. Give him something to do and of course pay him something to keep him going"

There was a slight pause. Then a loud chuckle came over the 'phone.

"Tut tut," said Clive, "Oh Maurice, you dear ol' thing. Yes, of course, a chance to redeem myself at last. Is he…"

"Excellent, and yes, Clive, without a doubt, as certain as I am of you and me," Clive heard Maurice laughing. "He'll travel down by the five o'clock. You will meet the train?"

"Great!" enthused Clive, "I'll be there personally to meet him!"

"Steady now, watch your pulse!" said Maurice laughing.

"And Alec, behaving himself?"

"Good Lord, Clive, my friend, that is not Alec's style. It's the wild beast that appeals, particularly when aroused, if you follow." Alec joined the laughter.

"What is Clive saying about me, Maurice? Give him my… my love."

Maurice grinned at Alec who was leaning on his shoulder listening. "He's just sent you his love, Clive, now ain't that quaint!"

"I'm getting to like this conversation, Maurice."

"Thanks a million, Clive. You will like the lad."

Alec turned to Maurice. "Clive, what a difference. Don't sound like the same bloke. All thanks to you, Maurice."

Maurice immediately dials another number. "Captain Benson, Please."

There was a pause, and then the loud voice of Maurice's friend was heard.

"Hello, who's that?"

"Benny, it's Maurice"

"Maurice, old chap," came a cheerful voice, "how are you?

Long time no see. How's the old stock market?"

"Fine, Benny, just fine. We're off to Greece tomorrow."

"Lucky fellow."

"Look, Benny," Maurice said sounding serious, "I have a favour to ask."

"Fire away!" came the cheerful voice.

"I met one of your men, a character named Trubshore, corporal I think. Nasty bastard. Earlier today we took a stroll in Hyde Park. Came across this Trubshore causing no end of trouble. Agent provocateur, young lad and all that rot. Read him the riot act and warn the bugger off, will you?"

"But of course, Maurice, consider it done."

"Thanks. How's Dorothy by the way."

"Wonderful."

"Give her my love."

After Maurice came off the telephone, Alec remarked, "You know a lot of people around here, Maurice. Wouldn't want to be in that soldier's shoes."

"He is a bastard, Alec, and can fry in hell. Benny? Great chum. He was up at Cambridge with me."

When they got back into the next room George and Robert were sitting at a table near the window.

"Maurice, you won't believe this, but Robert was at the school where I taught."

"My goodness that is a coincidence," exclaimed Maurice.

"Of course it was some time after I had left. Robert has just told me that he heard from an 'old boy' that the Head recently had a heart attack which, he gathers, saw him off."

"A darn good thing if you asks me," said Alec.

"Maybe, Alec, maybe," answered George, "though I doubt whether attitudes will change because of it."

"That will take another hundred years!" said John.

"God, how depressing a thought," remarked Maurice. "Gather round chaps," he said cheerfully.

"Now, Robert," Maurice began, "the proposition I have is this. A friend of mine has an estate in the country called Penge, which is near a small village in the West Country – give you details later. He can offer you work, albeit on a temporary basis, helping him run the estate, accounts or something of the kind, but, what is most important at this time, a room of your own in a house not far from the estate." He said feeling very pleased with himself.

"He will, of course," Maurice went on, "pay you a wage, which is very important. You'll be under no obligation to stay if you find it unsuitable, Robert, though I would be very surprised if you and Clive don't get on well together. So, Robert how does that sound to you?"

"It sounds, what can I say, just too good to be true," said a more animated Robert.

"After helping me over the most frightening day of my life, I'm lost," Robert said shaking his head, "I'm really lost for what to say. Gratitude? In the circumstances how can I do justice to the word? I'm already so indebted to you all, and now this. Why should I suddenly have such good fortune? This doesn't really happen in real life. Perhaps in some melodramatic play."

"Don't be too sure about that," said Maurice. "Fact is often stranger than fiction. So, you would like to give it a try?"

"Oh, heavens," cried Robert, "what better thing could happen to me? I've grown so unused to receiving kindness in this measure. What can I say, what can I say?" He looked as if he would cry.

"Good," said Maurice, hurrying on. "Now the practicalities of it all, Robert. You will need money, which I am lending you." He waved his hand when Robert attempted to protest. "To pay off your landlady, then to travel by the five o'clock train tomorrow afternoon. Clive, Clive Durham, that's his name, will meet your train." He then passed him an envelope. "All the details are there, Robert, and I have also enclosed a note for Clive."

Robert was obviously overwhelmed. Within the last few hours, his life had swung from the threat of prison to securing new friends and employment.

"You will be happy down there, Robert, I warrant," concluded Maurice.

"Why don't you stay and have dinner with us?" enquired John.

"Excellent idea," agreed George.

Maurice considered their position to that of conspirators secretly whisking an innocent victim away from angry and violent hordes of reactionaries.

Smiling at such a vision, Maurice, together with his fellow conspirators and fugitive, all descended on the dining room at the very stroke of eight o'clock.

Chapter Thirteen

Walking back to his house following the meeting with Maurice and his rewarding visit to George's cottage, Clive realised that from this very moment the direction of his life would have to alter. He had been shaken to the core by events over the last couple of days. His oscillation between one course and another, between pride and realism, between what in truth was the way forward for him, the only way.

As he moved across the meadow he talked aloud and determinedly to himself. There was no one else around to distract him or witness the new mood. "I am resolved," he said defiantly and appearing to address the sheep – the only other occupants of the field – "to take the horns of the beast and swing the blasted thing into an orbit of my own choosing for a change. Enough, by God, is enough," he said with renewed defiance, "and hell can have my soul if I deviate from this." The ferocity in his voice declared a new Clive, one escaping from the torture and misery of the recent past. This fierce determination followed the revival of his friendship with Maurice, and killed, once and for all, that metaphorical can of worms gnawing his destruction.

He decided that the totally unrewarding existence he had led for the last two years or more was now at an end. Now or never was the time to affect dramatic changes in his life. To drive a path which, even if he had to compromise slightly, would be – as he had just informed his woollen-clad audience – of his own choosing.

Clive gave thought on a most unusual subject, the chance spermatozoa, and one amongst millions to reach gestation, which had led to his sudden appearance on this orbiting planet. It was now that Clive latched on to the transparently obvious, the fact that there is but one entrance and one exit from this world, certainly no encores. Although at an early stage in youth, he knew that he must measure and savour each phase of what remained of his tenure on earth. He knew that there are no extensions or bonuses for time lost or past. This philosophic appreciation of life was not something new in Clive's thinking; it is just that he had been side tracked by allowing maladjusted aliens to trespass.

On the following night, in the drawing room after dinner he was alone with his mother.

He looked over at her and watched as she idly studied the design on a small piece of linen she had chosen for the tapestry she was planning to make. Her eyes did not reflect the beauty they once had. Where skin had been smooth there were creases which age had forced upon her. It also reflected the trials and tribulations life had marked out for her. As time raced forward it left the inevitable trail of happiness as well as tragedy in its path. Clive had experienced both of these. With his life set to change, he did not for a moment contemplate the mood of his parent, for what he had to say would bear no interruption or argument.

"Mother," he called.

She looked up. "Yes, dear?"

"Mother," he began, "As you know, Anne and I enjoy a friendship which is important to me." Mrs. Durham thought this an odd thing for her son to say.

"Yes, dear, I am sure that is so." She found this conversation somewhat pointless. She was tired and felt irritable.

"But our marriage is not a success."

His mother looked up, startled and fearing what would follow.

"To put it bluntly, Mother, it has degenerated into a marriage of, of convenience if you like."

"Clive!" She spoke this as if in response to someone having broken a sacred law. "Clive," she repeated, "this is absolutely terrible. Why, in heaven's name…?"

"I suppose the expression incompatible would adequately describe the situation." he said interrupting her. "It is not just one sided I would have you believe for we both have unalterable defects which flaw the relationship. One of significance for Anne, and which terrifies her, is what she terms the grosser side of marriage. It has reached a situation where she now views the whole of our marriage, in fact marriage generally, as something of a disaster, certainly not to be taken seriously in the accepted sense."

"Clive, my dear," said his mother sympathetically.

"And love doesn't come into it. She 'likes' me and that's where it ends. Likes me! That's what she said," Clive exclaimed, "and by that expression she excludes all marital vows and promises. I am possibly equally to blame for I sped towards marriage too fast, and with about the same amount of emotional purpose as Anne. Regrettably, it was a mistake we both made."

Mrs. Durham considered the time she had spent in trying to direct Clive towards marriage. Initially it had been very difficult, as Clive had shown greater obstinacy than she would have imagined.

'They must have had a disagreement over some marital problem; something that would soon sort itself out,' she reasoned, 'Clive is merely upset. All of this would blow over.' By this process of reasoning she had purposely blotted out the purport of what Clive was telling her. Within next to no time at all, however, Clive's original message began to sink in and she became overwhelmed by its true meaning and purpose. Now she became extremely worried and uttered the first thing to occur to her.

"But surely, Clive, Anne must be aware of her duty and obligations," she said tersely.

"That is an absurd Victorian concept, Mother," he said.

"Very simply, Mother, Anne has told me, and I quote her words exactly, that 'she will never allow me to intrude – stupid word – upon her person.'" Clive laughed at the recollection of her saying this to him.

"She declares that she is very fond of me – fond, I ask you, Mother, what sort of a marriage is that? To put it bluntly, Mother, she will not 'with her body me endow' to use that hackneyed biblical text." He said this with a smile then immediately hoped that it did not give away the truth of his own feelings. "In fairness to Anne, however, you must also know that my own feelings have fallen to a similar level. In a nutshell, Mother, 'tis finished and Anne and I have both come to recognise it."

Mrs. Hall gave an audible gasp. To her, Clive's smile was not only inappropriate, it frightened her.

"Heavens!" she finally managed, startled as the reality of Clive's news took shape. The finality of what Clive had said caused her confusion and panic. Hastily she withdrew from somewhere about her – as if by magic – a silver box containing her sal volatile. With an air of proclaimed distress she placed it, with great display, just beneath her nose then, with a deep breath, inhaled.

"I feel positively faint," she cried, "I am quite overcome, Clive."

Clive did not answer. He had absolutely no intention of continuing during his mother's sudden indisposition.

Absence of the expected courtesy from her son in this instance ensured that Mrs. Durham's period of revival was of short duration, much to her dismay.

"I am sorry, Mother, but you may as well know the truth."

"I am devastated. Oh, my poor boy." Now somewhat alerted to the future, she remarked. "The family, what of the family?"

"The family must take its chances as it has always done. I am sorry, mother but you had to know the truth." Clive paused, then thinking perhaps of the family's future said, "There's dear Pippa. She's already courting Hawk, what a terrible name, and is on the verge of getting engaged. She'll give you grandchildren, never fret – not too soon I hope!" he said with a laughs.

"Clive! Oh, how I wish you had married the Hall's daughter, she was such a sweet girl and much more level headed."

"Mother," he said sharply, "You make it sound like a cattle market. For God's sake, at least I didn't have to resort to selecting a whore from the harem of debutantes."

Deeply offended by this remark his mother rose to go. "I find your remark vulgar and very offensive, Clive."

"I did not mean it to be. Please sit down, my dear, I have not quite finished. I have to face facts, and the important fact at this moment is that neither Anne nor I can continue as before. Quite frankly, Mother, that is the way we both feel and nothing in the world is going to change it."

Neither of them spoke for several minutes. The silence was oppressive.

"When did Anne tell you all this?"

"To be quite honest, Mother, I have really known for some time. But the day before yesterday, whilst out riding,

Anne gave me a very clear picture of how she saw our future together or more accurately, how she doesn't see it."

"Maybe I should have a word with her."

"I wouldn't recommend it, Mother."

Mrs. Durham continued to shake her head, as if trying to dislodge the unpleasant implications of what Clive had told her.

"In view of what has happened," continued Clive, "it is obvious that there will have to be a number of changes. I would like you to hear what I propose, Mother." His mother waited.

"In the first instance Anne is insisting that I move out of the rooms we share. I have, therefore, asked Molly to prepare the Sedgewick room for me – as you know George Simcox is on holiday."

"Good gracious, but that is at the other end of the south wing," protested his mother.

"That is true but all the other spare bedrooms are about to be redecorated. No, I shall be alright in there for a while." "Oh," said Mrs. Hall accepting this with difficulty.

"Also, I would rather like you to continue with the responsibility of running this house." He knew this would please her.

"Does Anne know this?"

"Of course, I discussed it with her yesterday. She accepted it somewhat too readily I thought. Anyway the idea suits her.

"This means, of course, that contrary to father's wishes you will not be moving into the dower house down at Sellinge. I am personally very pleased at that. I never thought it a good idea anyway." Her feelings he knew corresponded with his.

"Perhaps in time Anne will take over the responsibilities," Mrs. Durham said, hopefully, meaning as well that maybe she will change her attitude to Clive. She conveniently forgot Clive's own expressed feelings towards Anne.

Clive did not bother to reply.

"There is one other thing you should know. I intend to use the dower house myself."

"Not to live there, surely?"

"Perhaps. I am not yet sure, Mother. It would certainly be useful as a base and, if I continue to be involved in politics, it is better that my office be removed from here anyway."

Unbeknown to his mother, Clive had for some time been planning to dispose of the property at Sellinge. Now, with the recent dramatic changes affecting his married life he viewed the dower house as positively essential to his future plans.

There was a local train to the small coastal town of Sellinge where the dower house was situated. His father had first of all rented the house from old Sir John Whitwell. In 1909 he purchased the freehold. Named Coronia, it had been built in the late 18th century. It was Georgian in every way, with slate roof, double fronted and with large rectangular windows. Including the basement there were four floors. Clive employed a permanent housekeeper, a Mrs. Winter – a widow. She lived in.

In the early days, when his father was alive, they would spend many a holiday at Sellinge. He still recalled with nostalgia the excitement when he and his sister Pippa, and the servants, were put on the train. They were always seated in a separate compartment from their parents. Father would not tolerate the endless babble of his children. Occasionally they were taken down in the motorcar, but to them it was not half as exciting.

For Clive, father had always been an old man. He thought this could be attributed to the drooping grey moustache he wore. On the other hand, his early recollections of his mother offered someone ever young and vibrant.

He looked over at her now. She had aged considerably. Her hair was now peppered with grey. He could only imagine his parents' relationship. Father, he remembered, was always gentle with her, ever considerate of her wellbeing and loathing the occasions when they had to be apart. Clive knew instinctively the extent of their love for each other. It reminded Clive of a quote from Disraeli –

"I cannot reconcile love and separation. My ideas of love, is the perpetual enjoyment of the society of the sweet being to whom I am devoted, the sharing of every thought and even every fancy, of every charm and every care – I wish to be with you, to live with you, never to be away from you – I care not where."

The shock of her husband dying so suddenly, of a heart attack, had made a profound mark. For several months after father died, he and Pippa worried greatly over their mother's health. She would eat very little and then usually in her room where she confined herself most of the day. The pain in her heart was reflected in her eyes, and was visible for over a year. Even now, whenever his name is mentioned, she retreats into sadness.

"Anyway, Mother, life must continue and all we can do is make it as tolerable as possible."

"This has been sad news indeed, Clive. I had such high hopes. I am thankful that I shall not be moving to Sellinge. This has been my home for so long. My memories of your dear father are here."

"I know, Mother, and it shall remain so for as long as you wish."

"Dear boy," she said sadly, "I feel suddenly very tired. I think I will lie down in my room." As she moved past the door into the hall she turned.

"Good night, Clive dear."

"Good night, Mother."

The call from Maurice had come as a complete surprise. That he had agreed to temporarily employ Robert was a sure indication of his own desire for change. At first, when Maurice, with considerable prudence, had given him details about the encounter in the park, he had felt the same fear as when poor Risley had asked for help. This time, however, his support came easily, there was no hesitation. The blemish on his conscience had now been excised.

Since the call Clive had done some rapid thinking. Obviously Robert would have to stay at Penge overnight. Then he would install him at Sellinge where, if he proved useful, could stay on as a sort of private secretary.

Clive informed Anne and his mother that they would be having a guest for dinner that night. He mentioned only that he was a friend of Maurice's. He did not feel inclined to elaborate further. In any event he was not quite sure what the chap would be like. 'How could I be, for heaven's sake, after all Maurice had only known him for a few hours.' he muttered to himself. That fact did worry Clive. Clive hated uncertainties. And this was one of them. He had at one time believed that everything had a neat compartment into which it belonged. This probably accounted for his removal into marriage. He would not, he decided, rely on that unsatisfactory principle ever again.

Although Clive did not want to make it seem a clandestine affair he still decided to go to the station on his own. It gave him some pleasure anyway to drive the new motorcar he had recently purchased. Anne had laughed when he first wore the leather driving tunic.

"It's not mandatory, Anne, just keeps me warm."

"I thought it was for the chauffeur."

"Perhaps it is. Tonight I am he," he said grinning.

"You know that I am going up to town to stay with Maud."

"Oh, yes, of course. I had forgotten. If you were to catch an earlier train, Anne, I could take you to the station myself."

"What a super idea," she enthused. "I'll have to call Maud first as she is meeting me at Paddington."

The evenings were drawing in, and it was dusk before they set off.

The car was thrown about considerably by the uneven surface of the driveway. "I shall certainly have to get them on to repairing this part of the drive," Clive remarked, "I don't want the car damaged." The car was travelling much faster than the usual horse drawn carriages for which the driveway had originally been designed. Once they reached the public high road, however, the journey became less bumpy.

"I'm sorry that I shall miss Maurice's friend," said Anne as they drove along, "What's his name by the way?"

"Robert." He said this with a sudden feeling of guilt. He thought about this as Anne continued talking to him. 'What the hell am I feeling guilty about' he said under his breath.

They drove in through the station entrance. The station was usually manned by two men, a deputy, who had gone off duty at four o'clock, and the Station Master who would be on duty until the station closed at midnight. From his office the Station Master heard the sound of Clive's car drawing up outside. He left his office and walked out through the booking hall and onto the road. He noticed Clive struggling to retrieve Anne's case from the rear seat of the car.

"Here, let me, sir," he said, lifting the luggage from the car as Clive moved away. Clive offered Anne his hand as she stepped gingerly down from the car. Once inside the booking hall Clive tipped the Station Master then retrieved the case.

Anne followed Clive as they walked across the bridge to the platform from which the up trains to London departed. They had not long to wait which pleased Clive. As the train drew alongside the platform Anne gave Clive a perfunctory kiss on the cheek. So lightly was it done that he barely noticed. He held open the door as she drew herself up and into the carriage then passed up her light overnight case through the window. He slammed the heavy door shut then waited for her to reappear, or make some further sign of farewell. She seemed disinclined to do either of these things. Instead, she moved quickly over to the far side of the dimly lit carriage. As the train pulled out of the station, Anne did not so much as glance in his direction. By this action, Clive instinctively knew that the gulf between them had irretrievably widened, the link broken. He suddenly felt alone, and the darkness of the night merely added to his gloom.

He looked at his watch. Twenty minutes before the down train was due. He walked back over the bridge to the other side of the station. As he walked into the building he noticed that the Station Master had retreated into his office. He looked comfortable enough as he sat before a blazing coal fire. This made Clive suddenly feel the chill of the evening. As he looked through the ticket office window he spotted a hand clasping a mug now raised to open lips. Clive stood for a moment wondering whether to wait in the car. He was spotted by the stationmaster, who called out.

"Are you waiting for the down train, Sir?"

"As a matter of fact I am," Clive answered.

"Well, it won't be 'ere for 'bout twenty minutes so would you like to join me for a cup of tea, Sir?"

"That is very kind of you, but…"

The Station Master was already filling the second cup so Clive had an enforced companion until the train arrived.

Their conversation was restricted to discussing the efficiency of the motorcar and the introduction of a new type of express train. Beyond that they seemed to have absolutely nothing in common. Here again Clive was reminded of the tragic difference between their respective social classes. In the very language they spoke; in their knowledge of things outside the horizon of their village. Nationalism with its waving flags, its kings and queens in undemocratic roles, emotive words against foreigners of whom the working class had little or no knowledge and hence could be manipulated into rousing passions of hate – the foreignness of the royal family was conveniently never stressed. He was reminded of the speech he had prepared for the election. It was all cliché, carried little of substance, and had nothing that would attend to changing the drab lives of the labouring classes. In other words, utter crap, he thought, from beginning to end.

Another vehicle arrived outside.

"That'll be ole Jack Boughton, come to meet Miss Spinney off the train," said the Station Master.

They heard a steam whistle sound in the distance. The stationmaster grabbed his hat hanging behind the door and with a lantern swinging in his hand, led the way onto the platform. Within minutes the white lights hanging from the engine got larger and larger, until finally, with bursts of steam hissing from a red painted funnel, the train crawled to a noisy halt.

Clive looked towards the first class carriages for opening doors. Only one person alighted and that an elderly lady carrying a covered birdcage. He presumed that to be the Miss Spinney.

"Oh, hell," he said to himself, "the blighter's not coming after all."

A voice behind pulled him up.

"Excuse me, but are you Mr. Clive Durham?"

Clive swung around and saw Robert standing there with a large case which was weighing him down. In the dim gas light of the station he could make out a tallish figure that wore a cap. The voice seemed pleasant to Clive's ears. He took the outstretched hand and immediately noticed its warmth.

"Yes, I am he. And you are Robert. Welcome. I have a car outside. Let me help you with your case."

The case had only one handle. They both gave it support, their hands touching beneath the leather. Even this seemed provocative to Clive though he dared not think it significant.

"Did you have a good journey?" he asked.

"Thank you, yes. I came third class as it was much cheaper. A bit rough on the serge. Anyway, beggars can't be choosers."

Clive laughed. "Come on, old chap, let's get your bag up. Fine, now hop in."

Along the way they chattered freely as though they had known each other for a long time. "All I know about you is the little Maurice told me on the telephone. Your name is Robert and you had an unfortunate adventure – I'm sorry if I make it sound inconsequential for I am sure the consequences could have been absolutely catastrophic – in Hyde Park. Tell me about yourself."

Robert had immediately warmed to this man. There was an informality in his manner, which made Robert feel comfortable.

"Well," began Robert, "I shall be 21 years old next month. My father is the Reverend Hopkins. I was expelled from school last year and similarly from home. I have no work nor money. My dear mother is dead and my father is a bastard." The finality of the word left little doubt of there being a reconciliation between papa and son. At least not in the foreseeable future.

"My, my, Robert, that is some condensed history. Anything more?"

"I can call you Clive?"

"Of course."

"I was to have gone up to Cambridge but I rather mucked up my chances. I would like you to know," Robert hastily added, "that I was expelled for the heinous crime of a hug and a kiss. Do you object to me talking on this subject?"

"Of course not."

"A master just happened to be passing," he said with a sigh. "My friend behaved rather badly I thought. Claimed I'd pushed him into it or some such nonsense. Untrue, of course, but in fairness he was very frightened." Robert hesitated, then quickly went on,

"There was the inevitable interview. Extremely unpleasant. First of all, the Head asked if I had had relations with other boys, which I denied." Robert chuckles slightly. "His language, heavens! Talk of sexual fantasy. Was I familiar with this or that? he asked. Evidently disappointment when I said no. Ever persistent, and judging from the expression on his face, and heavy breathing, he was getting, well, excited just talking about it. I hadn't expected this. I'd been nervous about the interview in the first place, but now I was really upset and in the heat of the moment accused him of being a miserable pervert." Robert laughed. "The words caught him off guard and his ardour cooled instantaneously. He swore and cursed me violently. I was given half an hour to pack and caught the early morning train. The rest is history."

"Foolhardy perhaps, but yes, I can understand how you felt," said Clive, recalling the risks he and Maurice had taken. "A rotten experience, nevertheless." Clive heard a sigh and turned to look at Robert but it was too dark to see the distress on his face.

"On the basis of what I saw at that school, half the masters and a great number of students would be eligible for the stocks. Does all this shock you?"

"No, Robert. Just makes one realise how uncivilised and inhuman some of our Victorian law-makers were. They are beyond contempt, but their evil spirits will be with us for years to come, sadly. There we are, it is all so difficult," he said. "I'm just sorry that this has caused you to miss out on Cambridge. What were you reading?"

"Languages and European history."

They were now running along the drive in front of the house. "This is Penge?" said Robert obviously impressed.

"Yes, this is the estate I inherited and which needs a lot of repairs."

The front door was opened by a young girl just as they were removing Robert's case from the car.

"Come, Robert," said Clive cheerfully "come and meet mother."

The introductions went well. During the course of the evening Clive's mother probed, in society's most delicate yet effective manner, into the guest's history and background. His stock was adequately marked with the revelation of the vocation of his father. Robert, needless to say, was none too happy in having to mention the name of his father's parish.

"Mr. Borenius will, I am sure, look forward to meeting you," she said, as if this were an enviable choice.

Clive later explained who the religious gentleman was, causing Robert to remark, much to Clive's amusement 'that his love of holy cows flew out of the vicarage on the day of his expulsion, or possibly much earlier.'

"We should get on well, Robert," he said laughing.

Robert was allocated the room where Maurice had first stayed. Robert's wardrobe was very limited and certainly did not extend to evening clothes. He offered no apologies nor did Clive seek any. Clive was quickly becoming impressed by Robert's unaffected manner. He seemed to lack the guile and pretence often evident in one faced with unfamiliar surroundings. His conversation was easy and fluent. Good, thought Clive, we shall not have to waste time tunnelling through each other's defences.

It was not until after Mrs. Durham had retired that Clive had Robert to himself and when both felt more at ease.

"Robert, did Maurice mention that I am married?"

"No," said Robert with evident surprise. "Indeed he mentioned little except that you were his friend."

"We once meant much more than that to each other," Clive said with meaning.

"Really?"

"Yes. And to use Alec's phrase, I fucked it up. I decided to toe the time-honoured heterosexual line, instead of following my natural feelings. The early Romans and Greeks had no such problems, nor, by and large, do they on the continent today. In these islands, however, IT remains unmentionable. Still, all is not lost," said Clive without expanding on what he hoped to recover.

"My wife is very charming – you shall meet her – but guileless? Well maybe not as much she would have you believe. Strictly off the record, Anne and I have agreed to separate. All a mistake. There have been no histrionics and we remain just good friends."

"Sounds very civilised," said Robert.

It occurred to Robert that Clive was taking something of a gamble in confiding in him. On the other hand, Maurice's telephone conversation, he knew, would have informed Clive of the nature and disposition of Robert's sexuality, nullifying any risk to either of them.

"Clive, may I ask why you tell me this?"

"Because, Robert, I hope that apart from working for me I shall be able to talk to you openly about other matters," here he hesitated, "things of a more personal nature. After all, we are both, according to the less informed, demons from hell. Will this bother you?"

"Oh, no. I am rather honoured actually, especially since we've only known each other for what, five hours?"

Clive warmed to his guest, the rapport between them seemed immediate and uninhibited.

"The job, for which I have a real need, is someone to act as my secretary. Someone to do some bookkeeping, to help me in the management of the estate. 'Tis a tall order. Do you think you will be able to cope with it?"

"I have no experience," Robert said frankly, "all I can offer are my wits, though they are not in too bad a shape."

"Excellent, excellent. By the way, you will not be living here, Robert, but at my house in Sellinge. I think you will find it very pleasing. A short distance from the sea. Tomorrow we will motor down."

Clive and Robert left the house shortly after breakfast. The day was fine and they found motoring along the country roads exhilarating. It was a journey lasting an hour. Against a fleeting landscape Robert secretly studied the side view Clive's face offered, from his falling fair hair, down the aquiline nose to full lips where he momentarily hesitated. That something which increasingly troubled him was active again. He felt a distinct change, a warmth, a sudden desire. He dared not let Clive become aware of it. He strove, successfully to dismiss these thoughts from his mind.

Out of the corner of one eye Clive was quite conscious of being scrutinised. It was only when Robert turned to look in the opposite direction that Clive allowed himself to smile. It was a smile of satisfaction, a satisfaction of knowing that the enterprise, initiated by Maurice, had turned out well. He did not dwell upon the other benefit that Robert's presence might provide, but at the same time saw no purpose in dismissing it either. Why should he? He knew the boy attracted him. He also knew that for the moment such ideas were come too early, but not taboo.

Chapter Fourteen

It is surely important that the very essence of a holiday should be to add to the reservoir of human knowledge and understanding as well as pleasure. At least that was the adult view fervently held by Maurice. He therefore derived great pleasure and satisfaction from Alec's continual if exhausting inquisitiveness. His observations and comments were, in general, very perceptive. It at once came home to Maurice that lack of enthusiasm for knowledge, in most of the poorer and less well placed in our society, was usually the result of their inherited circumstances. Freed at the beginning of their lives to enjoy the fruits of universal learning – available to the more fortunate in society – would show that their flight of imagination was just as capable of soaring the heights as any other. Equally, of course, he accepted that a panoramic vision of understanding was often lacking in the imaginations of a great many from the affluent classes, despite expensive tuition. That had to prove something or other, he mused.

The journey through Kent provided them with ever changing landscapes. First came the grime stained houses, huddled together in their squalor, which lined the route out of smoky London. Then followed the green and lush pastures of the Garden of England, as Kent is often referred to, providing a welcoming side of nature, a beauty not yet hidden or disfigured. Of course, to Alec, this was familiar stuff.

It was a fast train which stopped only twice. The first encouragement to excitement occurred when the train slowed down over a high viaduct, providing Alec with a view of the English Channel and the town of Folkestone. As the train reduced speed, he could make out the old Parish Church set right on the top of a high cliff. The church, St Mary & St Earswythe, built in the 12th century, was significant in that it had been painted by one or two famous Victorian artists, including Turner. From it led a road to the harbour, which, during the war, had carried troops joining ships destined for France. Because of its association with this tragedy it had been renamed Remembrance Hill. Alec could just make out the harbour quay and a single funnel ferryboat alongside.

The train travelled further along the coast until terminating at Dover Harbour station. It was not a boat train – another innovation which had been introduced in 1918 and which Alec found hard to believe when Maurice mentioned it to him. "A train on a ship? Damn dangerous I'd 'ave thought. Wouldn't they topple over if there were a storm?" he asked.

"Don't worry, Alec, they make sure that doesn't happen."

Embarking formalities were a small interruption. Alec followed Maurice closely as they mounted the gangway to board the ship, a large vessel by Alec's standards. This floating monument proclaimed the start of their foreign holiday. John joined Maurice and Alec as they watched the bows of the ship head out into the English Channel. As the white cliffs distanced themselves, the romance of it all came flooding in.

The sea was mirror calm, much to George's delight and relief. As they travelled further south all the vistas previously described by George became a reality and Alec bubbled with excitement at every stage of their journey.

They had been away from England for over a month.

Alec lay stretched out, naked, in the sun. Sand still clung to him following his last dive into the shallow sea. With Maurice's patience he had managed not only to float, but also to swim properly, and was now learning to dive. This was not achieved, at the beginning anyway, without gulping what he imagined was half the salty ocean. A paradise this must be. In his wildest dreams he had not seen the like. They had travelled on foot, by train, on horseback. They had all pummelled him with knowledge about the Greek civilisation, about the great Plato, Socrates and other great thinkers. He was introduced to Lord Byron's romantic poetry and taken to the suburb of Athens named after him. He had taken on an immense task in trying to absorb so much so quickly. Now, towards the end of the holiday, was a time for utter relaxation. Maurice lay alongside him on the same large towel, eyes closed as if in sleep. Alec sat up. He looked down at the sleeping figure. He marvelled at the face he had come to love so much, at the body he worshipped. Carefully he climbed astride him, then fell forwards seeking the lips he had kissed a thousand times. Maurice was not asleep and accepted this interruption with as much desire and pleasure as Alec.

"What a joy it is to be privy to such depravity," joked George as he and John came onto the veranda.

"It makes a change from mountain climbing," said Alec cheekily.

"'Tis a born rebel I have here," remarked Maurice "still, I was the first to teach him to float even though he was at risk from our feathered friends. That morsel is already reserved and not for the birds."

"My God," protested John in fake pretence, "are my ears to be filled with such profanity?"

"And, furthermore, if you're interested in anatomy, John, Alec here, given the slightest encouragement from me, can demonstrate how quickly his, er, helmeted warrior can reach for the skies. You could say that I have become completely addick-ted, if you'll pardon the pun," he said while attempting to breathe under the weight of Alec's body. This caused them all to laugh, including Alec.

"Want a demonstration?" offered Alec, grinning.

"No, we jolly well don't. I am to be the only witness to such theatrics." Laughter took flight with the sea breeze.

This banter carried on for some time.

"The post," cried Maurice, "I must catch the post," he said pushing Alec from him. "Promised I would let Clive know when we are arriving back" He then picked up a towel and began dusting the sand from his body. "I wonder how it all went," he said, a frown clouding his face.

"Do you think I was right to trust Robert?"

"I would stake my life on it," said John confidently.

"Oh, I forgot," said George reaching into his pocket. "A telegram came for you, Maurice."

It was from his sister. They were arriving that day from Paris.

Maurice began to write.

My Dear Clive,

By the time you receive this letter the chances are that we shall already be started on our homeward trek. My only regret is that time ultimately spoils things in that there is always an end. This time I know that our re-union will be less traumatic. The last five weeks have been immeasurably wonderful. One could never calculate happiness of this sort. I am still in a daze. It all seems too good to be true and at times I wonder if I will wake up to find it were a dream.

Looking back, I contemplate how fate and fortune have played tricks with me. How fortunate it was that you insisted that I continue my visits to Penge, even after your immersion, or perhaps I should say 'conversion', into things 'normal'. Were I not to have done so, my luck may never have turned. How, my dear Clive, I thank the Gods for the sheer persistence and audacity of my astonishing Alec. I am sure you will allow me the extravagance of continually counting my blessings. After my initial failed baptism I never expected to see Apollo again, at least not in this world. It was but a short time ago that I still ventured to hold on to the crazy notion that our ardour might be rekindled. You can have had no idea of the weight of the depression I experienced. Alec's sudden and forceful appearance that wet evening saved the day (or, to be correct, night and early morning!) and I responded, as one released from ancient bonds, willingly. The gift was mine. Without it I would not be here with my lover beside me, happy and contented as I pen this letter to you from Greece. The other day you say I saved your life. Well, my dear Clive, that blustery evening, Alec saved mine.

The holiday has been one enormous success. We have enjoyed the freedom, which seems to be ours to exploit. The language is a problem, especially for Alec, in fact for both of us. Here, none of us has to worry about contamination from the poisoned tentacles of rabid righteousness. If only the maxim live and let live... Ah well!

Of course we are all on tenterhooks wondering what I, perhaps in my innocence, have let you in for. Upon reflection, it was perhaps unfair of me to ask you to take on a complete stranger. There, my heart overruled me. Was it my persuasiveness or your innate humanity, which allowed you to agree to look after Robert for a while? I would never forgive myself were you to be intimidated in any way. My judgement tells me all will be well.

We are dining with Ada and her husband this evening. I think I mentioned that she is here on her honeymoon. The second one in the family, eh! – to quote Alec. As you already know, she is fully au fait with the situation, vis-à-vis Alec and me. Her complete understanding and acceptance of our situation was something I didn't fully expect. Remarkable isn't it? I am so glad that Ada and I are friends once again. It will be fun meeting them here. I am inclined to believe that they like Alec. Then who wouldn't? The world is a queer place, Clive. Who would have thought a couple of months ago that I would be writing to you in this manner and looking forward to meeting a sister who I thought I had lost. C'est la vie!

The body sleeping on the patio beside me has turned sepia. Poses, reminiscent of 'Poseidon', abound, and very provocative too. It is enough to turn the spirit pagan – though many a spirit would be glad of the chance to change places with me! There is one post collection that I would like to meet. We shall arrive in Dover midday on Friday next. For so many reasons, I am looking forward to seeing you soon for there is so much that I have to tell you. It is my sincere wish, Clive, that from now on we can exchange ideas and confidences without the intrusion of those false values which in the past have hampered us so.

It goes without saying, my dear Clive, that our love wings its way with this letter.

Always,

Maurice

Ada and Arthur were staying at the Hotel Troia in the middle of Athens. A call from Maurice and they arranged to meet that evening outside the rooftop taverna in the Plaka district. 'There, in the early evening, one can sit in the balmy cool and look up at the Acropolis' is how Maurice had described it to Ada that very morning.

The choice, in truth, had been John's.

With George and John leading the way, they walked along the narrow streets, with pavements full and heaving like a market day. They passed pastel coloured and whitewashed walled houses whose balcony gardens were seething with red geraniums growing from an assortment of boxes and ornate containers. Strung coloured lights decorated the shops and tavernas. At this very time, their world could best be described as a large panoramic canvas on which was painted, in many shades and colours, all the excitement of an old time pageant. Against a backdrop of antiquity and mountainous beauty bustled the traders in their shops or attending pavement stalls.

Varied were the throngs of leisurely strolling visitors. All appeared at peace with the world.

Maurice greatly looked forward to seeing Ada again. They had spoken on the telephone several times since they had last met. Her wedding had gone smoothly with the attendant doctor providing the respectability society demanded, much to her mother's delight. Accordingly, to Ada, Clive attended on his own, making excuses for his wife, who he claimed was feeling unwell. This excuse, according to Ada, lacked conviction and was said in such a light-hearted manner. She noticed that Clive was not in the least put out by his wife's absence. He even jokingly remarked, 'Oh, that's women for you'. Mrs. Hall had not been impressed. Subsequently, when thinking about, and having regard to her earlier conversation with Maurice, it occurred to her, the slightest suspicion maybe, that all may not be well with their marriage. She would ask Maurice, he would know.

A small white pony pulled an open carriage through the cluttered streets, the iron clad wheels noisily bumping over the cobbled stones. It finally came to rest outside the restaurant where Maurice and the others waited. Maurice and Alec vied with each other to help Ada down onto the cobbled pavement. She hugged Maurice, then turning towards Alec, and with an exceptional show of pleasure, she kissed him. George and John were introduced and were immediately captivated by the young married couple. In a chattering babble, fused with expectation, they climbed the stairs to the restaurant.

Following a very attentive if somewhat portly headwaiter and avoiding a young Adonis balancing a heavily laden tray who swept past them, they were finally and comfortably seated at a table affording them the magnificent views which had been promised. It was all very appropriate to the occasion, thought Maurice as he looked fondly across at Alec.

Alec was becoming accustomed to going into fine restaurants, but not with the high cost of doing so. He still equated everything with his experience of values. It was all so unreal. He had remarked one day to Maurice on how the decorative nature and size of a menu often reflected the price of the dishes it had to offer. Actually he put it more bluntly as, 'the posher they were the more bloody expensive.' He could not understand why the others seemed not to understand this attitude towards extravagance. But tonight, there was so much else to occupy his mind that he had, for once, not given it so much as a single thought.

There was much laughter as John, the more seasoned traveller, began to describe the origin of some of the Greek dishes. Alec, with his simpler tastes, had an ally in Ada.

George, Maurice, Arthur and finally Alec (pressed into this decision after the teasing, laughter, and finally the utter confusion) chose Moussaka. Ada ordered fish – a type of Greek bream called Sinagrida, and John had Kebabs.

John poured the wine then lifted his glass to propose a toast to the recently married couple.

"To the bride and groom," he said.

"I suppose I should blush," said Ada, "but for the life of me I just can't, which says something about my upbringing or Arthur's bad influence." Here she laughed, and, in John's words, positively sparkled.

"Bride and groom, your health indeed," said Alec again raising his glass. "Now, what about us, stallion, groom, whatever, all the same to me 'cept the actions are different."

"Alec," said Maurice genuinely shocked.

Arthur roared with laughter, more so because of Maurice's look of embarrassment.

"How about to the groom and groom," said Arthur, smiling and looking across at Ada. "We want to drink your health – so I say, here's health and happiness to Alec and Maurice," he said raising his glass a second time.

Ada put her hand on Maurice's arm. "Don't look so serious, Maurice. And it's no good you trying to hide that grin, Alec," she said trying to control her own fit of giggles. "Lord, if Dr Barry could see us now, your goose, Maurice, would be cooked forever."

"A year or two ago it would have mattered," remarked Maurice, "but not anymore. In fact, I would probably relish the opportunity of confronting Dr Barry. Point out the conspicuous inadequacies in his character. Which reminds me, I had thought of sending old Borenius a postcard, one on which the bronze figure of Poseidon is so beautifully displayed."

"You are positively evil," said Ada.

"I agree with you, Ada," said Alec, "though the old sod would probably enjoy it."

"Why not?" said Maurice.

"We don't know his address."

"We can send it care of Penge."

"What about Clive?" said Alec with some concern.

"For once I know that he would enjoy the prank."

"Well, if you say so, Maurice, but I don't think 'tis such a good idea," said Alec with caution in his voice.

Maurice looked over at Alec and caught the doubt in his voice. He loved him for his concern for others feelings.

"Perhaps you are right, Alec."

"Not worth the risk, Maurice, for they might just jump to conclusions that they haven't knowledge of at the moment," concluded George.

"By the way, Maurice, have you written to Mother?" Ada asked.

"Yes, I sent her a letter when we first arrived and a postcard last Friday," said Maurice.

"A respectable postcard I hope."

"Yes, indeed. Though I did send it with love from me and Alec!"

"Well!" grinned Ada. "Mind you, contrary to what you may think, Maurice, she might indeed be pleased. You never can tell with us women."

"That is a truly remarkable observation," said Arthur with a laugh. Ada joined in the laughter as she clouted him with her rolled up serviette.

"Seriously though, Maurice," Ada went on, "try to be patient with her, I know for a fact that she is trying so hard to come to terms with a situation very new and strange to her."

"Yes, I do know." said Maurice.

Ada turned to Alec. "Alec, you've caught the sun. You've got the most wonderful tan. Gracious, with your looks you could be in great demand on the Riviera, some heiress would... there I go, getting it all wrong again. My apologies, Maurice."

Alec grinned at the compliment. "She'd 'ave to be very rich and even then I'm not too sure. No, Maurice?" he said raising his eyebrows, and then began laughing.

"You're damned right. The demand rests here, with yours truly," said Maurice tapping his chest with his forefinger.

"Prove it then by giving us a..." Alec began provocatively and continuing to laugh.

"Don't you dare," said Maurice as Alec leaned towards him.

George raised his glass to salute this further demonstration of Alec and Maurice's mutual adoration.

John had been studying Ada and Arthur from across the table. He had been well briefed by Maurice on her reaction to Alec becoming a 'member' of the Hall family. It did seem remarkable to him that given her upbringing and society's current values, the so called moral ones in particular, that she had responded so sympathetically. He knew that she was associated with the suffragettes and had a husband whose leanings tended to be more progressive, but it still surprised him. An element which may have influenced her was her own involvement in affairs of the heart, and her recognition of a kindred spirit in Maurice. Whatever, he thought her a very charming person.

"Would you believe it, George," Ada said leaning across the table, "but I was actually propositioned in our hotel yesterday! Well, the nearest thing to it."

"Dear, oh, dear, whatever next," said George, unsure of how to respond.

"Did you witness this extramarital promise, Arthur?" said Maurice in mock sympathy.

"Oh, yes," he said resignedly, "rather flattering don't you think?"

"It might have been," continued Ada, "had not our Greek paramour made a similar overture to a young English boy staying at the same hotel," she said to their rising laughter.

"And," Ada went on "to compound my embarrassment they walked blatantly past me, arm in arm, on their way over to the stairs. I was mortified." she said with a sly grin.

"No you weren't, Ada, maybe a little disappointed, well, your ego didn't suffer, that I know, least hope I do."

"Arthur!" Then she considered it more carefully, "Maybe, but of course you can never tell in these romantic islands," she said softly, giggling once again.

"The lad was what they call bisexual, Alec," said Arthur.

"Is this the enlightenment you were telling me about, Ada?" Maurice asked mischievously.

"In a way it is," replied Arthur, "for without observation, knowledge has to be limited. Ask Alec. And with fewer prejudices, one's education will expand."

"So I am beginning to believe," said Alec.

"Bi means two, Alec," said George.

"By God!" exclaimed Alec, "don't think I could manage two. Maurice is more than enough I can tell you."

Ada nearly choked on the wine she was sipping. "Oh, Alec, you are such a dear," she said leaning over to kiss him.

"You encourage him, Ada," Maurice said joining in with the laughter. He felt a hand squeeze his knee. "Alec, don't you dare."

As they were leaving the restaurant Arthur drew Maurice to one side.

"Well, old friend," he started, "Hell, how do I start? Let me say that I was not unduly surprised when Ada first told me about you and Alec. Maurice, my dear friend, let me just say that I am the happiest of men right now and 'tis all down to Ada agreeing to marry me, a wish that really came true. If I've another wish, Maurice, then it shall be that you and Alec have the good fortune you both deserve. The environment here is right for you both, but be assured, Maurice, that the environment in our home will be as friendly. You and I have always been pretty close friends. Sharing in your new life, so to speak, will, I hope, make us even closer."

"Thank you, Arthur, I'll always cherish this moment. It is as if you and Ada had offered Alec and me a kind of benediction. I treasure your friendship. Ada deserves you and by the same token you have earned happiness in abundance. Bless you both."

Chapter Fifteen

Clive sat in his study poised over blank sheets of notepaper ready to activate his mind. His raised pen descended slowly to record, for the first time in a very long time, his most intimate and relished thoughts.

My Very Dear Maurice,

Although you are miles away at this time I feel as if you are here in spirit, ever cautioning, ever guiding. That's my Maurice. Rather like having a personal spirit. I only hope that I come up to your expectations. There are big changes in the wind, I can feel it. They will not all happen at once, I know, but I am resigned to being patient for as long as it takes.

I have been worked hard by Jake, my agent, and shall be glad when the bloody election and fighting are over. My enthusiasm for politics has, I regret to say, lost its charm and purpose, for, of the moment, other significant things of greater importance have been happening in this 'screwy old nook in the south west'. Nevertheless, Jake reckons that I stand a good chance. Well, we'll soon know. Over confidence is a thing of the past – look where it has got me!

I am sure you will be pleased to learn, Maurice, that Anne and I are agreeably reconciled to the inevitable. An announcement of separation at the moment would not be 'politically convenient', so, for the time being, we've agreed not to make any public statements; there will be plenty of time for that later. We both know that our marriage was a mistake. An understanding with Anne has resulted – I am more than pleased to say – in us remaining friends. I can hear you saying, 'how civilised'. After two years of agony I am naturally pleased to be released, freed, from my grand folly. Anne may have played the piper but I was close behind.

Robert duly arrived the day after you left. Well, what can I say? What would you expect to hear? As a secretary he has been good, very good. His abilities as well as his energy seem boundless. We are falling into a routine where I am beginning to depend on him quite a lot. That just describes his performance as secretary. He is also excellent company which is just what I need right now. I am eternally grateful to you on that account alone.

I am beginning to see a little further ahead, Maurice, and incredible though it may seem, there is in the air a feel of those Cambridge days when we first met. I tread cautiously, however. I expect you are wondering just what in the hell I'm going on about? Enough to say that I hold 'hope' as a friend, and a future with more promise. There have been no emotional trials. Let's just say that my 'heart' is on stand-by! Whatever the future, Maurice, if my starting point is now, or rather from our recent meeting on that sunny day in the field, then I have nothing to fear.

Events of the last couple of years have played havoc with my emotions, pushing one way and then another. I felt at times as if I were being dragged into the very centre of a hurricane where the only direction was down. Oh, God, the very thought of it all. Pray that is all in the past. I am myself again. I have recovered my will to really live and, this time, Maurice, the path I follow will be the one I desire to follow, not that conceived and imposed by someone else. The happiness I now enjoy makes me impatient to share. If I were with you in Greece, I should feel very inclined to climb to the pinnacle of one of the hills or mountains, up to Poseidon's temple, maybe, and inscribe my name alongside that of Byron. There I go, Maurice, with my fantasies, some of which I am hopeful will turn into reality.

It goes without saying that you, Maurice, have all the prime elements of happiness. Luckily, my depression and madness have been replaced by sanity once again, and Robert, unwittingly, has helped the process. I can live comfortably with the memory of our companionship and remember its passion. In precious moments like this I can sit back and enjoy thinking of you and Alec.

You may think me mad, Maurice, but believe me, I am rejuvenated, life is returning. Eternal thanks, my dear friend. I hope you return soon as I miss you all.

Cable me your arrival time. Affectionately,

Clive

Chapter Sixteen

"A letter for you," said Clive when he arrived at Sellinge, "I see it's been re-directed." he commented as he passed it to Robert.

He watched Robert as he unfolded the single lined sheet of paper and began slowly to read its carefully written contents. The frown on his face had deepened by the time he reached the end of the letter.

"Bad news, Robert?"

"Yes," he said without looking up. It's from father's housekeeper. I wrote to tell her where I was staying in London. Oh, damn," he said, "just when everything was going so perfectly. It's Father. He's been very ill with pneumonia and there is still some doubt as to whether he will pull through. She begs me go visit him at the rectory."

"Do you want to go?"

"No, not really. But I am reminded of happier times and if he should die, God forbid, then I would suffer a guilt at not being there."

The thought made Robert sad. He also realised that his father's death would leave him finally alone, joining the ranks of orphans. It made him shudder at the very idea.

"Mostly for the sake of my mother's memory, I feel under some obligation." He sighed. "Oh, this would have to happen. But I can never stay in his house again. Quite apart from anything else, there are far too many unhappy memories," he said with determination.

"Even before I was expelled," he went on, "father and I, in the latter years, were never very close. Now of course the situation has worsened. He will probably still be very abusive, though in his present state of health is unlikely to be violent. I had better go," he said looking miserable.

Clive looked over at Robert whose face reflected considerable sadness.

"Then I shall come with you," he suddenly decided. "Yes, Robert," he insisted when Robert started to protest, "we shall drive there together. If we start off early in the morning, we can be back by late afternoon. After all, 'tis only thirty or so miles to Farnham."

The St. Mary's rectory lay sprawled behind the church, in a typical setting of tall trees and croaking ravens. As Clive drove along the pebbled drive he could sense that Robert was apprehensive and nervous.

Any yearning Robert had had for the house where he lived for most of his young life was gone. Memories of happier days, with his mother alive, slightly mollified the mood of extreme depression. The sombre graveyard, with its flaking headstones, matched the stillness that surrounded it. On an impulse Robert leaned towards the open window of the car half expecting to catch the sound of his mother's voice. The mysticism of the moment soon passed. He sighed.

Clive turned and seeing the ache of despair placed his hand gently but reassuringly on Robert's arm. A soft heartfelt moan escaped, tearing away yet another memory from the past. Clive became concerned for Robert and wished the encounter quickly over.

With the support Clive now provided Robert felt more secure and a degree of confidence returned. Despite this, however, it was with some foreboding that he looked towards this meeting with his father.

The bleached oak door was opened by Ethel Crouch, the housekeeper.

"Robert, my dear," she said cheerfully, "I am so glad you came. As I mentioned in the letter, he has been very ill. The doctor was here only an hour since. He is now much more optimistic. We had begun to worry that your father might not come through it."

She led them into a dark room, which was lit solely by the daylight from three arched leaded-light windows. A small coal fire flickered aimlessly in the grate. Robert knew well the direction of his father's chair.

The figure of his father sat huddled in blankets.

Robert walked over to him. "Hello Father," he said cheerfully, purposely forgetting their last meeting.

"Hhhm," came a disgruntled voice.

"It is me, Robert. Mrs. Crouch wrote to tell me you had been ill." There was no reply.

"Father, if you are still of a mind to disregard me, or wish that I had not called, then, of course, I will disturb you no longer," said Robert, now beginning to regret his decision to call on his father.

There was a mumbled response, then a movement that disturbed the blankets around the sitting man. Then his father's face became clear. Finally he spoke, though he barely raised his head. His voice was weaker than usual yet carried a determination for which he was known.

"You sound very sure of yourself, Robert. I suppose that's what comes of living in London, that den of vice," he said accusingly.

"As it happens, Father, I do not live in London. I work for Mr. Durham, and he lives in Hampshire. This is Mr. Durham," he said introducing Clive for the first time.

"Hhhm," came the voice again, ignoring Clive completely. "Well," he went on, "I suppose that is something to be thankful for." He made no further comment.

Robert was amazed to see Clive stride quickly across the room and stand immediately before his father who had purposely not acknowledged his presence.

"I am truly sorry that you are ill but do you have to be as disagreeable and ill-mannered as this?" said Clive brusquely, somewhat aggrieved at being so obviously ignored.

"Who the devil are you, Sir?" said Robert's father, angry yet mildly surprised at the man's arrogance.

"Certainly not one of your miserable flock, that is for sure," said Clive mischievously.

The man made to move, then decided otherwise and fell back into the chair.

"Do you want me to leave, Robert?"

"Oh, no, Clive."

Turning to Robert, Clive remarked. "Obviously, your father doesn't want us here. Your concern shows courage, Robert, but is ill spent. He doesn't need compassion; you were unwise to come. He's not only ill-mannered but contemptuous to boot."

"You dare to insult me in my own house. Get out! Get out, the both of you."

"Clive, please," Robert begged. "Alright father, we won't stay or disturb you any longer. You should know, however, that we have travelled a long way as I thought you needed help. I do not believe that you deserve my pity. The last time we met you outraged my dear mother's memory, as well as behaving towards me, your own flesh and blood, with violence and unpardonable hatred."

His father stared up at his son. He was aware of the truth in Robert's words, yet his natural belligerence would not allow it to register. There was anger in his eyes as he said, "And does your employer, here," he said pointing to

Clive "know why you were expelled from school, eh? Answer that if you dare," he said maliciously. Almost at once he began to regret having spoken. But it was too late, the damage was done.

Clive was livid with anger. He moved nearer, presenting an awesome figure, his face alive with rage as he spoke in a forced but controlled manner, answering, as if of right, for Robert.

"You are utterly despicable," Clive said spitting out the words. "But never imagine, however much you try, that you will destroy your son, if that is your aim."

Robert's father was visibly shaken by the accusation, causing him to hesitate.

"Yes," continued Clive and shaking his head violently, "I do happen to know why he was expelled, and were the head master of that wretched school not now dead, then I would have made it my business to see that he suffered, many times over, for his abominable behaviour." Here Clive paused as the man in front of him glared angrily at him.

But Clive went racing ahead permitting no interruptions.

"Oh, yes, and your present attitude would have made me even more determined than ever. I can but hope that his trail of filth conveys him to hell. And let me inform you, Sir, that I am not without some influence," he said without giving ground to Robert's now protesting father. "And that influence could very well extend to making your tenure here pretty damned uncomfortable – if I so wished."

The Rev. Hopkins looked hard at Clive. Events had taken a turn, which was not to his liking. Who was this man? The way in which he spoke was either bluff or he had some standing in society. Judging from his manner and bearing he was inclined to opt for the latter. He looked at Clive briefly. A determined individual, he thought. He was not too ill not to recognise possible danger.

"You take advantage, Sir. I am a sick man. Your intrusion here is a trespass. I did not ask for your attention, nor do I seek it," he said in a muted but angry voice.

Robert moved towards his father.

"I came because you are my father. I realise that I have made a terrible mistake. Do not worry, Father, you may be assured that once I leave the rectory you will never set eyes on me again."

The Rev. Jackson looked over at his son. Inwardly he was towards softening his manner but his persistent stubbornness overtook him.

"Let me remind you, boy, that until you are twenty-one you are technically in my charge," he said with a touch of recklessness in his voice.

This was all too much for Clive and he interjected immediately. "And let me remind you, Sir," he said, his anger still evident in his voice, "that my previous threat was no idle one. I will see you in hell first."

"In the name of God, what am I hearing?"

"You are supposed to be ill yet it does not stop your vociferous tongue from having free range. And yes, you are hearing," continued Clive more outraged than ever, "what you should have heard years ago. You," he said raising his voice, "you, of all people, petitioning in the name of God. That is blasphemy of the highest order. I swear that one action against your son will invoke a wrath the like of which you will never have encountered. Damnation you will consider a blessing. Come Robert," he said walking away, "you have tried to do your duty, but the devil is not to be reconciled."

By this time the older man had risen to his feet and stood shakily holding on to a nearby table

He turned and saw the picture of his wife on the wall above the bureau. He gasped and began making moaning sounds which alert Robert and Clive. His head sank into open hands then almost immediately he rose, lifting up, extending hands imploringly towards his wife's picture. He cried out, a strained despairing voice and rocked his head from side to side. They heard a subdued, now pitiful voice.

"Rebecca, my precious Rebecca, I see you, oh God, your shadowy image follows me wherever I turn, you appear disturbed and angry. Please, please, my precious Rebecca, do not desert me. I cannot be without you any longer. Dear God, take pity on me, still my heart, let me be forever with my dear Rebecca. You move, Rebecca, you are fading, please God!" He lowered his head and covered them with his hands again. He began to weep.

Clive was startled, "Robert, what in heaven's name?"

"I think he's delirious."

Clive walked out of the room and left the house immediately, leaving Robert to follow.

"Father! What troubles you?"

"Her ghost, my constant companion, Robert," he says between sobs. "I care no longer, my time is long overdue. I get near but will not reach until I die."

His father rested quietly for several minutes. Robert watched him suspiciously until he noticed the difficulty with which he now moved. It was obvious to him that his father was still very weak from his illness. He considered that his mother would not have recognised this man for the tall jaunty figure he once was. A sadness held Robert. He could not help but feel compassion.

"Before you go, Robert," his Father said in a much calmer voice that attracted Robert's pity, "there is something that I wish you to have. It belonged to me and your Mother."

Robert stood a few paces from his father. He watched him walk haltingly over to the bureau. He turned the key of a drawer, and then finally returned to face Robert who by now was standing near the door.

"You are still my son, Robert, and I am still your father." He said this with difficulty, wanting, yet somehow unable, to get closer. "This ring, Robert, this beautiful ring," he was now more emotional than Robert had ever seen him before, and his eyes misted over, "was your dear mother's wedding gift to me."

Robert shook his head. "No, no, no, father."

"Robert, please, hear me out." His breathing was laboured, and he rested awhile. Robert was disturbed on seeing how much his father's health had deteriorated.

His father started again.

"If you will accept that which I treasure most dearly, because I loved your dear mother, and, if only for her sake alone, I promise there shall be peace between us."

Robert was hesitant, unsure of himself, not wanting to give his father any more satisfaction, yet aware that he might never see him again.

"Please believe me, Robert," he said slowly, "when I tell you that I loved your mother beyond all else, beyond, I am sad to say, even you. When she died I wished to have died with her." Here he faltered, his throat full. "It is very hard for me to say this for I have never spoken about my feeling for her to anyone. But, I have to confess, she was everything to me to the exclusion of all else in this world, even, yes, Robert, even more than my God. I have been in perpetual mourning ever since she died. I would like to claim that this has caused me to become intolerant, the reason for treating you the way I have; but that would be too easy, too simple an excuse."

"Why do you tell me all this now?"

"Perhaps because you are taking your final leave of me. I feel as if in a daze, with your mother's spirit telling me to make amends before she also deserts me. The power of her spirit, the love I bore her, can you understand?"

"Yes, Father, I can. If only you had confided in me, in one who also loved her so very much. We could have been of greater comfort to each other."

"Then, Robert, you will take the ring?"

"On condition that you will remain my father who will try again to find the son he so nearly lost."

"Robert," came a choked voice, "thank you, thank you. Thank you for saving a soul that had very nearly quit. Apologise to your friend. I am..." He sat down and began to weep for the first time since his wife had died. He offered no excuse for this unusual behaviour, he was making atonement in the most natural way, in tears of regret.

Robert was at loss. This sudden turn around made him ill at ease. His father mopped his eyes then, after lifting himself from the chair, extended his hand containing a box.

"Here, Robert, please wear it."

Robert took the ring from the box and was surprised that it fitted the index finger of his right hand.

"Show me," said his father. He took Robert's hand and held it for several moments.

"Yes it looks fine on you, son." He hesitated. "Will you ever want to visit me again, Robert?"

Robert looked over at his father, was this a repentant figure, one asking for forgiveness yet unable to offer up the words? He was looking at a man once beloved when his dear mother was alive. Robert was near to tears with the compassion he suddenly felt.

"Yes, Father, if that is what you really want." His father nodded.

"I must go, Father. I will write to you shortly giving you my new address."

When his father spoke again it was in stark contrast to all that had gone before. He spoke words, which were apologetic in tone and mellow with feeling.

"A weight has been lifted from my shoulders, Robert, which I do not deserve." Robert thought he heard a sob, a kind of cry for help. "Partly, I have you to thank for that. As the image of your dear mother comes before me I feel humbled. If only I could have been taken with her, none of this would ever have happened. If my anger should ever again appear against you, I pray to God that I be struck down. I deserve no less. To make amends for the past – how is that possible?" he said sadly. "I can but beg your forgiveness. It is always too late to rewrite the past, Robert, but if I live, and am permitted, then I shall pray for happier times." He was now very tired and paused to regain his strength.

"Take care, Robert, my son," he said with tears in his eyes.

In the next instant he moved close to Robert and fell forward to embrace him in his arms.

"Robert, Robert," he cried, his body shaking violently.

As Robert walked away from the house towards the car he suddenly turned. He saw his father, a lonely figure, wave from behind the window. He knew that his father was expressing feelings which, until now, had remained out of reach since the death of his beloved wife. Perhaps, in Robert, he saw the vision of her reflected. Robert prayed that the ghost of his mother would be witness to this revelation.

He returned the wave. In their separate ways, each tear they now shed carried with it a seed of reconciliation.

Chapter Seventeen

9a.m. on the 23rd October. Election day.

Robert caught an early train and arrived at Penge in time for breakfast.

"Well, Robert," said Clive between mouthfuls of toast, "this is it. I hope all the hard work comes to fruition today. I am quite hoarse. Thank God there is only one more speech to make and that, of course, is if I win."

"There should be no doubt, Clive," said his mother confidently. "Who best to look after their interests? The Unions have been trying to stir up trouble but these people," she said as if referring to some strange species, "they will have more sense than to listen to their socialistic prattle."

"I can't say that I agree with you, Mother. If I were one of them I think I would vote for Sam Horler." Clive saw Robert smile at this.

Mrs. Durham lifted her head in a show of displeasure. "That's hardly what we expect to hear from you, Clive. I hope you haven't expressed such sentiments to your voters."

"Heavens no," he said laughing nervously.

"Well," he continued, with noticeable cynicism in his voice, "either our propaganda will have been jolly effective or the voters are, after all, much more discriminating. Anyway the die is now cast and there is very little to do now except crawl along after dinner this evening to the Sellinge Town Hall. Such a drab building and I find the mayor really hard going – such a pompous ass. Anyway, it will soon be all over and I shall be glad.

"I had a letter from Maurice."

"Oh, that's jolly," said Anne. She had remained rather quiet since her return from London. Her interest, or rather the lack of it, in Clive's election campaign had displeased his mother more than Clive. The wife of a candidate usually accompanied her husband during the hustings. Anne considered the whole thing tedious. "All those common people," she had said with disgust, which convinced Clive that her absence was probably a blessing.

"Do I really have to come with you this evening?"

"I think you should, Anne," he said trying not to make is appear demanding. "You know what the papers are like. They'd make a mountain of newsprint out of it if one of the wives didn't turn up, more particularly the wife of the elected candidate."

"Alright then, but don't ask me to get involved with anything else."

"That doesn't seem very fair, Anne," said his mother frowning, "after all, you will be the wife of a member of parliament soon," she said having already decided on the outcome of the poll, "and that will involve you in a lot of entertaining, especially if Clive is to make his mark."

"Then he will have to make his mark without me," she answered petulantly.

"Please," begged Clive of the two women, "we will manage alright. Thanks, Anne, anyway," he said, grateful that she would at least be at the Town Hall tonight.

After the last hectic few days of campaigning, Clive decided to motor down to Sellinge with Robert.

Robert had now been with him for nearly five weeks. They had met every day. On a couple of occasions he had travelled with Clive to certain areas within his constituency and watched him giving a prepared speech. Obviously he had not been asked to contribute, that was the job of Jake, Clive's agent, though Clive influenced and approved the shape of them. Robert was not impressed, some he thought rather trite, some patronising and others agonisingly patriotic. No one asked his opinion for which he was extremely grateful. He would certainly never have volunteered one, particularly as his views slanted more towards Sam Horler.

Robert was utterly thrilled to be living at Sellinge and it goes without saying that Mrs. Winter fussed over him. She was kindness itself and could not have been more attentive if he had been her own son.

Clive had so far avoided staying overnight at the dower house. He preferred to allow the existing arrangement to continue, it suited him well – at least for the moment. There was also uncertainty in his mind as to Robert's feelings towards any other type of 'relationship'. He was just delighted that Robert had managed to grasp the intricacies of estate management so quickly. During the last two weeks of the election he had been of tremendous help. To Robert it had been a challenge, an opportunity to prove himself at last. He was beginning to recover lost confidence, to see some purpose in what he was doing. During the last few days he had given thought to that last meeting with his father. He derived comfort from its unexpected conclusion, the outcome of which had mellowed, very considerably, his feelings towards his father.

"You are far too generous to that 'religious gorgon'," Clive had remarked. Clive's support as well as concern over the matter made Robert conscious of being somewhat protected. This pleased him enormously, for kindness and attention from another had been missing for so long. In fact, since his mother had died.

They stopped off for lunch at The Stag, an inn situated at the top of a hill just outside of Sellinge.

"Well, my friend, here's to our success," said Clive raising his glass. Their glasses chinked. "It would seem that I stand a good chance. Jake seems to think so anyway."

"Do you think it is all worth it?" queried Robert.

"An odd thing to say, Robert, but now you mention it, I don't. Just another act to follow the last. By the way, I had a letter yesterday from the Home Secretary's office. They've appointed me a magistrate. The local court is in Sellinge so it will be very convenient."

"Let's hope that your interests don't conflict – if you know what I mean."

"Yes, Robert, you have a point there," Clive said with a chuckle.

"As you know, Robert, I heard from Maurice this morning. I couldn't tell you much at breakfast for mother would have passed out at some of its contents. Quite shocking, bless him. They return on Friday."

"Did he mention me at all?"

"Here, Robert," he said passing him the letter, "you may as well read it for yourself."

Robert took the letter and read it slowly.

After a while he asked, "I haven't let you down, have I?"

"Good Lord, no! Quite the opposite, in fact. You have been my pillar of strength, Robert," he said smiling at him. He would have liked to have added 'but I would prefer your strength on my pillow'. But the time was still not ripe for even the mildest approach.

"I do worry about Maurice." He paused as if considering some other problem. "I wonder if he would consider renting or maybe buying Coronia. Perhaps," he said answering his own question. Suddenly an idea came to him.

"I have a thought, Robert. Why don't we meet them all at Dover; how about that, eh?" Clive said excitedly.

"A super idea," said Robert, noticing and enjoying the collective 'we'.

"But there will be six of us," Robert said, questioning the car's capacity for that many persons.

"Maurice can jolly well sit on Alec's lap then," Clive said with a laugh, "though I don't normally encourage misconduct, if only for the sake of the driver."

"How could I not like working for you, Clive?" Robert said with utter sincerity.

"For or with, it's all one and the same, Robert, for I am having just one hell of a good life right now."

Robert thought about this remark and its possible meaning.

For some reason it made him a little anxious.

It was a very animated Clive who drove them leisurely on to Sellinge. Although Mrs. Winter had not been expecting them right then, she soon rustled up what is known in some parts of the country as 'high tea'.

As she came in with the tray, Clive asked her, "Mrs. Winter, how many bedrooms are fit to occupy on the second floor?"

"Well, Sir, I dare say I could make up two or three. I puts all the sheets and blankets in the airing cupboard — keeps 'em aired you know."

Clive smiled. "Excellent," he said.

"It's just that I have four friends arriving on Friday evening. Only two rooms will be needed for them. I shall also be staying over that evening. Can you manage that, Mrs. Winter?"

"Oh yes, Mr. Durham," she said with obvious pleasure. Entertaining a party of that number was a rarity, yet Mrs. Winter made light of it. "And of course your guests will want dinner?" she said as if this would inevitably be her responsibility.

Clive beamed at her. "Well, that is certainly a jolly good idea, Mrs. Winter. But do you think you can manage? There'll be six of us!"

"It will be no problem I assure you, Sir."

"It needn't be anything ostentatious. We will take potluck with whatever you come up with, Mrs. Winter. I could of course get someone down from Penge to help you."

"That won't be necessary, Sir," said an indignant Mrs. Winter. "I be quite capable of cooking for more than that. No, Mr. Durham, you just leave it to me."

At about five o'clock Mrs. Winter walked through into the hall to answer the telephone. Clive heard a slight tap on the door as Mrs. Winter returned to the sitting room.

"It's for you, Sir, 'tis Mrs. Durham."

"Thank you, Mrs. Winter."

What can she possibly want, thought Clive, I shall be picking her up in a couple of hours.

"Hello, Anne? Yes. Oh Anne, and you promised. No, no, of course you must go if he is ill. It's just that I am disappointed, naturally. Give your father my very best wishes. Yes, yes, alright then, telephone me from London tomorrow." Clive rejoined Robert.

"She's a selfish bitch," he said angrily.

"Whatever has happened?" asked Robert somewhat surprised at Clive's language.

"Anne. She's not coming after all. Her father is ill, or so she says, which I doubt very much. I knew that she loathed the idea of tonight, but you would have thought, just this once," he said annoyed at the thought of having to appear at such an important public function without her.

"I'll be there," offered Robert, "out of sight but I'll be there."

"I very much hope so – need some support," he said, then without thinking added, "Although Jake is handling everything, I really need you there as well, Robert." Robert felt that anxious tension yet again. Clive had not actually said anything to cause this anxiety but Robert felt a hidden agenda lay behind some of his words. His own thoughts and feelings towards Clive had changed to one of growing affection. Robert shrugged his shoulders as if to hastily dislodge any other ideas lurking in his mind.

They arrived at the Town Hall just before midnight. Clive's agent, who had been watching the count, came across to them. "How's it going, Jake?" asked Clive.

"It will be a close thing, Clive. Tories ain't doing too well which is a help. It's between you and the Socialists. Must say Sam Horler's put up a damn good show – no criticism of you of course, Clive, you worked like the proverbial horse. That fat pig of a Mayor has been imbibing again. Just hope the silly old bugger remains sober enough to congratulate the right candidate," he said making even Clive laugh. "And the Mayoress, poor woman, twisted her ankle just half an hour ago." His eyes then travelled towards the door behind Clive.

"Isn't Mrs. Durham with you, Clive?"

"No, 'fraid not Jake, her father's taken ill," he said guiltily.

"Oh, I'm sorry," came a forced reply. "You must not forget to mention it in your acceptance speech, Clive. Serious illness of father in law, devoted daughter, and all that rot."

"I never knew you were such a cynic, Jake," replied Clive with a smile.

"I'm a political animal, remember?"

Clive laughed aloud. "I had better move onto the stage, don't want to be absent when they announce the results. God, Jake, what a bore the whole thing is. I wish Anne was here." Clive's interest in her presence was purely to enhance his public image, and to avoid special interest by the newspapers whose editors behave like stoats and weasels, the throat being their main target. "I notice a few of the journalists looking my way. Ah well, to hell with 'em."

There was an appreciable lull in the activity of the room in which the counting was taking place. Then a procession of clerks made their way into the main hall. It was now a quarter to one in the morning. The returning officer, the Mayor – with help from his clerk – and other dignitaries climbed up the four steps onto the stage. Clive watched as the chief clerk handed the Mayor the results. Clive, and the other candidates with their wives, crowded onto the stage behind them. Clive felt conspicuously alone, and was sure that the absence of Anne would have been noted by everyone, including the press. He spied Robert who was practically hidden from view, a head amongst the crowd just visible, right at the back of the hall. Jake, his agent, was standing in front of the journalists and their cameras.

The blow came within minutes. He had lost – only a small margin of around 500 votes, but enough. Had his confidence not been so strong his disappointment might not have been so great. He smiled at Sam Horler, the winner, and in customary fashion moved over to congratulate him. He shook hands with the third candidate. For the sake of the local press photographer he posed before exploding flashlights. He strove to present an image of one who accepts defeat with grace and dignity.

Needless to say he did not feel any of this, which proves the maxim that looks can be very deceptive.

It has to be said that Clive fully expected to win. Never, throughout the whole campaign, had he really been in any doubt. Yet the fact remained, he had lost! In this state of disbelief, he moved, as in a trance, down the steps of the stage and into the partisan cheering crowd. Robert, equally disappointed, watched from behind a group that were cheering madly, obviously for the winner.

He saw Clive stop to speak with Jake, his agent. They shook hands then after a few moments Clive moved away and seemed to push forward at astonishing speed towards an overhanging red light marked Emergency Exit. Robert, easing his way out through the crowd, rushed after him.

Clive had no recollection of where he was heading or where he would now go. Then an arm took his and guided him towards the car. He put up no resistance. The passenger seat in the front of the car was unfamiliar to him and made him feel in a strange place. Robert was driving, driving his car!

"What the devil do you think you are doing, Robert?"

"I am driving you home, to Sellinge," he said firmly.

Clive, with some misgivings, accepted the situation without saying a word. He just slumped down into the seat. He closed his eyes to hide his disappointment and despair. Where was the justice? Now this on top of everything else. His head ached, his frown a leaden weight. He groaned at the pain of all this disappointment. He gave himself up to that altar of self-pity, permitting the floodgates to open. In the secrecy of the night he could be allowed to weep quite openly.

Once the car had stopped Clive remained slumped in the car, unwilling to move. He did not object, however, when Robert took charge of the situation. He allowed himself to be eased from the car. Robert took Clive's arm without comment, calmly walking with him into the house. Fortunately, or so Robert hoped, Mrs. Winter would have long since retired for the night.

"Whisky, Robert, for God's sake get me a bloody drink."

Robert brought the decanter and a glass and placed them on a table beside him.

"If you want me to go, I will," said Robert carefully.

Clive looked sleepily at him, and then shook his head. "Christ, Robert, don't you desert me too."

Clive sat quietly drinking, first one and then another, and another. Robert wanted to help but the question was how. His affection for this man had developed considerably over the past weeks but that was locked up in the privacy of his head. It made it all the more difficult, however, not to interfere. As before, he again reminded himself of his position here. This was Clive's house and he was Clive's employee.

"Would you like some coffee?" he asked tentatively.

"No thanks," Clive replied with difficulty.

Within an hour Clive had drunk a considerable amount, for little whisky now remained in the decanter. Its effect was becoming all too apparent. Robert noticed that Clive's speech was becoming more and more slurred. He had difficulty in rounding off his words. At the beginning it made Robert smile, but as time went on Clive became even more incoherent.

Fearful though he was, Robert knew that he had to act, if only in Clive's interest. Throwing caution to the winds he insisted, "Clive, you really must go up and lie down."

"Min you-r own b-bloody business."

"It is my bloody business, that's the trouble."

"W-what y-you say."

Robert walked determinedly over to Clive, who was in no fit state to resist when Robert hoisted him up from the chair. Amazed at his own strength, he literally carried him up the first flight of stairs to the nearest bedroom, which happened to be Robert's. With great relief he laid Clive carefully onto his bed. It seemed that Clive had entered or was entering the first stages of alcoholic oblivion. With considerable difficulty Robert removed Clive's jacket, then his tie, then loosened his shirt. He prised off Clive shoes and tossed them to the floor. Reluctant at first he finally decided to remove Clive's trousers. This was the easiest. The belt, the buttons, then a couple of tugs and they were gone. For a moment he stood looking at the fine muscular thighs, at the chest with very little hair, at this partially clad body drawing him nearer. Robert shook his head as if to remove the temptation, then quickly pulled a blanket over the resting figure.

He looked down at the drunken Clive, a Clive whose cares and worries were floating away on an alcoholic cloud. He presented a peaceful picture of repose, even allowing for the occasional grunt. Again that irresistible force and without realising it, Robert found himself bending over the prostrate form.

They had known each other for so short a time, five weeks or thereabouts. Robert was maturing fast, the liveliness of his mind, his feelings, his sexuality, all made the present situation so much more difficult. Although his sexual orientation was settled long since and the direction of his inclinations in no doubt, he had had little experience in exercising them. Apart from the school interlude, the ghastly experience from which Maurice and his friends had rescued him, there had been no other opportunities. Now he felt a tremendous force within him, something quite new, feelings that had not previously appeared. It wrenched at his heart, tore into his very being, created havoc with his physical desires, and it all turned towards the body lying so close, and over which he now leaned.

Speaking softly to himself he whispered, "Heaven help me, Clive, but I think I am in love with you. What curse is it that makes me this way? I can't stay here now. You've already suffered too much." He leaned forward and lifted

Clive's hand to his lips and kissed it passionately. He could feel the light hairs on Clive's wrist brush again his lips as he drew them lightly from one side to the other. He felt confident in the knowledge that Clive would never know. It was a supreme yet sad moment.

Robert sat in a wicker bedside chair intending to keep watch over Clive. He marvelled that he could hear Clive's steady breathing. His own heart seemed to keep pace with it, to sing a melody of love. He continued to look at Clive through the shallow lit room until, eventually, dreaming impossible thoughts, fell into blissful unconsciousness.

It was the sound of restless movements from the bed that woke him. He realised that he must have slept for several hours judging from the noise coming from outside. The morning chorus of the birds was gathering pace and he noticed over towards the east a break in the darkness. The lamp beside the bed still flickered and shone its soft yellow light. He looked towards to bed. He blinked several times. Robert was sure he could see eyes, wide awake, and angled in his direction.

"Robert, are you asleep?" came a clear voice.

"Yes – no."

"Robert, come over here."

"Clive, please go back to sleep," Robert pleaded.

"Robert, Robert, come over here this minute," demanded the voice.

"What is it you want?"

"Robert, is it asking too much for you to come over here for just one moment?"

Robert got up and moved over to the head of the bed. He stood looking down at Clive. It struck him as very odd to see him grinning.

"You are supposed to be drunk and by rights you should be fast asleep."

"Drunk my arse," came Clive's voice, "Do you think I didn't hear what you said earlier?"

"I don't know what you are talking about," said a nervous Robert. "It must be the effects of the whisky. I've heard that one can get hallucinations from it."

A laugh came from the bed, then a voice.

"Poppycock! Balderdash! Think I am deaf as well, Robert. Well I'm not."

Robert began to get that nervous feeling again. Events were turning out the wrong way.

Clive sat up. "Whisper in my ear what you said earlier." There was no reply.

"Come closer, Robert, I can't see you, closer."

Rather guiltily Robert crouched down until he was at Clive's level.

"You remember alright, nobody forgets speaking words like that," insisted Clive putting his face so close to Robert that he could feel his breath.

"Clive, please," he begged, his voice fading into a sob.

Hearing the change in Robert's voice Clive realised his teasing had gone far enough. He must tread carefully!

"It is alright, Robert. I just wanted you to know that I heard you say that you loved me. And by God, I really believe you do.

Wait, wait," said Clive as Robert began to move away. "Don't you see what I am getting at? Can't you read my eyes, my voice, my whole body? Can't you see how much I want you too, Robert?"

"Clive, you can't, that's impossible. You are just upset, what with the bloody election."

"What the hell do I have to do to convince you, Robert?" Here Clive grasped Robert with both hands and pulled him towards him. "If I had lost the election by an ever bigger margin it wouldn't have mattered one iota. But if I lose you, knowing now that you love me, then, yes, Robert, I would not be just upset I would be utterly devastated. Does that make it clear enough?" he said tightening his grip on the hands he held. "Come on Robert, give up this pretence, say to me again what you said earlier."

"Alright, Clive, I love you. Is that what you want to hear?" Clive didn't reply.

"That was unfair of me, Clive, for in truth, I know that I love you. My body, my soul, have been singing that refrain for some time now. Now you know, Clive. Are you satisfied?" Without giving Clive a chance to reply, Robert rushed on with a heavy heart intruding sadness in his voice. "It can never be, Clive. Please try to look at it rationally. Homosexual love's illegal; that's one thing. Your wife – yes, what about her? Your mother, she wouldn't exactly hold a celebration; your position here and in society; your appointment as a magistrate. Do I have to go on?" Clive heard a quiet sob, so near were their faces.

"No, Clive," Robert continued, "The cards are all stacked against us. We wouldn't stand a chance. If you really heard what I said earlier you will know that for your sake, as well as mine, it is best that I leave here as soon as possible."

Robert did not want to believe this was the end, and the despair he now suffered was unbearable. Why? Why, when all had been going so well. Why did he have to become caught up with these emotions? That thing called a heart was pulling him one way, his rationality another. For a moment neither of them spoke. Robert could feel the strength in the man's hands clinging to him. If only they would release him. Just a little to allow him to go free. He didn't want this but again...

Clive's clasp on Robert grew even stronger. He pulled him nearer.

"No, Robert, not this time, not again." Robert heard a voice which was new to him, a voice of determination, a voice which described a strength he had not yet experienced in Clive.

"No, Robert, can you not see what is staring both of us in the face. You have expressed clearly how you feel, you love me, Robert, you have said it clearly enough. Yes, there are always reasons why it cannot be but if we constantly meddle with the truth and follow a path which is a lie, then you end up as I once have. No, Robert, believe me when I say that I also love you, yes, love you, Robert. Is that so strange, eh? I will not let you go, you are mine and to hell with everything else. This is my life, my love, and my decision. If you leave me now, I swear the outcome will be something your conscience will really have to worry about." Clive paused for only a moment.

"Christ almighty, Robert, surely we are both mature and intelligent enough to find a place in our lives for the most important thing on offer. Miss this opportunity and we are both done for. Anyway, my dear Robert, I'm going to have you even if I have to chain you to the bloody bedposts." With that he pulled Robert over onto the bed with him and clasped him firmly around the waist.

In spite of his attempt to remain serious and sensible, Clive's last remark had caused Robert to laugh and this resulted in a sudden relaxing of his taut and tired body. His emotions pushed him further and it was then that he gave into the only choice, surrender and love.

As he crushed Robert to him Clive noticed the change, felt the response and knew he had won.

"And now, my dear darling Robert," Clive exclaimed, "we can be real for a change, sleep together under the protection of Eros, and this time, Robert, no turning back." They moulded their faces together, kissing tenderly, then, out of sheer necessity their movements took on an urgent need to satisfy their aroused passion, which set the seal to an irreversible alliance.

As they lay together, holding on to each other as if threatened from the world about them, Clive whispered, "For me, Robert, my future now turns on our relationship, which, as far as I am concerned will be as purposeful and meaningful as if we were married – which, to all intents and purposes, we now are. I am now finished with running away. There will be no more ifs and buts, just you and me. I keep seeing that rogue Alec, bless him. What would he say if he saw us right now? What was it he said to Maurice? Oh I remember clearly what it was, Robert, he said 'fuck all the others'. And what's more he is right. We have reached our Elysium, and at last all is right with my world, for you are part of it."

Chapter Eighteen

From outside of the barriers on the quayside Robert and Clive watched the cross channel ferry steam slowly towards No. 3 berth where the cranes arched above it. They watched and waited patiently as lines were thrown from the ship to the dock, then the thick hawsers were pulled ashore and secured. After what seemed an interminably long time, a gangway was hoisted into position and the passengers begin slowly to disembark.

Hurrying toward the customs shed Clive and Robert waited, and then purposely hid themselves behind a concrete pillar.

There was no mistaking the sound of Alec's voice.

"Hey, wait for me, Maurice."

Clive and Robert watched as two bronzed and beaming figures walked slowly towards them. Then they stopped. It was several minutes before George and John caught up with them.

Using his hands as a megaphone, Clive shouted out, "Maurice".

"I'd know that voice a mile away," Maurice said to Alec as he turned, in time to see Clive and Robert materialise from behind the pillar. He rushed over to them.

"Clive," he said. "Well, this is a pleasure to be sure. What on earth are you doing down here? Now that's a stupid question," he said going up to Clive and embracing him.

"Just a surprise, my dear Maurice," said Clive hugging him. "I see you have brought back one of the bronze figures," he said going over to Alec.

"At least I've my clothes on, all of them," Alec said with a grin.

"Pity," joked Robert slyly and without thinking.

Alec looked at him, gave a wide grin, and then shook him warmly by the hand. "How are you, Robert?" he enquired kindly.

"If I dare think about it too long I may be tempting fate. But, yes, Alec, I'm really fine, thanks to you all."

Alec looked searchingly at both Clive and Robert. There is something going on between those two, he thought to himself. From the look in those enquiring eyes, and the smile now creasing that browned countenance, Robert knew all too soon that Alec had deciphered their secret.

George and John arrived as Robert was recovering from Alec's enquiring eyes with their perceptive discovery. They all shook hands.

"Maurice, you sit between my legs, careful, Maurice, mind my balls!" Alec said shifting on the seat slightly.

"Heavens, Alec, behave yourself – for the moment at least," Maurice said as laughter ran round the car.

"Do they carry on like this all the time?" Clive enquired of John who sat next to him. Robert, sitting next to John, laughed.

"'Fraid so. I tell you Clive, I may not have made any great archaeological discoveries but, by God, my knowledge of mankind and some of its antics has been well and truly enhanced. Seriously though, Maurice and Alec have made this such a special holiday, it has been a delightful experience for us both. I hope and pray that they will always remain friends."

"Yes," interrupted George, "we've had a wonderful time, and meeting Maurice's sister, Ada, and her husband, was the icing on the cake."

"They're talking about us again, Maurice," whispered Alec in his ear.

Turning to face him Maurice replied "I know; you should be flattered, Alec. On the other hand, I think perhaps you deserve some of the nice things they say about you. Then of course I'm very biased, wouldn't you say?"

"I guess so, Maurice, but all of the nice things they say have to include you, my love."

Maurice now began thinking about the recent elections, especially Clive's part in it. He was sure that Clive would tell them, sooner or later, but on such an important issue as this he felt it should have been sooner. His instincts told him that Clive had been unsuccessful. He decided, however, to leave it for Clive to raise the subject.

"Say, chaps," said Clive cheerfully, "I rather hope that you will stay over at Sellinge with us for a couple of nights. You'll have to stay to dinner anyway because I've already asked Mrs. Winter to prepare it – for around seven o'clock. And before you say anything, Maurice, there is heaps of room for you all. Not, I might add, all in one room!" There is much laughter.

"We shall be lucky to survive as far as Sellinge," said George as Alec nearly dislodged Maurice from the seat, and in the process caused the car to surge to one side.

"Steady," said Clive "or we shall spend the night in a ditch."

Clive managed to get up a good speed despite the heavy load the car was burdened with. Conversation was difficult particularly as there were many voices competing to be heard. Much to Maurice's disappointment Clive had still not mentioned the election. Mrs. Winter spied them from the window. She was forced to smile as she saw the way they all tumbled from the car. "Youth," she said to herself, "Oh happy days." It simply made her happy to see the cheerful faces and to hear their laughter as they dragged luggage towards the front door.

Despite Clive's offer of providing help from Penge, which Mrs. Winter had cheerfully declined, she was determined to show them that her cooking was second to none. Apart from her soup, which always seemed to be simmering on the kitchen range, and which was well received, she had prepared a large steak and kidney pie, which she served with a range of vegetables.

"By, God," said Alec, as he finished a second helping, "don't do anything like that in Greece, Maurice."

"Of course not, Alec. This is England, remember," remarked Maurice. "Not that your appetite changes one little bit whatever's on offer or wherever you are."

Once dinner was over and they had moved into the drawing room, Mrs. Winter, flushed with all the well-earned compliments, retired for the night to her room on the top floor.

Maurice sat with Alec in one large armchair, George and John were opposite in separate chairs and Clive and Robert had placed themselves, as if strangers, at either end of a settee.

'They don't fool no-one' were Alec's immediate thoughts.

George and Maurice lit pipes. Clive chose a cigar.

Looking across at Maurice and Alec as they reclined lazily together in the chair gave George much satisfaction, a feeling of having contributed to their happiness and contentment.

During the next hour the talk centred on the holiday in Greece. What amazed Clive was Alec's sudden conversion to all things Athenian. He was rather intrigued by this urgent interest in learning and was proud, if only for

Maurice's sake, that Alec was shaping up in this way. The roundness of some of Alec's descriptions, particularly relating to some of the bronze statues would, without doubt, have raised a few eyebrows and sent many a matron into screaming or fainting fits. He smiled at the thought, as well as the language. There was no longer the smallest twinge of envy around. Robert had changed all of that. He wondered at what might have happened if he had won the election. The evening would have been entirely different, that is for sure. It is doubtful if their present situation would have come about as quickly and decisively as it did. Anyway, he reasoned, he had no control over the one race he lost. The one race he won he could partly thank the victor of the first, namely one Sam Horler. He sighed, "Such is fate" he muttered under his breath, "I am nearly jealous of my own good fortune."

There was a hubbub of voices as the returning holidaymakers described much of what they had experienced. Some of Alec's remarks were vivid in the extreme. There was much amusement in the various stories they had to tell and from time to time the room rang with laughter.

Clive, utterly relaxed in this unique environment, for the first in a long time, laughed until tears ran down the side of his face while Maurice tried to allay some of Alec's enthusiasm, especially the spicy reminiscences.

He had learned to swim, "And in the nude, Robert," Alec said grinning "got seaweed caught in me, well, was rough on the you know what."

"I don't know what 'what' is," said Robert cheekily.

Alec grinned, "Maurice calls them testicles, the hanging down bits, then," he replied.

This sent John and George into hysterics.

It occurred to Clive that this taboo or fear of mention of those human reproductive bits and pieces, although laughable in some ways, was really rather tragic. Small wonder, he thought, that there were people around, including women and wives like Anne, who lacked any understanding.

"Well, Clive," said Maurice, coming at last to the question which had been rattling around in his head since arriving at Dover, "What's been happening here?" It was clear to them all that this was an obvious invitation to hear of Clive's election result.

"Maurice, my dear friend," began Clive with a laugh. "I have watched your impatience ever since you landed at Dover. Well," Clive continued, in a voice hardly reflecting disappointment, "there is bad as well as good news. The bad news, I'm afraid, Maurice, is that I did not get elected. Not by much of a margin, but enough. Sam Horler won the day."

"Shame. I'm really disappointed."

"Don't be, Maurice. I'm now rather glad. Anyway Sam Horler will be much more use to the people than me. He's really dedicated. I have never been able to understand why so many of our people vote for candidates with whom they cannot possibly identify, socially or politically. I mean, Maurice, can you ever imagine Mother voting for Sam?" As he said this he was grinning madly.

"But you are a liberal and surely there is a world of difference?"

"Not really. It's often remarked that a Liberal is a Tory with a slight conscience."

"You're becoming cynical."

"Well, maybe I am, Maurice. Anyhow, its importance no longer matters. What is much more to the point is the really great news I have to tell. Great, great news," he went on excitedly.

Maurice looked searchingly at Clive.

"What on earth has been happening? You lose an election and the chance of going to Parliament and then you behave as if your shares have doubled overnight. Something dramatic to cause all this excitement, that's for sure, and to judge from the look on your dear old face, you're terribly pleased about something," Maurice said. He turned to George.

"This exuberant animal is not the Clive we left behind, is it, George?"

"I bet I know," said Alec sounding mysterious.

Clive laughed. "Of course he does, you've been so occupied nurturing young Alec here or you would have seen what has been staring you in the face, Maurice."

"What on earth are you talking about?" asked Maurice.

"Well, for a start," began Clive, "and to put things into perspective, Anne and I have agreed to separate."

"Oh, my God, you haven't..." began Maurice imagining danger signs.

"It's alright, Maurice, my dear boy," said Clive interrupting, "calm down. Everything has remained frightfully civilised. We are not going to get involved in a divorce – not for the moment anyway. Anne and I have merely agreed that marriage, in the accepted and fullest sense, is, to quote Anne, 'incompatible with our respective temperaments.'" Clive laughed. "Put that way it does sounds damned funny, I must say. To put it more simply, Maurice, we've agreed to go our separate ways. Anne is mighty relieved I can tell you. As for me, well, thereby hangs another tale."

"I bet I know the ending," said Alec smugly.

"Keep quiet, Alec, I'm the star of the show tonight," Clive said with a laugh.

Turning to Maurice, Clive went on.

"Of course, I told you this much in my letter. Did you not get my letter, Maurice?"

"Well, yes," said Maurice, "But I am really surprised at Anne's part in all of this just the same. I would have said that she thrived in the name of a Durham even if not in it's er... action."

Clive roared with laughter, as did Alec. "Really, Maurice, you put it so delicately. You should never be fooled by appearances. After all, Maurice, look at me. The very essence of respectability – ask my mother," he said laughing again.

"All I can say," said John, "is that you seem pretty satisfied with the new situation."

Satisfied, John? I'm ecstatic! Getting rid of the marital headache accounts for only part, an important part admittedly, of my euphoria. The real cause lies elsewhere," said Clive, looking over at Alec, then "and that cute little bugger, Alec, knows where," he said with a wide smile.

"If that's what you want," said Maurice, still unaware of what Alec was being 'cute' about, "then of course I am pleased. But you will lose the support a wife gives you, even if in name only. You previously attached so much importance to it. Remember, Clive, how you once described marriage as one of the crutches of respectability. A prop prescribed by society, albeit one, which in your case, I always considered to be totally inappropriate. Sorry Clive, it is unkind of me to drag up the past."

"I remember it all, Maurice, you don't have to remind me. But I am much better at making judgements now."

"So," asked Maurice, "what will you do? Of course you can count on us, that goes without saying, but..."

Looking directly at Maurice, Alec began laughing, as did Clive.

"What," Maurice asked, "have I said that is so frightfully amusing?"

"Maurice," said Alec, "why don't you give Clive a chance? Surely you must know what he's on about, what he's trying to tell you? The same as you and me, darn it."

"You and me?" Maurice paused. "Preposterous."

"No, Maurice," said Clive "it is perfectly true."

"I don't understand. Who? When? Where?" he rattled off in quick succession and with a touch of impatience.

"You tell him, Alec," said Clive smiling, "Although he ought to have guessed it from my letter."

"Absolutely right," said Alec, "'twas writ clear enough even for me to understand."

Robert, sitting in the corner of the settee moved and seemed to shrink back into the upholstery.

Alec leaned over and kissed Maurice, then, laughing, got up and walked over to the settee.

"Come on, Robert," he said with a broad grin, "out of the wilderness and let the dog see the rabbit."

Robert's embarrassment was all too much. Clive quickly moved next to him, then, putting an arm affectionately around his shoulders, drew Robert towards him.

"Now do you understand, Maurice?" said Alec with a broad smile.

It is fair to say that Maurice was dumbfounded. He stared at Clive in disbelief.

"You see, Maurice, I have, as Alec would say, fucked things up in the past. Now I have been given a second chance. You needn't worry, Maurice, this time there will be no going to Greece to clear the mind. All is as clear as it could ever be and that instructs exactly where we are going. Only one word describes it. Together. Yes, Maurice, me and Robert. And the lucky thing for me is that I have Robert to thank for it all – well, not exactly all, for you played the fairy 'godmother' in the first place."

"Shouldn't it be godfather?" said Alec, quite innocently.

Laughter filled the room and it was some time before Clive could continue.

"My electoral demise merely added to the number of downs in my life. Now I am glad that I lost, though I did not feel that way at the time. Simply, Maurice, after the results, and I had been so confident that I would win, I staggered out of the Town Hall in an absolute daze. Robert, thank the Lord, offered the help I needed right then. When we got back here I started to drown my disappointment. Because of the significance of events which followed, and I hope Robert will forgive me for telling you, that after a while, when I was somewhat glassy eyed and staggering, Robert took charge and carried me up to bed." Clive hesitated then, "Is it alright, Robert if I tell them the rest?"

For a moment Robert looked embarrassed, the colour in his face brighter.

"If you must, Clive."

"Would you rather I didn't?"

"No, no, you want to relive the event, and therefore, so do I. Do carry on Clive."

"Well," continued Clive, "partly drunk maybe, but not so that I was totally unaware of Robert putting me to bed. Actually, to be helpless, partially at least, and have someone, well not any old someone, undress you, someone you wanted as desperately as I did, was really very exciting." Here Clive gave a chuckle. "Seriously, Maurice, I wanted to tell Robert then how I felt but coherent words just wouldn't form. Then, even through my alcoholic haze, I could not fail to experience amazement, as well as delight, when I heard Robert quietly express what I desperately wanted to hear. He made the mistake of thinking me asleep. But I heard, and later in the early hours, made, no forced him to repeat it. Obstinate as a mule he was but, finally, we made it."

Robert smiled and moved even closer to Clive.

"If that is luck, then it is long overdue," said Clive. "Of course I have you to thank, Maurice. For this alone I shall be eternally grateful."

"Well, I'll be damned," said Maurice after Clive had finished. "I just can't believe what I hear. Pleased would be an understatement. Of course I'm pleased. Well, Clive, you have been on both sides of the fence, now for my peace of mind will you settle down where you belong, with Robert."

"I began to think that you might disapprove, Maurice," said Alec, "I was ready for you if you had," he joked.

"How could I possibly disapprove when I look at you, you sun baked under-gamekeeper you?"

They all laughed as Maurice and Alec moved onto the settee beside Clive.

"I know I'll never catch you poaching, Robert, which is just as well," he said, grinning, "for I've a way with poachers." "And you can take my word for that," laughed Clive.

"I am so very pleased for you, Clive," said George earnestly, "such good fortune is long overdue. I wish both of you, with all my heart, a long and happy life. I view this as yet another victory over the hoard of unseasoned humans with their scarred vision."

"I view your luck with equal pleasure" agreed John.

"That sure was a smashing meal, Clive," remarked Alec, "Can't say I liked all those funny dishes we had over there."

"Funny?" said Maurice, "Well, all I can say is that your appetite didn't suffer one jot in Greece. In fact, you put us all to shame."

"I thought you were very ambitious, Alec," said George.

"Wait until you go to France and sample their snails."

"Snails?" said Alec in astonishment.

"Well if you can eat octopus, snails will be a luxury."

"Octopus! I didn't eat octopus, Maurice," he said, horrified, "did I?"

"Yes, you did," said Maurice laughing, "Remember the pink chunks of fish? That was octopus."

"Oh, my god," said Alec, squirming at the thought.

Maurice looked at his watch. "Clive, we really must go up.

Come on, Alec, I want you fresh and bright for the morning."

"You'll get me fresh and bright tonight, young Maurice."

Laughing, George and John followed, leaving Clive and Robert alone.

Once on their own Clive leaned towards his lover.

"Robert," he said lovingly, "I'm glad I got drunk that night. So I lost the election! But what a consolation prize! Tonight, however, shall be another celebration, a night together surrounded by friends, well not literally." They both laughed. Clive looked serious for a moment. "Tell me, Robert, that you have no regrets?"

Robert, sitting taller than Clive, moved nearer. Using both hands he turned his lover's face towards him so that they now faced each other.

"Would I be here?" he answered softly.

Clive looked into eyes which gave expression to that supreme moment. He studied the blond hair, which strayed over a high forehead, the faultless skin with just a trace of whisker, but above all else, to the utter sincerity in those few words. It was the answer to any lingering doubts. Momentarily, Clive thought of his relationship with Maurice. Why, he pondered, had he previously not been able to navigate correctly even though the route was so painfully obvious. 'Well', he thought to himself, 'that, thankfully, is all in the past.'

"I suppose history might charge me with careless irrationality, Robert. But this time, Robert, I swear to God, my heart is for you and you alone. This time there is no uncertainty on my part. I just want to be sure, Robert, that you have no doubts."

"What more can I say to convince you, Clive? Five or more years ago, or even longer, I was quite sure of what I really wanted, of how I felt towards my own sex. I also had a pretty good idea of the consequences of displaying such feelings – as my recent experiences bear witness," he said with a shudder. So I ended up trying to shut them out, hoping perhaps to be left in peace. But, of course, 'tis like refusing to accept the world is round, or significantly, to deny the evidence of nature. There is a disability in this debate, it rests in the blighted minds of those who cannot accept the reality of nature.

"My life, some of it meeting with danger enough to last a lifetime, has had its moments of sadness. I am not complaining for look at me now! My real life began when I met your friends, and through them, met you. You are now my life, Clive" he said clasping his hand. "There is little more to say except that, yes, I love you, Clive. Now can we at last go to our bed?"

They embraced as if to seal a 'partnership' just beginning and which they prayed would last throughout their lives.

Chapter Nineteen

They had finished breakfast. The sun was strengthening as Clive and Maurice walked out into the garden.

"Maurice, I can't thank you enough for staying over. I rather hoped that you would, there is so much I have yet to tell you."

Maurice glanced at his companion, seeing reflected the same happiness he saw when up at Cambridge.

"I am truly amazed, Clive. In less than a month you have discarded a wife and taken a lover, this time of the right orientation! What on earth motivated such changes?"

"Primarily, you, Maurice. You couldn't have known of the problems Anne and I were having, and pride, bloody pride, stopped me telling you. Then, when we met that night and you told me that you were going away with Alec, I knew right away that I was losing the greatest friend I would ever have. I saw myself clearly once again, the first time since you and I first met at Cambridge. I was very depressed, Maurice and could see no future.

"Then chance came to my aid. You re-appeared, and that seemed enough to sustain me for the future, unknown though it was at that time. And then came that final glorious act — even if by accident — of you sending Robert down here, to me. Maurice, I shall love you for that alone."

"Clive, you do exaggerate. However, I am very happy for you."

"Stay for a few more days," he pleaded, "George and John are still on holiday and Alec, well, he is now part of you." Maurice looked at Clive, then smiled.

"What about poor Mrs. Winter?"

"Oh, she'll be alright. I've arranged for some help to come in from the village."

They strolled on for some time then,

"Are you happy, Maurice? Is Alec all you imagined?" he said cautiously.

"In this very imperfect world, Clive, nothing could be more perfect. It is an incredible feeling to experience the quite frightening sensations that loving someone brings. If I could scream out every morning for the world's ears, I love you, Alec, it would still not express the true extent of my feelings. Does that answer your question?"

"Yes, my dear old comrade, it does."

"And what about you – are you sure of Robert?"

"Oh, yes, Oh, yes," Clive said quickly for fear that the truth might somehow be missed. "I shall never ever again attempt to change the unchangeable. I can still remember our first meeting, Maurice, oh, how easy it is to recall. I first spoke those magic, loving, yet forbidden words to you for the first time. Remember the difficulties you had at the time, Maurice, in accepting your homosexuality. You rebuffed me, remember? An unhappy moment. Might call it our growing pains. To your credit, Maurice, you had the guts to ditch those infectious prejudices, which cling to one like parasites. Because of your strength and honesty, you retrieved a situation and my love. That first intimate moment with you was like an awakening and is and will always remain engraved on my memory. I only wish that later on I had had the same strength, the same determination, to... well." Clive paused. "That's all in the past. My courage, Maurice, unlike yours, took a hell of a time asserting itself, but at last it's here." Shaking his head, he went on, "I have Robert, who is now my life, and you and Alec as my best friends. There is nothing more that I ask except that we may look upon each other, as do the stars in the sky, from now until eternity." Maurice moved to Clive and they embraced in a long and emotional hug.

As together, arm in arm, they walked slowly back into the house, nostalgic memories from the gardens and spires of Cambridge came flooding back, reminding both Maurice and Clive, not only of the responsibilities knowledge brings, but of the very birthplace of their experience in the divine nature of man's love for man.

| W1 | 2/17 | AB | 03/18 | D1 6/19 | |

DIDCOT LIBRARY
THE BROADWAY
DIDCOT
OX11 8RU
TEL. 01235 813103

7 Last item

To renew this book, phone 0845 1202811 or visit
our website at www.libcat.oxfordshire.gov.uk
You will need your library PIN number
(available from your library)

**OXFORDSHIRE
COUNTY COUNCIL**
SOCIAL & COMMUNITY SERVICES
www.oxfordshire.gov.uk

3303270867